MIRACLES A

• Lori
When nurse-turned-investigator Pauline Sokol decides to bring a bit of Christmas cheer to a helpless old man, she unwittingly discovers misdeeds of a Scrooge-like local dentist.

• Dana Cameron •
Modern detection techniques are called for on Christmas Eve in an elegant eighteenth-century English manor when murder and grand theft get thrown in amidst the Christmas cheer.

• Mary Daheim •
All the wacky relatives are together for the holidays at Judith McMonigle Flynn's bed-and-breakfast—but a murderous, uninvited "ghost" may dampen the Christmas spirit.

• Cait London •
When a well-meaning do-gooder lets a mysterious man into her life, she must discover if he's protecting her—or stalking her.

• Suzanne Macpherson •
A handsome hero's plucky late fiancée won't leave him be until he completes her unfinished mission on Earth.

• Kerrelyn Sparks •
Coming home for the holidays takes on new meaning when a newly turned vampire discovers his own Christmas miracle.

LORI
AVOCATO

DANA
CAMERON

MARY
DAHEIM

CAIT
LONDON

SUZANNE
MACPHERSON

KERRELYN
SPARKS

Sugarplums
and
Scandal

AVON BOOKS
An Imprint of HarperCollinsPublishers

AVON BOOKS
An Imprint of HarperCollins*Publishers*
10 East 53rd Street
New York, New York 10022-5299

"All I Want for Christmas Is My Two Front Teeth" copyright © 2006 by Lori Avocato
"The Lords of Misrule" copyright © 2006 by Dana Cameron
"The Ghost of Christmas Passed" copyright © 2006 by Mary Daheim
"Partners in Crime" copyright © 2006 by Lois Kleinsasser
"Holly Go Lightly" copyright © 2006 by Suzanne Macpherson
"A Very Vampy Christmas" copyright © 2006 by Kerrelyn Sparks
ISBN-13: 978-0-06-113695-5
ISBN-10: 0-06-113695-6
www.avonmystery.com

First Avon Books paperback printing: November 2006

Avon Trademark Reg. U.S. Pat. Off. and in Other Countries, Marca Registrada, Hecho en U.S.A.
HarperCollins® is a registered trademark of HarperCollins Publishers Inc.

Printed in the U.S.A.

10   9   8   7   6   5   4   3   2

Sugarplums
and
Scandal

All I Want for Christmas Is My Two Front Teeth

Lori Avocato

According to the druids, mistletoe was traditionally considered to be the semen of the gods.

I looked at the *Hope Valley Sentinel* article and wondered if the editor of our local newspaper had gone nuts. "Semen of the gods"? They had the nerve to print such sexual innuendoes in this ethnic, moral, home-spun, Wonder Bread suburban Connecticut town?

With my jaw down to my chest (a very common occurrence when I am stunned), I read on that the liquid of the berries looked and had the texture of semen. Geez. They actually printed that in a newspaper where folks like Mrs. Kaminski, the local gossip, Mr. Gansecki, the local over-eighty stud, and Miss Nawrocki, the local moral majority would read it? Yikes.

Slowly I looked up to see the ball of mistletoe hanging from my mother's foyer ceiling. Then I scrunched up the newspaper (only the semen/berry article) and stuck it into the pocket of my jeans.

Stella Sokol would rather die than hang *those* kinds of berries from her nineteen sixties ceiling.

And to think I'd kissed Jagger, The Delicious, under it last Christmas Eve. He was my sometimes partner in solving crimes, my all-the-time fantasy man. Yum.

I gulped.

"Pauline? Pauline Sokol, what is taking so long?" my mother yelled from the kitchen.

Even as a nurse, a thirty-something, and as her only single adult child, I couldn't tell her the truth. "Just reading the paper, Mom."

"What is so darned, excuse my language, important that you can't come help your mother make *pierogies*?"

I blew out a breath. For one thing, I hate making the little pillows of Polish dough, and each year put in my vote to buy ready-made ones, much to Stella Sokol's horror. And each year I end up taking time off from work to stuff the suckers with cabbage, mashed potatoes or cottage cheese, a process which takes about twenty hours since my *married* siblings have toys to buy for their kids and don't have time to help.

I shook my head and told myself that I had no life.

Since I'd given up a thirteen-year nursing career to switch to medical insurance fraud investigating for Scarpello and Tonelli Insurance Company, things haven't been going too well for me.

"Pauline!" Mom's voice was so loud I could swear she was—

I swung around—"Oh! Hey, Mom"—then I knocked the rest of the paper onto the floor.

She'd snatched the paper up as if I were some male teen who'd been reading *Playboy* (okay, nowadays all they had to do was boot up the Internet for peeping, but Stella wouldn't know that).

She looked down at the paper. "Toothless Holiday? Oh my."

I said a silent prayer to Saint Theresa for letting me have the foresight to pocket the berry article.

"Pauline? Are you reading about this poor man who doesn't have his front dentures yet?"

Lying never came easily to me. Catholic school induced conscience and being raised by *her,* I guess was the reason. I looked at my mother waving the paper at me. "Yep. Very sad, huh?" and wondered why the hell the guy didn't have his front teeth yet.

She snatched my father's reading glasses from the top of his head. Daddy had been napping within snatching range in his favorite La-Z-Boy recliner.

He never even stirred.

Guess that's what over forty-four years of being married did to a couple. Me, I wouldn't know.

The paper crinkled and *crackled* in her grip. She stuck on the glasses and read for a bit.

"Oh, my. How sad. How awful indeed. This poor man's dentist is holding his dentures hostage. *Do* something about this. Be a Good Samaritan for the holiday season. Or, you could, of course, go back to nursing. I'm sure they have those fill-in kinds of jobs at all the hospitals. Go back to Saint Gregory's where you used to make a decent living."

She never failed to remind me about the gigantic, nationwide nursing shortage. "Actually," she continued, "since you are not snooping around for the next week, go help this man so he can eat his Christmas dinner." With that she shoved the newspaper at my chest and gave me one of her "motherly" looks. "Seems right up your alley."

Now, none of us five kids could ever duck fast enough to avoid one of *those* looks. If "When E.F. Hutton talks, people listen," then when "Stella Sokol tells her kids something, they *better* damn well do what she says."

I grabbed the paper, held it in one hand, and knew that my Christmas vacation plans of R&R, overdosing on chocolate, and maybe dating a few hot guys had come to a screeching halt.

Seemed, for me anyway, the "you know what" of the gods was going to stay in the little white mistletoe berries this year—yet again.

As I stared way too long at the now-fascinating mistletoe, the doorbell rang.

Mother yelled from the kitchen, "Come in, Mr. Jagger," My heart did a one eighty in my chest. She'd once again invited him over without my knowledge. And he'd never corrected her when she called him "mister" either.

And how the hell did she know his phone number?

The door opened, Jagger nodded at me, and then came forward.

Oh . . . my . . . god.

His kiss landed on my right cheek. Cheek? Cheeeeeeeek?

Semen schmemen.

My hands ached from stuffing a gazillion pierogies with Lord knows what. My mother would stick a bowl in front of me, and I'd spoon it into the dough robotically. I looked up to see Jagger sitting across from me as if nothing on his body pained him—even though he'd been the official dough roller. Mother'd had her wooden rolling pin since the dawn of light, so it didn't exactly roll like Teflon; but with the strength in those arms (I took a deep breath for a Jagger moment), rolling a gazillion pillows of dough didn't seem to bother him in the least.

"I need some Tylenol, Mom. Do you have some?"

She eyed me as she waited for the batch of dough pillows to float to the top of the boiling water to signal they'd had enough. "What's wrong? Menstrual cramps?"

Cramps gripped my insides at that very moment. Talk about the power of suggestion. Of course Stella Sokol's power came from me nearly dying of embarrassment in front of Jagger.

"No," I said with a sigh. "My *hands* hurt."

Now *she* shook her head. Mother and Jagger, at times, were like two peas in a pod. Both had a way with their eyes that I didn't even want to ponder. "Daddy's baby aspirin are in my medicine cabinet. Someone your size should take two."

"Two? I'll need about six," I mumbled as I stood, brushed flour from my jeans, and turned to go.

Was that a snicker from my buddy?

Once the seven baby aspirin kicked in, and I didn't bleed out, I felt much better, so I decided to sit next to sleeping daddy and read the tooth article. At first I thought it was a joke. I mean they had printed about semen. Why not fake missing teeth? But the more I read the more credible the article became.

Jagger strolled in and sat next to me on the couch. He leaned over to read what I was holding. "What's so interesting?"

At first I wanted to say, "You can bloody well see for yourself," but, thinking that would be rude so close to Christmas, I said, "Sounds like dental fraud."

Did his expression change?

Jagger had this "thing" for medical insurance fraud, yet to this day I had no idea what it was. All I knew was that he was the Robin Hood of catching medical insurance fraud criminals. I mentally shrugged and said, "One Mr. Leonard Niski doesn't have his front dentures from a Dr. Elfin Santana, and his insurance has already paid for them."

I looked up. "What?"

Jagger grinned. "You're kidding. Right?"

I reread the last part of the article. "Nope. All paid for and no choppers."

Jagger shook his head, which was, I'd learned by now, his rather obvious way of showing annoyance at me. Two shakes and I was in big trouble. Three and I had to hightail it out of his sight. Not sure if I've ever suffered a three yet, though. At least not unless it was behind my back.

Which would not surprise me.

"Pauline, Elfin? Santana?"

"I'm guessing he's Mexican. You know, like Carlos Santana? I—" The look continued. "What the *hell* is wrong with you?" I asked.

Perfect timing.

"Pauline!" Mother chastised me as she came into the room. This from a woman who thought "darned" was cursing.

"Jagger is annoying me, Mother."

Now he really did smirk.

He got up and helped my mother get seated. Geez.

They'd become real buddies. No wonder she invited him and always took his side. I gasped inside when I realized—she must have invited him for Christmas Eve again too! That was more important to our family than Christmas Day (a day of rest and prayer), being the Polish celebration of *Wigilia,* which meant the Christmas Eve meal.

Last year was my first Jagger-kiss under the . . . mistletoe.

"Pauline? . . . Pauline? Jagger asked you a question."

I looked up from my daydreaming. "Hmm? What?"

"What are you planning to do about Mr. Niski?" Jagger repeated.

I wanted to say, "You interrupted my mistletoe-kissing daydream for *that*?" But I kept quiet—mostly because it had been about him. Business always came first with Jagger.

Learning to think quickly on my feet, I said, "Well, for starters, since I don't have a case for Fabio, I'm going to visit the old man and offer my assistance."

Fabio was my greasy, very unlikable boss—although he hadn't fired me yet, so there was at least one positive about him.

I knew I should have come alone, I thought as I rang the doorbell at the Twilight Hills Apartment complex, all the while ignoring Jagger with the hopes that he'd disappear like some magical Santa's elf. Twilight Hills? I still couldn't get over that name for senior citizen's housing. Someone had a sick sense of humor.

I looked at my buddy Jagger, and thought, he's got *no* sense of humor.

Earlier he'd made fun of the dentist's "Santa Claus"

name, but there wasn't anything funny about a guy who would take advantage of the elderly as Santana'd obviously done. I loved the elderly. My favorite person in the world was my Uncle Walt, who was pushing eighty-five. We watched Steelers games together, read about cars in his magazines, and shared a laugh or two when he wasn't napping. Seniors had so many wonderful life experiences to share.

Early on I'd decided I needed to keep fit so I would age gracefully and more importantly—*slowly*.

"Yeah?" a scratchy kind of voice asked through the intercom.

"Oh, hi, Mr. Niski?"

"None other."

I smiled even though he couldn't see me. "You don't know me—"

"Then beat it. Fixed income here. I can't buy what you are selling."

Of course, selling sounded more like "shelling" because of the no denture fiasco. I winced. "I'm not selling anything, Mr. Niski. I'm here to help you with your teeth."

I could feel Jagger behind me shaking his head.

"You got my tweeth?"

"Um. No. I will try to get . . . please let me in. It is cold out here. I'm a private investigator who specializes in medical insurance fraud."

No way was I going to turn around and see Jagger's reaction to "specialize."

After a few minutes, the door started to open—and a thin, very short (I'm guessing below five feet) elderly man appeared dressed in brown pants, way too big for him, a white button down shirt, way too big for him, and fuzzy black slippers, also way too big.

My first reaction was—I want to hug him.

Instead I held out my hand and introduced Jagger and myself. Mr. Niski's handshake was weak to say the least, and suddenly I felt sorry for him and very glad my mother had "suggested" that I help him.

We followed him into a tiny studio apartment with brown plaid furniture, a kitchen table that would only fit two, and a radio playing "White Christmas" by Bing Crosby. The place smelled very much like my Uncle Walt's bedroom. Not an unpleasant scent, merely an elderly scent. I was thinking Old Spice.

I explained to Mr. Niski, who now wanted me to call him Lenny, about how I'd read the article. He'd told us that he'd worked in a factory all his life, making rubber tires. Never married, but had two sisters and five nieces and two nephews. I felt as if I'd known Lenny all *my* life because I knew hundreds of older Polish men exactly like Leonard Niski.

I noticed there was no Christmas tree in Lenny's apartment, but he assured me there was a huge one in the dining room of the complex, where he went to eat each night if he didn't want to cook for himself.

"Mostly can only eat swoup anyway."

I winced again and looked at Jagger who'd remained silent the entire time.

Lenny must have noticed too. "You with her?" he asked, as if Jagger had come in off the street by himself. "Wife?"

I choked on nothing. "Um. No. We . . . sometimes we—"

Jagger interrupted with "Work together" as if he was afraid I was going to say, "Sometimes we have hot, wild unforgettable sex." With that he started to question Lenny and before I knew it, we had a case to work on. Lenny, being a very organized bachelor, had found all the bills and paperwork for his denture work and now had a sparkle in his eyes.

He was going to get his teeth.

On the way out, Lenny gave me a hug, shook hands with Jagger, and said, "All I want for Christmas is—"

I laughed. "I know, Len, your two front teeth."

He gave me an odd look. "I was going to say to eat my sister Helen's baked ham without having to stick it in the bwender."

I nodded and smiled, or at least pretended to smile.

Once in the SUV, I heard Jagger mutter, "Your two front teeth?"

Choosing to ignore him to save some dignity on my part, I said, "Drop me by my place. I feel a toothache coming on and need a dentist appointment."

From the corner of my eye I could see a slight grin on Jagger's face, and knew—I'd done good.

"Oh, my God, Suga'! What's the matter with your tooth?" my roommate Goldie Perlman asked. Goldie was a six-foot-tall, darling guy who bought his Armani in the best of men's departments—and the most fashionable of women's departments. He put me to shame when he dressed female. Don't even get me started on his flair for putting on makeup.

Nevertheless he was a whiz at investigating. He was also the loving partner of our other roomie, Miles Scarpello RN, who worked the OR at Saint Greg's, the hospital where I had my career meltdown several months ago.

"Relax, Gold. My tooth is fine. I'm working a case." I sat on the white couch and watched Jagger head into the kitchen, where I knew he'd help himself to a bottle of Coors. No need to wait on Jagger. He'd do whatever the hell he wanted to anyway.

"If you really had a toothache, you'd need to go see my doctor. Dr. Francis Perlman, no relation, but a wonder at teeth." Goldie smiled.

"Your pearly whites are spectacular, Gold, but I need to go see a Dr. Santana."

"Elfin Santana?"

It actually didn't surprise me that Goldie knew the "in question" fraudulent dentist. Gold got around and that was partly why he was a star investigator at Scarpello and Tonelli. "You know him?"

"Word on the street is that he can give you the best deal on Da Vinci porcelain veneers. Cheap."

"And probably hot."

Goldie gasped. "Several of my friends have gone to Elfin and had no problems."

"Really?" I settled back on the couch and petted Spanky, our joint-custody Shih tzu–poodle mix's squirrel-sized head.

"Yeah," Goldie said, then paused. "Wait a minute."

I sat upright, setting Spanky on a pillow so he wouldn't fall. "What?"

Just then Jagger walked back into the room and handed Goldie a glass of Chardonnay, me a bottle of Coors (I didn't drink out of cans, but liked a bottle instead of a glass), and a Coors for himself. Like some freaking clairvoyant waiter. What a guy.

Goldie took a sip of his wine then said, "Now I remember. Marty Poston. He never got his veneers finished. We all figured he couldn't afford to have the bottom teeth done, but he swore he'd paid for them and never *got* them."

· 2 ·

I looked from Jagger to Goldie. "Marty Poston never got his bottom veneers done by Dr. Santana?"

Goldie shook his head as he sipped.

"Hmm. I'll just bet there's something fishy going on here. I'm guessing Santana doesn't do some of the work he submits claims for." I looked at Jagger.

No head shaking. No grin. No smile.

A nonreaction by Jagger was sometimes just as good as an "atta girl." Not being too proud, I took what I could get.

"Okay. So we have someplace to start." I sipped my drink and looked at Jagger.

"Where?" he asked. Looking at him, I once again thought of how I should have taken Body Language 101.

"Well, we get into Santana's office and check out his files. Then we make a few calls to patients to see if they've had all the work done that he's sent in claims for, and Santana gets busted while Lenny gets his choppers by Christmas Eve and enjoys his ham."

Goldie looked at me.

"Don't ask." I waved my hand and noticed Jagger glaring at me. "What?" I sighed. "What now?" I refused to look at him and instead focused on the all white room, Miles's impeccable taste, and the gold clock ticking on the mantel.

"Nothing. Sounds like a plan. A damn good one."

I looked back. My grin went from the clichéd ear-to-ear until I noticed him still staring as if he had more to say.

"Go ahead," I said.

"Damn good plan. How do you figure you're going to initiate it?"

Details. There had to be an easy way. But *no* way was I going to tell Jagger that I didn't have any ideas at the moment. To stall, I took a long, slow sip of my beer. Then I cleared my throat and started to cough. I kept that up for a few minutes longer while I brainstormed.

Jagger was still staring.

One thing I figured was that if I went in as a patient, I wouldn't have much time or opportunity to snoop. "Okay. Here goes. Now realize that this is only a start. A beginning plan. A—"

"You have to get a job working for Santana and look in the files," Jagger said.

Goldie's eyes widened, and I think he gasped.

The reason I wasn't sure was because *I* had gasped at the same time.

"You are nuts if you think I'm going to . . ."

"I have to wear *what* to work this week?" I asked as I looked at the dentist glaring at me from across the desk, which was covered with a miniature Christmas village the likes of Hope Valley. It even included lit-tle, teeny, tiny lampposts and mailboxes and kids skating on glassy-looking ponds.

The thought of the damn outfit aside, it was a perfect Christmas gift that Doc Santana was looking for temporary help.

He chuckled. Sounded as if it came straight from a Santa CD. Very authentic. Despite his suggestion of work attire, I kinda liked the guy or at least liked his holiday spirit and dress, although I wondered what his patients thought about his red suit, with white trim, and his black boots.

Too bad he was a crook.

"Pauline. Can I call you Holline? You know, for Holly?"

"No."

He shook his head. "Too bad. Well, I'll call you Ms. Pauline Holly, and I insist you wear the Christmas outfit. That is, if you want the job. While my regular girl is off on her honeymoon, I only need you for the next week."

I nodded and thanked Saint T for the early "gift," and decided it was in my best "eternal rest" interest not to mention the outfit.

"What if it doesn't fit, Dr. Santana? The stupid . . . the outfit that is. Then can I wear my scrubs? I have red and green ones with little tiny squiggles that could pass as reindeer on them. Real cute. And professional-looking."

Dr. Santana leaned back in his black chair, tugged on his real white beard, adjusted his wire-rimmed glasses, and said, "It'll fit. Amazingly enough, you and she are about the same size."

I contemplated eating an entire batch of high-calorie pierogies tonight.

Dr. Santana got up and walked to the door. I shook my head as I watched him go.

How could you take a guy, who is going to drill your teeth, seriously when he was dressed like that? Then again with the never-ending Christmas music around here, and the festive decorations, he probably put a lot of his patients at ease.

"Be right back, Ms. Holly."

I rolled my eyes, sank back in my chair, and looked around.

His office was by no means fancy. Actually it was very homey. He had pictures of what I guessed was his family—including seven children. Seven! There was a fish tank on the shelf filled with little goldfish, the inexpensive ones. No pretentious saltwater, thirty-bucks-per-fish kind. On the wall near the window was a pedestal with a gigantic white tooth on it, and draped across it was the old-fashioned kind of toothbrush—big enough to clean King Kong's teeth.

Sitting there, I chuckled to myself.

Then I thought of Lenny and Marty.

I sat straight up in my furor as the doc walked in, carrying the dreaded outfit, covered in plastic from the cleaners.

"Freshly cleaned. Take it home and try it on. Then I'll see you at nine tomorrow. Don't be late. My wife always comes in at eight forty-five with hot apple cider and donuts during this season."

I cringed and said "Sounds delicious, I'm very punctual" as I took the stupid outfit from his outstretched hands.

Amazing what I would stoop to for a case.

* * *

Since I'd spent about a half hour tugging, pulling, yanking, and bending over until I was dizzy to hide most of the cleavage that the Miss Santa outfit revealed, I was nearly late for hot cider, donuts, and getting a load of Mrs. Claus . . . er . . . Mrs. Santana.

"My, dearie, you look lovely. Elfin has such nice taste in receptionists," his wife said as she smiled at me, her damn blue eyes twinkling from behind *her* wire-rimmed glasses. Yes, she wore a Mrs. Santa Claus outfit that looked way too real on her. No cleavage involved, and the length went down to her ankles.

It was hard to believe she was married to a crook and probably helping him out. I mean, I really got a motherly feeling from her, and I was usually an expert on *those* kinds of feelings—having been raised by Stella Sokol, Mother of the World.

After Mrs. S gave me a crash course in Receptionist for Dummies 101, I watched her bustle about the office as I sat down at the desk, sipped on hot cider, which I hated, and realized that Mrs. Claus/Santana didn't seem flustered about her husband's choice in receptionists or, more importantly, the sexy outfits he had them wear.

Clearly that's why *seven* kids.

I yanked at the bodice of my top again and pulled up enough white fluff to cover some exposed flesh. Before Mrs. Santana could say another word, the door opened and in walked a couple that appeared to be in their seventies. The guy winked at me. She nudged him and chuckled.

"Merry Christmas, dolly. Where's the other one?" he said, leaning over way too far.

I backed up and said, "Honeymoon. And you are?"

"The Shepherds." He chuckled again. "Appropriate for this time of year. Huh?"

I mentally shook my head and looked at the appointment book to see that there was, in fact, two appointments for them. As I contemplated the strangeness of working here at the North Pole, I told them both to sit and wait, grabbed their charts and took them to stick in the holders outside each of the exam rooms.

Just then the back door, used by employees only, swung open. In walked a guy. But not just any guy. A hot, sexy guy about an inch taller than Jagger but with hair the color of spun gold. Wow. He looked at me.

I looked at him.

One of us sighed.

"Hey. I'm Jay North, dental hygienist extraordinaire." He laughed.

I couldn't help but join him. He had on jeans and a brown leather jacket with a lambs' wool collar. Made a great first impression.

Nothing Christmasy about this guy. Thank God.

"Pauline Sokol, temp receptionist."

"I see you are about the same size as the receptionist, Holly Lightly."

Holly? I should have known. I nodded and felt as if I stood there naked. Okay, maybe just wishful thinking.

Dr. Santana came out of one of the exam rooms. "Oh, morning, Jay. I see you met Ms. Holly."

"Pauline," I corrected.

Jay winked at me and took off his jacket to reveal a dynamite chest of muscles honed to perfection. However, covering said muscles was a green felt shirt, and before I could blink, he'd donned an elf hat—which amazingly made him look even sexier.

Even though it bordered on perverted, he looked *hot*.

The doctor left us standing alone in the hallway.

Speechless, I could only force a smile.

"I know," Jay said and put his arm around me. "We do this each year for him." He nodded toward the doctor's office.

All I could think was, his arm is around me. How pathetic was I? Slowly I eased free, so I could get some work done.

"Doc grew up in an orphanage. Some children's home in Mexico, where his American mother'd left him. Thus the name. Never had a real Christmas so it means a lot to him." With that he turned and walked into Exam Room One.

I could only stare and nod. At least the last name now made sense, and despite my belief that the doctor was as crooked as a candy cane top, I felt sorry for him.

When I heard a tapping sound coming from Santana's office, I got up and stuck my head in the doorway. "Um, sorry to interrupt—"

Dear old Elfin was hammering a wooden horse together.

Oh . . . my . . . god! This was becoming more like a Tim Burton version of *The Nightmare Before Christmas*. Orphanage or not—this was all way too weird.

It's all right, I told myself. Everything is just coincidental. I got the Shepherds settled in the exam chairs, and decided it was time to take a peek at the files. Mrs. Santana wasn't around. Maybe she had some shopping to do for her seven offspring—unless their presents were always homemade.

Back at my desk, I looked around to make sure the coast was clear, and bent over to pull out the desk drawer where a section of recent files were kept. I took out A–L and set them on my desk. First I had to get myself acquainted with how the files were set up and what they covered. I started with Acorn—and didn't even think twice about the name.

My nursing background did, in fact, help with my investigating. Very quickly I found out how to read the treatments each patient had received and check the billing section to see what their insurance covered. Before the next appointment showed up, I had a list of ten patients to call later in the day.

Damn. This was going to be a piece of cake.

The door swung open to the sounds of "Jingle Bells" and a guy walked in. Wow. I thought Jay was a looker. This patient was built a tad better, had aviator sunglasses on, a moustache, and also wore leather, but black not brown. He had the same shade of blond hair as Jay, but wore it much longer and under a baseball cap. Guess Jay kept his short to be more professional, and maybe to keep it out of patients' mouths.

I swallowed and tried to make my voice come out steady, but to no avail. "Um. Hi. May I . . . may I help you?" I had to go on a date soon. *Real soon.* Suddenly the mistletoe crept into my thoughts. White berries. Teeny white berries. I felt my face burn as the patient came closer.

"Name?" What difference did a guy's name make when he looked like this one?

He hesitated.

I looked at the appointment book to see a new patient listed. A Mr. John Winters at nine forty-five. "Mr. Winters?"

He nodded.

"A toothache?"

"Uh-hah."

I reached for the clipboard with the new-patient-chart information form on it. "Please fill this out, sir. The doctor will then be with you shortly." I think I sighed, but Mr. Winters politely didn't notice or at least comment.

He walked to the chair by the Christmas tree and sat down.

Yes, I did stare at his butt on his trip over. Snug jeans worn out in strategic places hugged a firm, muscular backside.

Wait a minute!

Oh . . . my . . . god.

It looked *familiar*.

· 3 ·

Through clenched teeth I muttered, "Jagger. Jagger!"

He didn't even look up but kept writing.

Damn. Jagger was a master of disguise as evidenced by several of the other cases we'd worked. However, I had also been wrong about him a few times and accosted innocent victims, thinking they were Jagger in costume. This time I'd be more cautious—although I'd bet my next paycheck I was correct. I was getting better and better at recognizing him.

I got up, walked toward Mr. Winters and pretended to fix a few ornaments on the tree.

He didn't budge.

I tried to look at the handwriting—oh yeah, I'd always noted the small things about Jagger. But I couldn't see the form too well, and upside down it really didn't look that similar. For a few seconds I just stood there to see if any pheromones would waft in my direction.

Mistletoe, I thought and felt rather hot inside.

Ah-ha! There was my proof. This *was* Jagger in disguise!

"How's it going, Mr. Winters?" I asked, deciding I'd play his game to see why the hell he was here.

He looked up and held the clipboard out toward me. "Fine."

With shaky hands (this because of the stupid mistletoe thought) I managed to take it and head back to my desk, where I sat down with a thud. I looked up and smiled.

Jay came to the doorway. "Hey, Pauline, the Shepherds are done. I'll take the next one in for you."

I held out the form, then said, "Hold it. Let me fix the chart." I stuck it into a new-patient folder and then gave it to Jay while the Shepherds came bustling out, eating donuts and sipping on hot cider.

Could Mrs. Claus be far behind?

I watched "Mr. Winters" follow Jay through the doorway and mumbled, "I hope you have a cavity. A Grand Canyon one."

After I'd successfully ushered out the Shepherds— once the hubby got tired of talking to my chest, I might add—two more patients came in. One was sent into Exam Room Two and the other sat quietly in the waiting room. I noted how no one seemed very nervous waiting in a dentist's office.

Me, I'd be kneading and rekneading my fingers over and over. I hated dental work—even with Novocain. Of course, my old dentist, Dr. Scklagen, never even offered us Novocain for fillings. He'd say, "This doesn't hurt," while my father, who always took us kids there, would stand by and watch.

I often thought Daddy looked as if he wanted to slug the dentist. Thank goodness for fluoride.

I tucked the list of patient names and phone numbers from the files into the pocket of my skirt—which barely covered my thighs. Luckily I'd had green tights at home to at least give myself some modesty. Geez. Oddly enough I didn't miss the fact that I wasn't getting paid for this investigation—the season of giving must have hit me smack in the face.

I had to go see Lenny and get more info from him. Jay would show the remaining patients, including "Mr. Winters," out.

Thank goodness it was nearly lunchtime. I'd make a little home visit to Lenny—despite my outfit. Then again, if he were a long-term patient of the doc, he probably would *expect* me to be dressed as a Victoria's Secret Santa girl a few days before Christmas.

"I'm on a fixed income. Not buying what you are selling," the disembodied voice said through the intercom.

"It's me, Lenny. Pauline." I shivered, standing outside in the cold. To top it off, it had started snowing when I left the office for my lunch break. Since the doc gave me an hour, I grabbed a turkey sub from the nearby deli and headed to talk to Lenny.

"Pauwine who?"

I curled my lips. "Pauline Sokol. It's freezing out here. Let me in, Lenny."

"Don't think I know any Sokow. I'm on a fixed income—"

I'll fix your income, I thought, but didn't want to sound mean during the holidays. Actually with my Catholic-school induced conscience, I never wanted to sound mean. But Lenny was becoming a real pip.

"Please buzz me up, Lenny. I'm the one who is going to help you get your teeth before Christmas."

Buzz. Buzz.

Thank you Saint T.

When I got to the front door of Lenny's place, I juggled my sub and bottle of water and managed to knock on the door.

It opened slightly and Lenny poked his head out— which landed smack at my chest level.

Oh, Geez.

"Hey, Lenny."

He stared at me a few minutes. If he mentioned his fixed income, I was going to bop him on the head with my water bottle.

Slowly the door opened. "Hi, Miss Sokow. Are you working for Dr. Santana?"

Suddenly Leonard Niski sounded like a genius. I figured maybe he was one of those savants who was a whiz at math but everyday life kinda escaped him. Or, he was a typical sweet old Polish guy who eeked out a living and got ripped off along the way.

"Yeah, Len, I'm working for the doc. Are you hungry?" I made myself at home and walked into the kitchen section of his tiny place. When I went to the table and pulled out the chair, a fat black cat sprung up and flew past me. "Oh!"

"Midnight Clear. She's very particular," Lenny said, sitting down next to me.

About what? I wondered, but didn't really want to know. "Do you want some of my turkey sub? There's plenty."

He eyed the sandwich but shook his head. Poor guy was probably thinking it'd be hard to chew.

"I think the bread is very soft." I ripped off a piece of the sandwich and held it out toward him.

Lenny gingerly took the sub as if it were some poisonous snake. Then he fiddled with it, trying to chew on the right side—without luck—then the left. I stared down at my own food so I didn't have to watch the painful sight of Leonard Niski trying to eat sans his front teeth. Actually, from what I could see, he was missing more than just the front ones. Maybe about five in a row.

"So, tell me, Lenny, how long ago did you pay for your teeth?"

With a piece of bread poking out through the gapping opening, he managed to say, "Thwee months."

Wow. "Okay. You know, I am working just this week at Dr. Santana's office to see what I can find out. I have to tell you, though, all the patients I've seen today seem very happy with him."

"Hot cwider and donuts will do that to you."

"I'm not sure that menu would take away the fact

that I thought my dentist was a crook, Len. I'd be more cautious and suspicious and not act as if he were a real-life Santa Claus."

Lenny merely stared at me.

For a few minutes we ate in silence. I figured he had enough to do to get his lunch masticated, and I could observe dear Lenny in the interim.

He chewed and nibbled as best he could, but what started to bother me was that Lenny kept looking to his right side as if someone were there.

"Midnight Clear is in the living room," I said. "I can see her off to the left curled up on that brown stuffed chair."

Lenny looked at me as if I was an idiot savant only minus the savant part. "Who cares?"

Oops. "Well . . . I thought you were looking for her. Never mind." I shut up and went back to observing.

Again Lenny looked to the right and this time mumbled something. Great. Either my star client was talking to himself or he really saw someone there.

Suddenly Leonard Niski was not a reliable font of information who could help his own case.

What the hell? "Len, are you sure you ordered teeth from Dr. Santana?"

His eyes darkened. His forehead wrinkled. His lips curled.

I held on to the table but looked across the room in case an emergency exit was needed—fast.

"You read about it in the newspaper, Ms. Sokol."

As if *that* would make it true.

Once I'd excused myself from my lunch "date," I hurried out and into my car, where I promptly called

Jagger and left a message that I thought one Leonard Niski might be missing a bit more than just teeth.

When I got back to the office, I sat at my desk and pulled the Niski chart out.

Sure enough, Lenny was correct. He'd been measured and fitted for a dental bridge—which would surely help him eat much better than he could now. So it was true. I fiddled through the pages but part of the chart seemed to be missing!

Great.

Had someone been trying to cover up the fact that Lenny, in fact, had been ripped off? There was an insurance claim submitted and from what I could tell, the claim had been paid—to Dr. Elfin Santana.

"Miss?"

I looked up from Lenny's chart to see Jagger as "Mr. Winters" standing at cleavage-viewing level. I leaned back and smiled. "You're here again?"

"The doc hadn't finished, and I needed to go do something."

Mid teeth cleaning?

"I'm back now," he added.

Yeah, to spy on me.

Jagger could make a living disguising his voice. If I didn't know him so well, and that pheromone thing and all, he probably would have fooled me again.

"Oh. Fine." I looked at the appointment book. "Someone penciled your name in." That annoyed me since I wasn't informed, and I was supposed to be the receptionist. Even in these fake jobs, I took my work seriously. If nothing else, Pauline Sokol was a damn good worker.

"Mr. Winters" was staring at me.

My insides suddenly warmed and knotted all at the same time. The anger started to well inside me. I was about to let him have it, when Jay popped his head out from the back.

"Hey, Miss Holly," Jay said. He laughed. "Send in Winters before the two o'clock filling shows up."

I took Winters's chart, handed it to Jay, and whispered, "Even in this North Pole office, it's Pauline."

Jay laughed.

I joined him.

And "Mr. Winters" looked pissed.

Good.

The afternoon got busier than this morning because it was after-school hours. Damn if the kids all didn't look thrilled to be here, especially when each one walked out of the exam room carrying a little Christmas-wrapped gift.

I had to shake my head at that.

For some reason, I felt as if this case was not going to be the piece of cake that I thought earlier—more like fruitcake, with darling Lenny as the main ingredient.

Jagger had once again mysteriously disappeared, and I half expected "Mr. Winters" or some other Jagger–disguised patient to pop in that afternoon. But he never came back.

After I cleaned up my desk for the day and made sure the last patient had left, I grabbed my coat (the long gray one, to hide as much of my "outfit" as

possible) and said goodbye to Jay, the doctor, and
Mrs. Santana, who had a knack for popping in and
out of the office all day.

So she could assist in the crimes?

· 4 ·

I walked to my car in the parking lot, glad the snow
had stopped and there was only a dusting on the
ground. I hated to drive in the slippery mess. But as
I looked around, I had to admit it was like a winter
wonderland.

The Santana dental practice was located in—what
else?—a huge Victorian house, with sparkling windows of tiny white lights, snowcapped turrets, pink,
violet, and mauve painted details, and a sign shaped
like a Christmas tree that held Dr. Santana's name.

It was hard to believe this Christmas-addicted man
was dishonest; however, I'd learned in this business
that no one was squeaky clean—least of all the quiet,
innocent-looking ones.

When I stopped looking at the decor to stick my
key in the lock, I felt someone come up behind me.

Suddenly my body zoomed into heightened alert.

Adrenaline shot through my system.

Self-defense techniques surged through my brain.

I held my keys with one sticking out of my fist in
case I needed to shove them at my attacker's eyes.

Before I could touch the now unlocked door handle, someone grabbed my arm.

"No!" I swung around and held the keys toward . . .
"Mr. Winter's" face!

"You!" I pulled my fist back and eased out of his hold. "Are you crazy?" My voice sounded surprisingly calm despite the fact that my gut felt as if I'd swallowed a gallon of barium and it stuck mid-stomach and, oops, I'd nearly gouged out Jagger's eyes.

He stood for a few seconds looking at me. And when I saw him grin, something snapped inside me. Without a thought, I reached up and took his face in my hands. Before he had a chance to pull back (thank God he didn't) I stood on my tiptoes and planted a kiss on his lips!

I was not sure who was more surprised, me or "Mr. Winters." However, he hesitated, kissed a bit longer, then pulled back.

"What the hell was that all about? You in the habit of kissing strangers? Don't you know how dangerous that could be?"

Now *I* grinned. Dangerous, yes, but remarkably so. I looked him in the eye. "Yes, I do, *Jagger.*"

For several glorious minutes, Jagger was speechless. Finally he said, "Okay."

And I wanted to hug him.

Ever the guy, though, he leaned closer and said, "Lesson one-o-one in self-defense. Never trust anyone and let your guard down like that again." His lips came dangerously close to mine.

My eyes widened. He sounded so lethal. Threatening. Sexy.

And was he talking about my real safety . . . or the kiss?

"It's just . . . I . . . stop sneaking up on me. You do that on every damn case!" This time I steadied myself with the car door behind me.

But Jagger looked so delicious and harmless—two qualities I realized I couldn't trust in a guy.

So I pulled my shoulders straight and held on to the door handle to keep my wits about me.

Right then I felt less vulnerable.

"That's a hell of a lot better . . ." he said as he turned to leave, then over his shoulder said, "*Sherlock.*"

Sherlock? *Sherlock*? Why did I melt when he called me that?

It took several minutes for me to revive myself, then I started yelling at Jagger before he could make it to his SUV. Damn it. I was annoyed that he'd just given me a lesson in self-preservation—and he'd probably been at the office to make sure I was safe—and then the kiss and *poof,* he was gone.

I tried to tell myself he had good intentions—about the making-sure-I-was-safe part.

Across the parking lot, the lights of his SUV blinked on, the engine purred, and the vehicle soon zoomed past me—with Jagger looking straight at me.

And damned if he wasn't grinning.

All the way home, I told myself that I was going to get even with him, knowing full well that that was probably wishful thinking. But there would come a day when I would pull one over on him—I'd start my novena tonight to make that happen in the upcoming new year—and not feel one iota of guilt for involving St. Theresa in my revenge scheme. She was probably used to it when it came to Jagger anyway.

And I'd had a damn good start today when I'd taken him by surprise with my kiss.

I was in such a festive, holiday mood.

* * *

After I'd soaked in a tub of Goldie's jasmine-scented bubble bath, I dressed in my jeans and a black long-sleeve T-shirt, stuck on my fluffy red slippers, decided to forgo any makeup, and headed to the kitchen.

There was a note on the fridge from my roomies that they were off on a romantic dinner at the exclusive, expensive Madeline's restaurant on the banks of the Connecticut River.

I leaned against the door and sighed.

Ain't love grand?

Ding. Dong.

"Saved by the bell," I said to Spanky, who was now barking like the proper five-pound attack dog that he should be.

I almost said through the door, "Go away. I'm on a fixed income and can't buy anything."

I swung open the door . . . and cursed.

First, I cursed because Jagger stood there.

Second, I cursed because earlier he'd thought I needed his protection and now had the nerve to stand there oh-so-lusciously nonchalant.

And third, I cursed because I noticed my reflection in Miles's gold-leaf trimmed mirror near the door. No *makeup*.

Jagger had brought a pizza and six-pack of Coors in bottles. Half cheese, my favorite, and half mushroom and sausage for him. No call first. No are you hungry. No nothing.

The perfect meal.

After I took a few bites of pizza, having realized I

was actually starving, I looked at Jagger. "Saw Lenny today on my lunch break."

"I know." He took a sip of his beer and really didn't have a smartass look on his face. More a normal Jagger look. Well, truthfully, sometimes the two were indistinguishable.

"Why does that not surprise me?" I really didn't want an answer so I continued, "He's nuts, Jagger."

Jagger set his beer bottle down and wrinkled his forehead. "Come again?"

Men that look like Jagger should not use those kinds of multi-use terms with women like me. I suppressed my teen mentality and said, "Yeah. He sees people that aren't there. I stayed with him through lunch, and, unfortunately, I think he's crazy."

"Well, you should know."

I slammed my pizza onto the plate sending a wad of cheese flying onto the floor. Spanky was there at the speed of light to gobble it up. I looked at Jagger. "He'll probably have indigestion tonight because of you."

Suddenly Jagger smiled. It really was a genuine smile. Not a grin.

As I said "What?" he touched my hand.

"What I meant, Sherlock, was that if anyone could diagnose Lenny's illness, it would be you with your nursing background and talent for noticing things with your sharp observational skills."

Christmas had come early to Pauline Sokol tonight. Against my saner judgment, I sighed.

For a few seconds I remained still with Jagger's touch, and then decided we only had a few days to get Lenny his teeth and, now I was guessing, some mental health care. So, I eased my arm free. "Thank . . . thank you."

Jagger nodded.

"I looked in his chart, and it does confirm his teeth issues, but part of the chart is missing."

"Hmm. Interesting." Jagger finished his piece of pizza, breaking up part of the crust and giving it to Spanky on the sly as if I couldn't see.

"He's going to get fat," I said.

"Walk him more."

I had to laugh. What kind of guy remains so mysterious, sexy, smart, and still has a soft spot for a teeny, tiny dog? "I'm going to call a list of patients that I found today to see if all their work was done."

Jagger nodded and lifted the pizza box. When he took out one of my plain-cheese slices and chivalrously set it on *my* plate, I had to get out of the room—or the kitchen table would be used for something *other* than eating pizza.

"Thank you so much, Mrs. Pinefield. And you have a wonderful Christmas too." I set down the phone and looked up to see Jagger standing in the hallway, holding Spanky.

"He looks as if he's gained a pound already. Miles and Goldie are going to kill you."

Jagger merely sat down on the white sofa near me. "What did you find out?" Spanky curled up on Jagger's lap.

I rolled my eyes at the little traitor and said, "Well, seems as if our doc is not really Santa Claus after all. After making a few phone calls to patients, I smell fraud in about half of these cases. I guess only half are fraudulent, so it's not too obvious and helps the doc not get caught. Or so he thought. The others all seem fine. All work done and accounted for."

Jagger rubbed his finger across Spanky's little head. The damn dog purred like a cat.

"Tomorrow when I go to work, I'm going to recheck their charts and compare what I learned from talking to the patients with what is written in their charts. That'll tell me if the insurance paid up. We may just have Santana in jail by the twenty-fifth."

Then I thought of his seven kids.

· 5 ·

After Jagger had helped clean up—what a guy—and left last night, I'd headed off to bed to get up bright and early for work and, in fact, made it in just in time for hot cider and a donut. I had actually started to like the stuff.

I almost choked on a bite when I noticed Mrs. Santana, dressed to the holiday hilt, give the doc a big hug as he came into the reception area. "You are my Santa, Elfin. And the kids are so excited again this year. No one is a better father and makes this holiday so special as you."

I managed an "Excuse me" and hurried to the bathroom where I washed the cider and donut out of my mouth. Being in this environment, I did everything to avoid cavities. As I looked in the mirror, I tried not to think of the touching scene I'd just witnessed.

The man could be arrested by Christmas Day and

those kids would be fatherless as they opened their presents.

Tears formed in my eyes, but I sucked them back and told myself that crime is crime. No one is above the law. Sure it was a tough sentiment to swallow at this time of the year, but I did and promptly went out to resume my investigation.

The reception area was filled with smiling, happy, laughing, and even singing patients, which made my intent to prove Dr. Santana a crook all the more difficult. But after I ushered them in to Jay, one by one, I stuck my nose in the five charts of the folks I'd talked to on the phone last night.

Each and every one had been charged for work that they said was not done. All involved dentures too, which made proving this case much easier. To give the doc the benefit of the doubt, especially after his two youngest (twin boys) came in "just to see our daddy and have him ask Santa for a rocking horse," I checked and rechecked several more charts until my vision blurred.

Finally it was lunchtime. I closed up the reception area, declined a lunch offer from Jay (although I'd much rather have been eating with the "eye candy" instead of what I had to do), and hurried out to my car.

After I got in the car, I called Jagger.

"Hey." Jagger's voice, even on a cell phone, always had the power to cause a hitch in my breath.

"We've got him," I said. "I've made copies of the files for you to take to Lieutenant Shatley."

The lieutenant was a buddy of Jagger's, his main connection to the local police, and, I'm sure, the reason

Jagger himself didn't do time for some of his unortho-
dox means of investigation.

"Meet me at our place now," Jagger said.

Pressed for time, I didn't even let the "our place"
cause a phone-induced orgasm. I acted very professional and headed to "our place"—Dunkin' Donuts
where I gave him the files and turned to go.

"Atta girl, Sherlock."

The words usually made me feel on top of the
world, but after seeing the eyes of the Santana twins
sparkle at the mention of their daddy—I felt like crap.

Some days fighting crime was more exhausting
and emotional than nursing.

"Wesolych Swiat, Bozego Narodzenia!" my mother
shouted to Goldie and Miles as they came in the door.
Then she explained the greeting meant Merry Christmas in Polish.

Both hugged her, looked up at the mistletoe, and
kissed her on the cheeks.

"We hang that on *Wigilia* to ward off evil," she said.

I choked on nothing and thought, *She has no idea
how deliciously evil it could be.*

"Go get some beer, Pauline," she said to me. "And
get a shot and beer for your roommates too."

Goldie, all decked out in a sparkling silver-and-red
dress with silver panty hose, chuckled. Tonight his
hair was styled in a sexy, Meg Ryan kind of messy
look with golden strands covering one eye. I could
only imagine how it made the ever-sophisticated Miles
feel. He, too, was all decked out, but in a suave navy
suit with red tie.

"I'll get some Chardonnay for us," I whispered and winked at them.

Goldie grabbed my arm. "Did she put condoms in our Christmas stockings again this year?"

We all laughed. "I'm sure my mother only has the best intentions in mind. Even if they are ridiculous sometimes."

Miles looked into the dining room. "Who's the extra plate for?"

"Polish tradition. We set it on *Wigilia* for an absent family member or unexpected guest."

They looked at each other.

"Stop it you two. This year my mother *swore* she did not invite 'Mister' Jagger."

Goldie smiled. "Phew. Hey, I hear they busted the Santa-wielding dentist."

My insides knotted. "I know." Tears formed in my eyes. "This case doesn't sit right with me, though."

Before I could get our wine, the doorbell rang. I looked around the room to see all my siblings and their families, Uncle Walt, Daddy, Mother, and my buddies. Who the heck . . . oh, no.

"May I help you?" I heard my mother say.

She wouldn't ask "Mister" Jagger that.

"Merwy Cwistmas."

I froze on the spot then defrosted fast enough to hurry to the door. "Oh, hi, Lenny."

"I didn't get my tweeth yet, Miss Sokol. Tomowow is ham day."

"I know, Len. The cops are shorthanded during the holidays and it seems your case is going to take a bit longer. I'm so so sorry."

Just as I said it, Jagger walked up behind Lenny. "Merry Christmas everyone. Going in, Len?"

My mother grabbed his arm. "Of course, we have our extra place set."

I leaned toward Jagger. "Oops. That means there's no room for you."

"Miles," I heard my mother say, "get another place setting for Mr. Jagger, please."

And she didn't sound at all surprised that he'd shown up.

He took my arm and walked me to the other side of the porch, where we stood for a few seconds in the freezing cold. Snow had started to fall, making the festive atmosphere of *Wigilia* all the more joyful.

"Let's go in, Jagger."

"Look, Shatley just called. Seems there's been a mistake."

I felt my knees buckle.

"I worked all night with him to find out that the doc was telling the truth. Seems old Lenny really is a bit off kilter."

"Oh . . . my . . . god. He lied to me? To the newspaper? Made fools of us?"

Jagger nodded. "The good news is, Santana is home with his family and wanted me to pass along that he harbors no ill feelings toward you or Len."

I shut my eyes for a second and thanked Saint Theresa for that. "I feel horrible."

"Don't. Lenny did a job on all of us. Even Shatley believed his story. Turns out that in the other cases, the guy who makes the dentures was hospitalized and never told Santana. All along he thought his patients were all set with their choppers."

"So no fraud. But what about Lenny?"

"Jay was there when Lenny was fitted with dentures."

Christmas was going to be very melancholy for me this year.

"Let's go inside," Jagger said.

I felt like throwing myself into the snow to freeze for punishment.

Once inside, I noticed Goldie walk down the hallway, headed for the dining room.

"Oh, Gold," I said, taking his arm. "What ever happened to your friend Marty? About his veneers?"

"Geez, Suga', with all the Christmas shopping, I forgot to tell you. The rat lied to us about them. He really couldn't afford top and bottom work but didn't want to be embarrassed, so he lied about paying for both. The shit."

"So no fraud again. Thanks." I patted his arm and stood in the hallway looking at Lenny.

Maybe my anger was palpable enough and that's what made Lenny look up.

He waved his hands in the air. "Pweeze, let me say something."

Daddy nodded at Lenny then held the *Oplatek,* a blessed sheet of bread to represent communion that we shared with each other on *Wigilia,* in his hand. "Go ahead, Mr. Niski."

Lenny stood up. "I . . . feel terrwible. I've lied to you all and mostly to Pauwine. I'm sworry that the dentist got awessted. He didn't do anythwing."

I stepped forward. "Did you misplace your bridgework, Len?"

He nodded. A tear ran down his cheek, landing on

his way-too-big white shirt that was tucked into over-sized brown pants. I noticed he was wearing his fuzzy slippers too. "I'm on a fixed income," he whispered.

"And your insurance wouldn't pay for another set so you thought you could get one—"

"My friend came up with the idea. He made me cover it up by taking part of my chart when Jay didn't see." Lenny looked to his side.

I cringed.

As my heart tore in two, Jagger took me by the shoulders, which seemed to help a little. Poor Leonard Niski, a forgotten, down-on-his-luck mentally ill man who just wanted to eat his sister's ham tomorrow.

Ding. Dong.

I looked around the room, as did everyone else. No one was missing. Jagger let go of me and turned to open the door.

"Ho! Ho! Ho!"

My nephews' and nieces' eyes widened and some squealed with delight—actually it may have been Goldie who squealed. A jolly man, dressed in Santa garb (but looking nothing like Santana . . . hmm) handed Jagger a tiny, gold-wrapped gift.

To Leonard Niski it said. From Santa.

I couldn't move as Jagger took the box to Lenny and helped him open it since the poor guy's fingers shook so.

"My tweeth," Lenny whispered, then shouted, "My tweeth!"

I turned around to see "Santa" gone.

My family began yelling, talking, singing, and passing every bowl and platter on the table around. Lenny was so excited that he stuck his bridge in upside down, but corrected it when Goldie pointed it out.

Instantly a warm feeling passed through me, and I felt as if this Christmas wasn't going to be a bust. Lenny had gotten his Christmas gift after all. . . .

Suddenly Jagger swung me around and leaned forward. His lips touched mine softly, gently, then—hungrily . . . and just like that, I'd gotten a damn fab Christmas gift as well.

I looked up at the tiny white mistletoe berries . . . and smiled. Maybe the druids were onto something. . . .

The Lords of Misrule

Dana Cameron

London
December 24, 1722

"I detest Christmas." My mother swept into the parlor, making the pronouncement with all the venom of a curse. "The perceived license turns the whole world upside-down, and one would think my house kept by the lords of misrule for the entire season instead of Twelfth Night."

I looked up, afraid. Had she seen what I was doing?

"I grant you, a bit of merriment among the servants on Boxing Day, or even Christmas as well—I leave it to Michaels to keep order, and God knows I am a fair mistress—but these excesses. . . . "

Almost as if she noticed me for the first time, Mother said, "Margaret, you must tell me why Mrs. Baker is in a fury, Mrs. Billings is beyond civil speech, and the maids are rushing about as though the Dev–" Mother caught herself; the world would indeed be upturned before she uttered *that* oath. "As though the Furies were after them?"

"Mrs. Baker, the cook, is in a fury," I said, carefully slipping the book I'd been reading alongside the cushion of my chair, "because Father did not present himself along with the rest of us to stir the mincemeat for luck, and she fears catastrophe. And the tradesmen, footmen, and indeed, her own kitchen maids are in a riot, one inspiring the next, to take advantage of the coming holiday. Indeed, to judge by the footmen's flushed faces, the drinking and carrying-on began at least a week ago." I paused to consider the rest of her query, and my heart slowed its frantic racing.

"Mrs. Billings is vexed by the housemaids, who are tearing about because I've just had a note from Tommy that he will be coming home and will be bringing a gentleman from Oxford with him. And since Betty left us, they are still shorthanded."

"Mrs. Baker is an excellent cook, but the woman is ridiculously superstitious." Mother sniffed; she and Mrs. Baker were in a state of uneasy alliance, as both were strong-willed to a fault, and both believed she knew best. However, since Mother's reputation as a hostess relied on the excellence of Mrs. Baker's cooking, and Mrs. Baker's standing in the world was in great part tied to Mother's, there was generally very little open strife between the two. "And Tommy's arrival—with or without guests—should occasion no more fluster than usual amongst the maids, even if we are short one."

"I believe that Sally is more than usually giddy," I said, "though Mrs. Billings has promised me that the girl has sworn she will be less excitable from now on. It is not only the fever of the coming holidays: She suspects the maid is infatuated with Simon, and has taken steps to remind them of their respective places. Sally is now outside sweeping the front stairs, giving consideration, I am sure, to Mrs. Billings's words."

Mother sighed. "Thank you, Margaret. There really is no point in training a girl if she'll run off to get married as soon as she's been taught to be an adequate servant. Just as Betty did!"

I bridled at this, true as it might be. Maintaining a staff was a constant struggle.

"As for Tommy," my mother continued, "indeed, I am delighted the boy will be coming, as I miss the young menace dreadfully."

"Yes, Mother." Whenever Tommy was home, she often wished him back at Oxford.

"With the rest of your brothers and sisters safely in the country at Carisbrooke, all we have to do now is pray your father eventually finds his way home." Mother's lips pursed. "Excellent man, your dear father. I explained that when he left this morning, he must fetch Mr. Fairchild, who will be staying with us, and be home promptly. He assured me that they would be no more than an hour or two. But since he has apparently decided to visit friends on his way home, and will no doubt be carousing with each one of them, it is indeed considerate of him to keep his jollity out in the street, rather than adding to the disturbance at home."

It was now midafternoon. Mother did not need to mention that one reason for her impatience was that today, Christmas Eve, was also her birthday. I nodded gravely and kept my mouth firmly shut.

Quite apart from my mother's just complaints, I liked Christmastime. I looked forward to the chance for Christian reflection, fellowship, and charity. Most years I anticipated the sociability and dancing, but this year—

A great hullabaloo in the foyer forestalled more thought or discussion. A tumultuous crash, the front door slamming open, was followed by shouts, and we both ran to see what the matter was. Dash, my father's morose spaniel, gave several halfhearted barks at the company of servants and gentlemen who fairly exploded into the house. The sound of men's laughter, fueled, no doubt, by congenial company and a great deal of wassail punch told it all: Father was home.

And he was not alone. More than a half dozen household servants—man and maid—were required to get my father and his guests through the front door. Cold air now mixed with the smells of baking apples and roasting meats. I discerned that there were four other gentlemen with my father, two of whom were unknown to me; one in fine clothing in the current London fashion, the other, a hulking brute in decent but travel-stained clothing. Their valets also added to the chaos of baggage and cloaks and mud and boots.

The other two gentlemen were familiar to me, and welcome faces. One was Mr. John Fairchild, a great friend of my father's, and the other, looming suddenly before me, was my brother Tommy.

Tommy swooped down and swept me up, twirling me around with a cry of "Mags!"

An unwilling cry of "Tommy!" was torn from my lips, as much from glad emotion as from dizziness and protest. "Put me down, you wretch! You stink of horse!"

"Say you're glad to see me!" he said, crushing me all the harder.

I could barely breathe. "My dress . . . the . . . guests . . . awk—glad to see you! Now put me down!"

Fortunately, Mother had been too distracted by Father's bellowing—a capacity he had developed from years of shouting orders in his father's coffee shop in one of the busier streets in London—to see Tommy's unseemly display. Unfortunately, Tommy set me down abruptly, so that the very tall gentleman, pressed back from the confusion, immediately trod on my foot.

I yelped, unable to control myself. Even several years of dancing with a wide variety of inept partners, including the very fat Reverend Grantley, had not prepared me for the oaf's crushing weight.

My late fiancé Richard had been, among other things, an excellent dancer.

The oaf noticed immediately and stepped away, bumping into Sally, who was flushed with the outside cold and now laden with cloaks. He stammered an incoherent attempt at an apology to me. Dash woofed in protest at the confusion, and then turned tail and escaped, his footing none too steady on the slick marble floors.

"Careful, Chandler," my father said, laughing. The aroma of nutmeg and cloves and brandy punch perfumed him. "Or have your travels in America already unfitted you for polite company?"

I bowed, casting my eyes down as much from modesty as to ascertain how my poor slipper had fared under the heel of Mr. Chandler's riding boot. It appeared intact, though I could not say the same might hold true for my toes; my brother owed me an excellent

Christmas present to make up for them. Tommy appeared to be no better in his judgment in choosing friends than he ever was: University seemed to have no other effect on him than draining Father's purse. An excellent boy, but sense could not be purchased.

"All of you, into the parlor!" Father bellowed. "Drinks, Michaels! When will dinner be ready? Tell Cook, Lamb will be joining us! I couldn't just leave him in the street on Christmas Eve!"

"Mr. Chase." My mother tried to rein in my father's ebullience with the polite harness of civility. "Perhaps some introductions?" She cast her eyes meaningfully at me: My parents barely disguised their conspiracy to get me back onto the marriage market.

"Oh—? Right. I don't believe you know Mr. Lamb, though you may have heard me speak well of him. Found him in Town on business with Fairchild, and insisted that he spend the week with us. Lamb, my eldest daughter, Margaret."

I curtsied and watched surreptitiously as Mr. Lamb made an elegant bow back to me. "Miss Chase." He had a very fine leg, and his coat was beautifully cut, though not ostentatious. Mr. Lamb knew the ways of society, I deduced in a moment.

"You know Fairchild, of course," my father said.

"Mr. Fairchild, it's a pleasure to see you again." As we exchanged courtesies, I realized that my father's old friend looked a little worried. An excellent businessman—he had in fact saved my family two years ago by warning us about the South Sea Bubble, when so many lost their fortunes—I wondered if he was well. I found myself surprised at the depth of my concern for him, and promised myself the chance to examine it further.

"And this is Mr. Chandler. Came from Oxford with Tommy." My father clapped his hands, now that he'd satisfied courtesy, and said, "Now for punch! Michaels!"

"I think that you forget that our guests might like a moment to collect themselves after the afternoon's . . . sociability . . . and that Tommy and Mr. Chandler would in all likelihood wish to wash the roads from themselves." The way Mother said it was more of an order than a suggestion to Father and the other gentlemen.

"Very well—but no dallying, none of you!" Father stomped off toward the parlor. "And you—Fairchild and Lamb! You've not been ahorse, so you should be there the faster."

My father might be one of the wealthier men in town, but in his cups, he showed the manners my mother had worked so hard to impress upon him were naught but a pretty veneer over a nature used to the rough and tumble of the streets and wharves. His heart, however, was as large as his voice, as everyone who came into contact with him—business competitor or new acquaintance—had to concede.

My mother sighed as she watched him track mud down the hall, which was beautifully bedecked with evergreens and holly in honor of the Yuletide. She then turned to the assembled gentlemen and curtsied. "Welcome, sirs. If you would care to join us after you've seen your rooms . . . ?" With a nod to Michaels, who gestured to several quick footmen, a semblance of order came into our house, and I followed Mother down the hall.

A short time later, when everyone was seated and tea was poured, Father erupted from his chair, impatient to reveal his surprise.

"As you all know, today is Mrs. Chase's birthday. And no man could ask for a better helpmeet."

Indeed, I thought. My parents' marriage had been a successful one, uniting his fortune in trade with her family's distant but definite connection to nobility, resulting in six living children. Both parties were mindful of their God-appointed roles and kept discreetly to themselves. I could not hope for a better arrangement, I thought as I refolded my handkerchief.

"And while Christmastide is a time for giving gifts—and a good wife is a true gift to a man—I hope I may also give her a gift, to mark the happiness—the gift!—of a happy house. A mark of my high esteem. Happy birthday, Mrs. Chase!"

The guests and family smiled as they tried to work out what Father was saying—an able and generous man, his tongue had not learned to keep pace with his kindly heart—and clapped politely as Father made his best legs, stumbling only a little. With a flourish, he presented my mother with a small velvet bag.

"Mr. Chase, thank you! You are the most thoughtful of husbands." Mother smiled with genuine pleasure as she removed a small leather box from the velvet— she recognized the trademark burgundy leather of Mr. Hillwood, the jeweler. As careful a housewife as Mother is—always vigilant regarding the finances of the household—she delighted in baubles as much as any woman alive. In fact, no matter how magnificent a present she received, she would still look forward to the small gifts the family exchanged on Christmas morning. My father, in fits of affection that only sometimes vexed my mother (who treasured her reputation for modesty and moderation), called her "a little magpie."

She opened the box, and her face was transmuted from delight to unhappy surprise in an instant. "Mr. Chase, I . . . I do not understand. Is this . . . some sort of drollery? Brought on by the day's entertainments?"

My father, pleased with himself and perhaps distracted by an agreeable amount of punch still coursing in his veins, was not as alert to my mother's sudden change in mood as the rest of us. "It is my pleasure, Madam."

"But . . . is this how you prize me? And if so, husband, could you not have found some way to . . . communicate your rebuke . . . in some more private fashion?" Tears welled up in her eyes, and her blushes were the match of the box in her hand.

I rushed to my mother's side.

"What rebuke? What prize?" my father said, puffing himself up, though he didn't know the cause. "If the color does not please you, Madam, I am sure that I can find a better. My taste is not as elevated as your own, but surely my good intentions should excuse any fault you might find."

"Good intentions? Mr. Chase, if I have not made you happy, surely my care of your house must be worth more still than this!"

She thrust the box out, for the entire company to see.

Tommy gasped. Mr. Lamb and Mr. Fairchild were on their feet immediately.

Lying on the white satin lining was a collection of small, dirty pebbles.

"Damn me!" my father roared. "What does that rogue Hillwood play at?"

"Mr. Chase!" Whatever else of hurt and confusion my mother must have felt, she would not tolerate Father swearing so in the house. I tried to appear shocked, but it was the very sort of thing I would have said had I been in his situation. And I was so very used to Father expressing his feelings candidly that I would have been more surprised if he had not used such bad language.

"A very expensive pearl and garnet suite should be there! I don't know what Hillwood means by this, but I'll have it out of his hide!"

"Henry, I'm sure there is some innocent reason for this . . . confusion," Mr. John Fairchild said, and I was grateful to him for his calm and comforting presence. "Hillwood is the most reliable man in the world, and never has such a taint of dishonor been laid at his door."

Out of the corner of my eye, I saw Tommy dart a worried and questioning glance at the giant brute who sat silently in the corner. A bare shake of the head was his only reply. "Father, what did the suite look like?" I asked, determined to ask Tommy later about his pantomime with Chandler.

"Margaret Amalie Chase! What the Devil does that matter?" Father's temper was getting the better of his sense, to swear a second time in front of company and Mother, whose composure had fled, had now begun to cry. She left the room, her lady's maid scurrying after her. "Just like a lady, to worry about the fashion of some ornament, when there are weightier matters at hand!"

I bit my tongue; to protest would solve nothing. He'd think of it himself in a moment, I was sure.

"Perhaps Miss Chase wishes to know so that we might be equipped to identify the pieces, should they have been mislaid," said Mr. Lamb. "For surely . . . pebbles? 'Tis a childish prank, no more."

I said nothing, but inclined my head to Mr. Lamb, pleased that he should come so quickly to my assistance.

Father waved his hand, a dismissive gesture that was certainly made to hide his ignorance of such things. "There were garnets, principally, and some pearls of a good size. Set in gold. Hillwood had showed me some other, lesser pieces, newly made in the best fashion, but I told him, I care not for fashion and will not have French paste or newfangled Pinchbeck, no matter the taste of the day. If they cannot be melted down and got into gold and gems again, I will not have them. Fairchild, Lamb, you of all men take my meaning: in an uncertain world, you cannot store wealth in such things, and the Devil take mode and Hillwood's silly novelties! I'm a rich man, I don't care, and an honest one, and will have the best!"

I waited for Father to finish; his views on the practicality of everything, including the ornaments that he was so kind to give to us, were as well known to me as Reverend Grantley's one Christmas sermon. "I'm sure Hillwood did not mean to imply you could only afford paste, and such things are also useful to foil robbers, both pickpockets and highwaymen." I wished I could have seen what Mr. Hillwood offered, as his trinkets were always the height of taste and fashion. I loved them for the cunning that went into their making, for he was no mere goldsmith.

"Bless me, girl," he said, pinching my cheek, which I bore as patiently as I could. "As if I would let my daughters go out into any wilderness so adorned, without me to protect them."

"You have told us the substance of the jewels, but not the style, Chase," Mr. Fairchild said, admirably to the point.

Father waved his hand. "How the Dev— why, I am sure I don't know. I had Hillwood's assurances that they were modish, and I saw myself—as did you and Lamb—that there were no prettier things in the shop." Father might know the language of ship and ledger, warehouse and coffee shop, but other than the raw materials that went into clothing and jewelry and such, he was unschooled.

"I saw them only for a moment," said Mr. Fairchild, "as did Lamb here, but even he was absorbed in picking out shoe buckles."

"But they were just as you said," Mr. Lamb agreed.

Father huffed and puffed, racking his brains. "There were earrings, two of 'em, of course. A fine pearl at center, garnets around it and three more goodly pearls dangling from it. Gold setting."

Girandole earrings, I thought to myself. A central piece with ornaments hanging from both sides and beneath.

"And there was a brooch. In the form of a sort of . . . a knot. A sort of drooping bow, if you will, as if it lacked starch or the substance to hold itself up.

The sort that might adorn the, er . . . front . . . of a gown." Father held his hand up just below his collarbone, then, fearing he might be indiscreet, went red and moved his hand away. "A good size, but not the sort of armor plate that some ladies wear there . . . though it could be fitted to other pieces if Mrs. Chase wanted."

A brooch *à la Sévigné,* I imagined he meant. Where another lady might have a ribbon bow at the front of her gown, my mother would have had a toy in gold and garnets. Father had been more than generous with Mother's gift, and now it was stolen, a double blow.

"But to the matter before us," Father insisted, "I have had the box tucked safely in my pocket this entire day." His face was growing redder by the moment.

"Surely, Father, that cannot be correct," Tommy said. "For you only had it of Hillwood's boy as Chandler here and I met you, and that was just at The Sun. That was three hours ago, and we met several of your friends, stopping at various other establishments on our way home. Caroling, at times."

"You are right, my boy; I remember it now. I met Fairchild and Lamb, and we stopped by Hillwood's to retrieve Mrs. Chase's present. I noticed that one of the links on an earring did not sit quite right, and asked him to repair it. He apologized and allowed as his journeyman must have caused the flaw in the final cleaning. He assured me it was no great matter, that he himself would repair it and send it with his boy after me. I'm sure the boy is to blame: Servants are unruly this time of year—which seems foolish, with

Boxing Day so near, and their tips and perquisites at stake—or perhaps he bore some grudge against Hillwood and sought to repay him thus."

"It is a very grave thing, to steal so much. And there was no hope that the change would go unnoticed," Tommy's friend Mr. Chandler, the oaf, said suddenly. His voice startled me, it being so deep and coming so unexpectedly.

"And Hillwood is known as a fair master, there's no one who will say otherwise," Fairchild added.

"Did you inspect the box, Father, when it was delivered?" I asked.

Mr. Chandler started at my question. Perhaps he was surprised that I should speak up again, perhaps he was surprised that I was here at all, but with Mother taken to her bed, someone had to preside over the tea. And my family being somewhat used to my forward manner was no reminder; I vowed I should be less obvious in my attention, using my place behind the teapot to observe everything. After all, Father had no doubt brought his guests home for me to inspect for possible husbands, and I could not put that off forever. This was, after all, the season to contemplate the many forms of Christian fellowship. But perhaps he would be distracted a little longer by his . . . present . . . concerns.

"Let me see . . ." Father scrubbed at his face, the better to drive off drink and ire. "No, I did not look at them, for upon my life, I was not willing to show such a thing about in a public house, and then there was the surprise of seeing Tommy and . . . er . . . Chandler there, arriving just as the boy did."

"We did meet several gentlemen who were also out

wassailing. We ourselves stopped for a quick pot at several other public houses after," Mr. Lamb said.

My father enjoyed sociability, and the holidays provided an ample opportunity for him to indulge his gregarious nature. It was a blessing that he was so addicted to company, for a man in commerce finds his business in his circle of friends, acquaintances, and more distant connections, and his good name and character proceed him into the marketplace.

And if punch, wine, or good, plain beer was to be found in such visits, then so much the better. But Father was merry, not witless, in his drink, and I'd never met a man so unafraid to walk the streets. Not through some foolish ignorance, but a strong arm to his own defense and a familiarity with London in all her guises led him, always, safely home. Even during the commotion—and thievery—that always attended the holidays.

Father was decided. "I'll send to Hillwood immediately. He'll make this all clear, or I'll have him clapped in irons."

"But . . . Henry." Mr. Fairchild set his teacup down carefully. "By now the shop is closed up tight, and the jeweler visiting his relations. Do you not remember? That was the reason to go yourself, this afternoon."

"Blast!" Father began to pace again.

"He will be back tomorrow morning; but I'm sure, on Christmas, you would not . . ." Mr. Fairchild paused, hoping Father would take the hint. We exchanged a glance, and I realized just how adept that excellent gentleman was at managing my father's precarious temper.

"I'll see him if it's Christmas or Easter or he's on

his deathbed!" Father rumbled, but faced with the facts of his situation, he consented to sit and have another cup of tea.

We dined later, but hardly doing justice to Mrs. Baker's excellent food: beef and veal, goose, pies, and puddings, a merry surfeit in honor of the holiday. Mother having retired for the evening, I pride myself on having done my best, taking her seat and turning the conversation away to more pleasant topics as often as I could lure Father out of his sulk. He was drinking steadily, and what was meant to be a birthday celebration and the eve of a holy day was a sorry, hollow sort of occasion for us.

A small corner of my heart was glad that Mother was away, for it made it much easier for me to observe the gentlemen without her orchestrating things in her determined way. And Father was so upset that he had quite forgotten why he'd filled the house with gentlemen in the first place.

But as the evening drew on, I found myself stifling a yawn: I would have liked to stay up a little later, for Mr. Fairchild's conversation was always very pleasant, and there were moments where it was almost as if we were alone in the room. I found Mr. Lamb very knowledgeable about roses, and even Mr. Chandler made an effort and was not so dull as at first I supposed, or perhaps it was Mrs. Baker's superb beef setting the doldrums aside finally, or the last of several glasses of wine Father pressed on us. I withdrew and left the gentlemen and Tommy to their talk, having extracted the promise that they would retire shortly: The sooner they were asleep, the sooner the morning would come, and all would be resolved.

The gentlemen, weary from the day's business, pleasure, traveling, and—it must be admitted—unpleasant excitement, were as good as their word, and each went to his room shortly. I heard them preparing for bed as I assured myself that the house was locked up, the kitchen in order, and the servants accounted for by Michaels, and tended those affairs that must require a lady's attention at day's end.

It seemed I had no sooner said my prayers and was asleep, when the whole house was roused, not with preparations for church to celebrate the birth of our Savior, but with alarms and barking dogs and cries of "Murder, murder!"

Having pulled on a dressing gown and shawl against the chill and lit a candle to find my way through the dark hallways, I hurried toward the source of the noise, in the kitchen. There, I found Michaels and two sleepy-eyed footmen already there, staring at something on the floor at the bottom of a flight of stairs. The warmth of the room by day had fled, though the heady smells of pepper and cloves remained; the fire was banked and gave off little light, this augmented by two candles on the table. The men looked up, their faces ashen in the shadows when they saw me.

"Miss Chase . . . do not look," Michaels begged.

"Is someone hurt?" I said, pausing. "For if he is, I must see to him, as my mother is ill and not to be disturbed on any account."

"He's beyond any help we can give him," Michaels said. "A dreadful accident, and no sight for a lady."

I held my tongue, knowing that Michaels was only thinking of me, but if a lady is given the care of her household, and has the stomach and the brains to manage it, her obligation is to her duty first, and niceties after.

"It's Simon," Michaels said. "I've already seen that it was him."

I nodded, and out of respect to Michaels—the poor man looked as though he would be sick in a moment—I left the jacket over the face of the dead man. I took the man's wrist in my hand and felt that there was no pulse, though his skin was still warm.

The footsteps I heard behind me were halted abruptly by the horror on the floor before them. I looked up.

"My God!" Tommy said. "Mags?"

"I'm afraid so." I sat back on my heels, rocking back and forth. As I bent my head to say a quick prayer, I was shocked to see Michaels's coat pulled away from the dead man's face. Mr. Chandler was gazing impassively at Simon's corpse.

I gasped, but took the opportunity to look myself, quickly, so as not to disturb Michaels's sense of propriety. Simon's face was still caught in a fearful contortion, blood had trickled from his brow. There were no other marks on his face or hands.

At my gasp, Mr. Chandler was suddenly aware that I was watching him. He at least had the decency to blush, after his too rough handling of matters not his business.

Mr. Lamb arrived, pale and sweating, his jacket thrown hastily on, his shirt untucked. "He is dead, isn't he, Chandler—?"

"It's as Miss Chase says," Mr. Chandler said slowly. With no more consideration than to uncover a dead man when he was a guest in a strange house, he had come into the kitchen dressed only in a shirt and britches. He turned to me. "What lies up that set of stairs?"

I gave him a look that I hoped was full of my unspoken rebuke. "One of the maids' rooms. I'm sure it's their cries that drew us here."

"But Mags . . . how did it happen?" Tommy whispered. He was shaking, though he tried to hide it.

"I heard the maids' noise, Mr. Thomas," said Michaels, "and, thinking to silence their untoward frivolity, an effect of the holiday celebration, came to find Simon here."

"Have you spoken to the maids?" I asked.

"Not myself, not yet, Miss Chase," Michaels answered. "I'd hardly gotten here when you arrived yourself. I believe Mrs. Billings is up there now."

"You gentlemen should return to bed," I said. "I'm sorry that you were disturbed by this unpleasant matter, but we would prefer that we address our house's problems in private. Indeed, you've been exposed to too much scandal already and you have my apologies for it. I am certain we will have this resolved by morning."

"Miss Chase, I would hardly feel comfortable to leave you alone in such circumstances," Mr. Lamb said.

As frustrated as I was with this universal refusal to accede to my request, I kept my tone mild. "Hardly alone sir, in my own house, with my own people around me. Please, do not trouble yourself. I'm sure my father will be here presently to relieve me of this burden."

"Perhaps I might stay until that time, Miss Chase?" Mr. Lamb said.

I shook my head. "I thank you for your pains, but I would prefer you leave us to this. It would not be kind to the servants to expose them to unfamiliar faces on what must certainly be a terrible occasion for them."

He withdrew, reluctantly I thought, and that left only me, Tommy, Mr. Chandler, Michaels, and the footmen there.

"Mr. Chandler?" I said. "I think that you would be more comfortable in your room. Thank you for your concern, but please, for the sake of our people—"

Tommy was looking out the kitchen door to the darkened house beyond. He turned to me and said sharply, "It is my desire that Matthew stays, Margaret."

My brother's stern tone of voice and use of my proper Christian name was a slap in the face. I was so unused to this peremptory manner in him toward me that I found myself unable to answer.

I drew myself up, blinking back tears. "As you will, Thomas. I will be in my chamber, if you should need—"

"I do not want you to leave, Mags," he said, quite his usual self. "Only . . . I need you to talk to the maids. It would be more . . . seemly . . . if you are there with us."

I blinked again. Tommy was as changeable as spring weather, which was unlike him. Clever enough, but foolish quite frequently, his temperament was equable and mild, and he seldom made anything of his role as eldest son. But now, something was troubling him, for I had never heard him so, and he and

Chandler looked even more anxious than required by our present situation. As for the seemliness of him being in the maids' chamber, surely the presence of Michaels and Mrs. Billings was more than enough.

Or perhaps Tommy wanted me there for another reason. He knew, better than anyone in the house, of my peculiar interest in the well-being of the maidservants. He was the only one in my family with whom I'd discussed the revelations that had come on the death of my fiancé, and perhaps that was his reason.

But why insist on Mr. Chandler's presence? Surely the man was an impediment—the thoughtless clod—and would scare the servants into silence by his imposing presence alone, when we needed them to be as open as possible. And, it was an embarrassment to us Chases, who, I may modestly say, enjoyed a character for generous hospitality: To have a man present who'd not only witnessed the outrage of the theft—or misplacement—of Mother's gift, but to find a dead footman to boot? It was the disgrace of the age, the food on which Dame Rumor thrived upon.

I bowed my head in assent, unable to read anything from Tommy's face and unwilling to ask him in front of a stranger. I bade Michaels and the footmen to remove the body to some place where it could be tended, took my candle, and led the way to the maids' quarters, the steep wooden stairs dancing with shadows from our flickering lights.

In the chamber she had shared with Betty, the giddy maid Sally was sobbing hysterically. Mrs. Billings the housekeeper was by her side, and cast me a look of desperate fear. She knew better than anyone what this might mean for the staff: They were, traditionally, the first to be suspected, innocent or no.

"Mrs. Billings, did you see what happened?" I asked. Tommy and Chandler, for all their eagerness to play a part, stayed well in the background.

"I did not, I came when I heard her screams. And I can barely make sense of what this fool Sally is saying, she blubbers so. Too much Christmas ale, I'm sure. She said a man came into her room, and then . . . I can get nothing more from her."

Surely the girl had had a terrible fright, I thought, to be so incoherent. Mrs. Billings was too harsh with her. "Perhaps . . . thank you, Mrs. Billings. You may go. I'd like to talk with Sally, if you please."

The woman left reluctantly, and I felt a surge of dislike for her. She was an admirable housekeeper—scrupulously honest, meticulously organized, and a scourge to dirt and disorder—but a notorious gossip and a tyrant with the housemaids, if we let her.

I pulled my shawl closer over my dressing gown, all too aware of the cold wind banging a branch against the outside of the house. Sally's bed was pushed up against the chimney for warmth, and she was wrapped in a quilt, her face streaming with tears. Her cloak was spread over the bed for additional warmth, and I was glad that we did not stint on the stuff we gave the maids, whether new or castoff, gift or perquisite.

"Now, Sally, my girl," Tommy began, "tell us what happened. How did Simon end up at the bottom of the stairs?"

His words were meant kindly, but Tommy had about as much understanding of the womanly mind as he did of waistcoats: He had all the best intentions in the world, but his aspirations were far beyond his grasp.

Sally took a look at him and promptly burst into even louder sobs.

I gently pushed him to one side, indicating with my eyes that he should stay in the shadows. A glance at Mr. Chandler told me that he understood as well.

I picked up a stool and sat next to the bed, waiting for Sally to catch her breath. Perhaps she was worn out, perhaps she was unnerved by having three of her betters watch her, but the girl's native modesty won out and she composed herself.

"Sally, can you tell us what happened?"

The girl took a few more hitching breaths, and then stammered, "He came into the chamber. I wasn't yet asleep."

I bit my lip, frowning. "Then Simon came up here?"

"No! Miss, he would never dare! He only did to-night because—" She broke off, white as a sheet at what she had just admitted.

I knew what she was afraid of: Fraternizing between the male and female servants was frowned upon, and an . . . intimate visit . . . absolutely forbidden. We were, after all, responsible for the well-being of our maids, or why else would their parents allow them to come into our service?

"So Simon . . . did come up here?" As soon as I said it, I recalled that the reason Sally had been rebuked for giddiness was that she had been mooning over Simon for several weeks now.

"No, Miss! It was a gentleman!"

As bad as a footman might be, this was worse. "Who was it?" I asked.

"I could not say, Miss. It was dark as dark can be, it was."

"Then how do you know it was a gentleman?" I insisted. "Sally, this is a grievous charge to lay before anyone, but to make such a claim when you do not have even the evidence of your own eyes?"

At this the maid had the decency to blush, and I feared that I'd caught the girl in a lie.

"It was . . . he didn't smell like no footman!" she blurted out.

I blinked, horrified. "I beg your pardon!"

Sally looked deathly afraid, but continued. "He . . . well, Miss, even if my eyes are shut, I can smell the difference between boot polish, firewood, and the kitchen as opposed to perfumes and fresh laundry, Miss. This was a gentleman, unwanted and unwelcome, in my room."

"I think you must be mistaken, Sally," I said, my heart sinking. "Or perhaps it was some trick of being still asleep. It was *Simon* we found at the foot of the stairs."

"That was after, Miss!" Somehow Sally had found her composure. "I screamed, being startled so, realizing that there was someone in the room. The man . . . he put his hand over my mouth, but I kicked at him and scratched at him and screamed again—"

Good for you, I thought. Not many would have been as brave as that, footman or gentleman.

"—and it was then I heard Simon shout below, down on the stairs. The gentleman ran out. I heard a struggle, and a cry . . ." Here she began to weep again.

If Sally was telling the truth, then this was more than an accident. . . . I exchanged a horror-struck glance with Tommy, who'd gone pale.

I was about to protest again, when I was struck by a chilling thought, a reason for murder. "Sally, did you know that a very valuable piece of jewelry was stolen today?"

She nodded. "Yes, Miss. I'd heard. It was all over the kitchen. A terrible shame that the jeweler's boy should play such a prank."

She said it so disarmingly that I believed her instantly.

"Mags?" Tommy motioned for me to come aside. "What ever makes you think there is a connection?" he whispered. "Isn't it bad enough that the girl's got caught meeting her lover—he must have fallen down the stairs in the dark and broke his neck—that you've got to accuse her of worse things as well? Even if she didn't steal a thing, well—meeting a man? She's bound to lose her place, and with this blemish to her name, she won't get another. It'll be her ruin."

"But I don't think she's lying," I whispered back. "She seemed genuinely affrighted, when we came in—"

"Yes, afraid she'd been caught—"

"Thomas, a moment, please." Mr. Chandler had been so quiet that I had forgotten he was there at all, something of a miracle, considering how large he was. "Miss Chase, why did you ask about the suite? The two seem to be unrelated."

I prepared to snub the man: Who was he to ask me questions, and to decide what was related to what? It was only for Tommy's sake that he was here at all, and most improperly, too. It was too much. And the sight of a few golden hairs and his collarbone peeping through his good lawn shirt was unnerving, to say the least.

It was not for him that I answered, but Tommy should know my reasoning, in any case. "It . . . it's worse than an accident or possible assignation, I fear. Sally's an honest girl, and . . . I . . . there was a moment, when I wondered . . . whether the theft of the jewelry might also have occasioned murderous violence."

Tommy caught his breath and Mr. Chandler's expression was very grave.

I continued, before they could protest. "If the jeweler's boy did not take the earrings and brooch, then perhaps . . . well, there was a moment when Sally, Simon, and my father were all together. On the occasion of the arrival of you gentlemen, she was outside, sweeping, and then came in to help. There was such a . . . tumult, that perhaps the box with the gift might have been removed then. If so, wouldn't the worth of the gems be motive enough for murder?"

"There was some confusion, was there not?" Mr. Chandler scratched his head, remembering. "I'm sure matters were unnecessarily complicated by the . . . high spirits of the party."

"Quite so," I said. "There's also . . . I have reason to believe that Sally is telling the truth. Her manner is entirely open, despite her tears. I think she was first afraid because she was being . . . attacked . . . and then because she heard that Simon was dead. Not because she imagines that she'll be held responsible for the man's death, or for the loss of the jewels, or both."

I hesitated, not wanting to follow my thoughts to their logical conclusion. "If Sally is lying, we shall find out soon enough. But if she is not, it means that someone else attacked her, for Simon certainly did not."

"Why is that?" Tommy demanded.

"Because there were no scratches on his arms or face," I said. "I noticed nothing besides those hurts that might have come from his fall down the stairs."

"Neither did I notice anything like that," Mr. Chandler said.

Was that approval I saw in Mr. Chandler's face? Or surprise that I should notice anything at all?

"But Mags," Tommy said, his whisper more urgent now. "What if Simon was in league with Sally, and came to claim the trinkets—?"

I nodded as if in reluctant agreement, taking the opportunity to observe Mr. Chandler's hands and face. I never would dream of asking our guests to show their hands to determine whether the maid was telling the truth, but that did not mean that I wouldn't make the most of a chance that presented itself. And Mr. Chandler's excess of curiosity and his very quick arrival on the scene—in a state of undress—did make me wonder.

His were very nice hands, I had to admit, unmarked, save for evidence that he made copious use of pen and ink. They were not smooth, and it was clear to me that he rode often, without gloves. The side of his face (for I could only observe his profile) was also unmarred, strong, but well made, and though I am not especially partial to light-haired gentlemen, I was surprised to find that he was very good looking, in an unpolished sort of way. He was the sort of gentleman, I noted, who would be careless in his dress. He was clean enough to be decent, and dressed to fit his station—though it suddenly occurred to me that I had no idea what that might be. From Oxford, was all I knew, and whether that was the town or the university, I had no more clue.

Since he was good looking, I immediately hardened my heart. I know what a fair face can hide.

"Then we are at an impasse," Mr. Matthew Chandler said suddenly, and I blushed, aware that he'd caught me staring.

"Unless we get more information to illuminate our ignorance, or we find the jewels, we have no way of determining what went on this evening. Or, rather, corroborating what the maid's told us."

I was grateful to him for that, in spite of myself. Rather, I decided, it was decent of him to not immediately judge Sally.

"I suppose that the easiest thing to do is turn out the staff and search their rooms," Tommy said. I could tell that his spirits were quite low, and that the very thought of such a thing was abhorrent to him.

My eye lighted on the cloak, which I recognized as my sister Lydia's from several years back. That sparked a thought in me, and it was so strange, so wonderful, that I knew the Almighty had inspired it. I tested each part of it, much as a seamstress tests her work, to ascertain a garment will stand under the weight of its fabric. The excitement rising in me, I pulled Tommy aside to the far corner of the room, where we could confer privately.

"Given your pransterish nature, Tom," I whispered,

"and your sometime lapses of judgment regarding personality—here I think of your foolish attachment to the empty-headed Caroline Denbigh—I must ask you: How much do you trust Mr. Chandler?"

I could see the thoughts flying through Tommy's head at my curious question, and although he almost drew himself up to protest, the earnestness of my demeanor and the urgency of the situation won out. "I trust him with my life, Margaret," he said simply. "And I will tell you why you should, too."

What he related briefly to me was so extraordinary that I could not but be amazed at my brother. I looked at Mr. Chandler, seeing him in a new, more favorable light, and was profoundly disturbed to see the man watching me closely as well.

"And so you see why I could not tell you before," Tommy concluded.

I nodded.

"And what's wrong with Caroline Denbigh?" he blurted, all trace of his new-found maturity fleeing on the instant.

I sighed. "At the conclusion of this ordeal, I will make a list for you. But now, Tommy, if we are agreed, we must move forward with my plan."

A few moments later, Tommy was at his most authoritative when he addressed the servants, who were waiting for us in the kitchen. "Where's Simon now?"

"In the cellar, sir," answered Michaels. "We wanted to wait until we had word from you before we rendered him the last offices of a friend."

"Excellent. There will be a service for him tomorrow, but for tonight, you should all return to your rooms."

A sudden wailing from the upstairs maids' room drew every eye, and Tommy's face was grim. "Cease your noise! Sally, I will not tolerate this. I'm certain that when my father hears of this, you'll be turned out of the house in the morning. Only consider our shame in being forced to take such action at Christmastime!"

Muted sniffles were heard from above, and Tommy turned to the rest of the servants. "I won't have such goings on in this house! And if I find that any of you had any hand in the theft, it will be the worse for you!"

I don't know where Tommy learned to behave like this, but if Mother or Father had seen him, they would not have recognized their son. I hope they would have been appalled. But it was not my place to say anything now, so I bit my lip and lowered my eyes.

Tommy pounded the table with a ferocity that made us all jump. "To bed, all of you!"

Servants stared, then scattered. Two remained behind, uncertain what to do.

Tommy turned on them. "You, men!"

The visiting gentlemen's valets jumped out of their skins. "Yes, sir?"

"If your masters don't require you awake and abroad, then I suggest you get to your room as well. I'm not in a mood to be dealing with anyone else's people tonight; I've had a stomachful of my own!"

The valets bowed: Mr. Fairchild's man followed Michaels upstairs, and Mr. Lamb's man took a glass of wine and a biscuit on a tray and hurried back toward his master's room as if a lit fuse was hanging from the back of his britches.

Tommy, Mr. Chandler, and myself were left alone in the kitchen. Tommy puffed out his cheeks. "I hope never to have to do that again. If there is nothing else, I believe I shall retire for the night."

"God keep you, Tommy." I kissed him on the cheek. "Mr. Chandler, I wish you a good night. With any luck, this will be behind us by tomorrow morning."

I returned to my room, my feet quite freezing despite my thick stockings. I thought of the appeal of my bed, but was too wakeful after the night's events and revelations. There was no sleep in me, and I would feel more than useless abed while others kept a lonely watch. My heart went out to Sally; I could not imagine what thoughts tormented her now, at what should be a time of peace and goodwill.

My book, however, was down in the parlor where I'd left it hidden, and so resolved to see in the dawn, I dressed hurriedly, took my candle, and returned there. I poked the ashes until I found the sleeping embers and added some fuel; no point in calling a maid, as I suspect they were cowering in their beds, amazed at Tommy's display of anger. The little fire sprang up, reminding me of the Yule log we kept burning through the twelve days of Christmas at Carisbrooke, lit with the remains of the one from the year before. For luck, or so Cook had it.

Or so it was supposed to be, I thought, frowning. Father had neglected that tradition as well, using new kindling, much to the superstitious Mrs. Baker's dismay. Between the mincemeat and the Yule log, there was plenty of ill luck on us now.

A blaze going, my candle close at hand to keep the shadows at bay, I settled in to find my book.

It was not tucked down next to the cushion where I'd hidden it.

My heart stopped: I had been very careful to hide it—had I succeeded in hiding it from myself? Or had I grown too careless lately, and left it somewhere else? What if someone had discovered it?

I cast about, desperately, and finally found it on the other side of the walnut wing chair, stuck between the cushion and arm. Sighing deeply, I turned to sit, clutching the book to my bosom, only to look up and see Mr. Chandler watching me, a candle in his hand, casting grotesque shadows on the wall.

"Ah. Did I replace it incorrectly?" he asked. "My apologies. I had thought to return it to the library, when I found it there earlier, but then I realized that whoever had put it there would come back for it, eventually. Inevitably, I should say, because it is altogether impossible to leave Mr. Swift's provoking arguments alone until they are concluded, I find."

"I—I . . . the book . . . is not mine," I stammered. I could feel myself redden to the brow; it was not entirely a falsehood. I had taken it from my father's library.

Mr. Chandler bowed. "Miss Chase. Good night."

I sat for a few minutes, clutching the ridiculous book for a moment more, feeling my heart pound as if it would break through my stays. At least the man was wearing a coat now, and I was no longer clad in my nightclothes. There had been nothing improper about our last encounter, but it had left me unnerved.

Unfortunately, there was nothing about being fully dressed that made me feel less vulnerable now.

I began to tremble: Surely Mr. Chandler knew it was none of his business to mention my reading habits to my family? What if he should—?

A blast like the roar of a cannon came from the other end of the house. I secured the book in my pocket, safely under my gown, and hurried to see what had transpired.

A few servants were emerging from their rooms into the kitchen just as I arrived. I hiked up my skirts and ascended to Sally's room, as quickly as I could, stumbling only a little on the well-worn stairs.

What I saw at the top made my blood run cold: Mr. Chandler was at the doorway, a grim look on his face and a pistol in his hand. The acrid smell of burnt powder still hung in the air.

A few steps more and I could see what I feared most: Tommy was clutching his arm, his white linen sleeve blossoming red, roses on snow.

He was dressed in the maid's night garments, complete with mobcap.

The cloak that had served as a coverlet was pulled off the bed, now on the floor, and a small fortune in garnets, pearls, and gold spilled out of the hood, glinting in the candlelight.

I looked up at Mr. Chandler, horrified. He kept his pistol steady on its intended target, Mr. Lamb, who was cowering in the opposite corner. A spent pistol was lying on the floor before him, and Mr. Lamb clutched his jaw, as if hurt. A graze reddened the knuckles on Mr. Chandler's left hand.

Scarcely knowing what to do first, I heard Tommy moan. "Get Mother, Mags. I'm dying!"

"You're hardly dying," I said out of habit, for I

have remarked that a positive outlook is as good as a tonic, and men are too prone to overexaggerate their hurts. I climbed onto the bed. "I'm sure it's no more than a scratch." I seized the fabric of the sleeve and tore it, so I could ascertain the nature of the wound.

As I worked, using the hem of his nightshirt, I recalled the time one of Father's friends had shot himself in the foot at one of our hunts. The blood had been so copious then that even Mother had been forced to concede the need for a physician. But, to my great relief, this was nothing of that sort.

"No, Tommy, no need for Mother," I said with satisfaction. "I'll bind it up, now, and then make a poultice when the dust has settled, to draw the poisons out. You won't even miss church tomorrow."

"I might," Tommy said, seeing an opportunity to avoid Reverend Grantley's special two-hour Christmas sermon, a tradition he'd inflicted on us for each of the past twenty-some years.

"Caroline Denbigh will be there," I said, knotting the cloth. "Imagine what a story you'll have to tell her."

Tommy went silent, deep in thought.

I got off the bed, strode up to Mr. Lamb, and slapped him in the face. "That's for Simon," I said. "And that"—I slapped him twice more—"is for scaring poor Sally, and that for shooting my brother!"

"Nice to know that I hover within the bare periphery of your good wishes," Tommy muttered from the corner of the bed.

I raised my hand again, but Mr. Chandler coughed. "Perhaps, Miss Chase, as just as your punishment is, it would be more effective—for the moment—if you stayed out of my line of fire."

Mother arrived then, emitting a little shriek. Her dressing gown was belted tightly around her, and her hair in rags under her cap. Her personal maid followed behind, rubbing her eyes.

"Thomas! What monstrosity is this? You in the maid's bed—in the maid's garments! What have you done? Where is the maid?"

Then she saw Mr. Chandler with his pistol aimed at Mr. Lamb. "I take it, sir, there is some good reason for this unseasonable breach of courtesy?"

Before he could answer, Mother saw the jewels on the floor.

She scooped them up, instantly, and was temporarily silenced, her mouth forming a small *o.*

"I believe I owe Mr. Chase an apology," she murmured. Mother shook the gems to watch them sparkle in her hand under the candlelight, then she rummaged in the hood to ascertain she had them all, and stowed them in the bosom of her dressing gown. Then she turned to Tommy.

"I am sure that I raised you better than this! Please tell me that you have not sunk so low as to . . . *tamper* with the maids! And then to be making such a mess! And wearing a maid's clothing! What a disgrace you are, Thomas. Take that cap off! I'll have no riotous mummery here!"

To her credit, however, even as Mother castigated Tommy for his sins, real and imagined, she examined the bandaged wound. "This will need a poultice, and quick, but there's no pus, and nothing left in the wound to fester." She nodded to me, approving my handiwork.

"If you would permit me, Madam," Mr. Chandler said. "I believe I can explain everything."

"I think I would like your explaining better if we had one of our London magistrates to hear it, too!" Mother replied. "I like not this crush of people in the servants' quarters, nor this display of weaponry in the city, in a quiet, civil, and respectable house. And on Christmas morn, too! And you, Mr. Lamb, have you nothing to say for yourself?"

"I am sure this is all some mistake," Lamb began, his jaw bruised.

Mr. Chandler, who had so far managed to suppress any inappropriate emotion he might have felt at my mother's outraged sense of propriety and list of grievances, frowned and raised his pistol again. That effectively stopped Mr. Lamb's words as effectively as my bandage had stanched Tommy's wound.

"I believe that your wish is about to be granted," Mr. Chandler said. "If that noise below marks the arrival of my good friend from Lincoln's Inn. I sent my man with Sally to fetch him, telling him to keep her safe there tonight, while Thomas took her place. I hope this will satisfy you, Madam, as he is as forthright a magistrate as any alive, and will take all the evidence as quick as you like."

"Well, that is very satisfactory," my mother conceded, "but why should you be receiving callers here, and at this time of night—or morning, should I say?"

"Mother, you know that Mr. Matthew Chandler is my very good friend," Tommy said, "and before all else, he is a gentleman, through and through. Besides that, he is a magistrate himself, lately come from his home near Oxford."

"If it had not been for the excitement of Mr. Chase's announcement, and sudden discovery of the theft, I would have revealed my occupation to you," Mr. Chandler said. "My profound apologies: I did not want to conceal anything from you. Rather, at the discovery of the loss of the jewels, I kept my identity secret—with Tommy's help—so that I might better help recover the treasure. And, as it happens, Simon's murderer, I'm sorry to say." Here he gestured at Mr. Lamb, who made no reply.

"Murder!" Mother gasped. She turned to Mr. Lamb. "You brute! Poor Simon! And I am already so short-handed."

Mr. Chandler continued. "However, it was your daughter, Miss Chase, and her keen observations that were chiefly responsible for revealing the truth tonight. The vindication of an innocent maid, vengeance for an honest man, and the apprehension of a dangerous villain."

With that he inclined his head to me, and I curtsied in return. I did not, however, lower my eyes. I was so caught up in his gaze, I could not bear to do it.

"Well," Mother said finally, "my Margaret's not without her faults, but she's a good girl. And if she did have a hand in resolving these dealings tonight, I'm sure no harm was meant by it." She heard the arrival of the magistrate below. "And now, we have guests to welcome, servants to calm, and Tommy to bind up. It seems Christmas morning has come beforetime, but I will not be caught unprepared. Mrs. Baker! Mrs. Billings!"

* * *

Most of the carriage ride back from church the next morning—or later that morning, I should say—was quiet. Father never roused the whole night, not even waking early in the morning, when as a family we exchanged small gifts. He was in a sad state, his aching head made no easier by hearing that one of his guests was a thief and murderer.

Finally, Father erupted. "Damn me—your pardon, Mrs. Chase—"

"Not at all, Mr. Chase." My mother was so enthralled with her birthday present—and the opportunity to show off her pearls and garnets at church—that she would have forgiven my father a good deal more.

"—but the man was buying fancy buckles at the same time I was. We had no idea of his recent financial troubles, and certainly, he was dressed well enough and made no complaint of being ruined."

"No, Father," I said, "he was buying on credit. And he used his case—emptied of his buckles and filled with pebbles—in order to swap it with your own. I'm sure he planned it on the way home—you did wander a bit, you know—and seized on the confusion of your arrival with your guests—and with Tommy and Mr. Chandler—to hide the gems in Sally's hood. Such a small weight would hardly be noticed under the heaviness of her own cloak, indeed, or under the burden of garments she bore into the house. His plan was to slip into her room and retrieve the jewels later."

"But that seems such an awful risk, Mags," Tommy said. He'd woken out of his daydreams, wherein I'm sure he was revisiting Caroline Denbigh's squeals of affected and ladylike horror when he offered to tell her how he had been hurt. He would cherish it as a token to his heart for weeks to come, or until the next false hope presented itself. "What if Sally found it? What if she'd kept it for herself, or told us of her discovery?"

"If she found it and kept it, he'd only have to blackmail her into returning it to him," Mr. Matthew Chandler said. "If she'd found them and returned them to you, why, the puzzle would remain but no harm would be done. It was a risk worth taking. With that stake, Lamb might parlay it into a bigger fortune, either at the gaming tables or on the seas."

Mr. Chandler sat comfortably in the rear-facing seat of the coach. "A gentleman with good credit and reputation can live on those for a long time. Lamb didn't want to wait to see whether he could change his fortunes. Now, I daresay, he'll be living the rest of his life in the colonies, transported for murder, instead."

Mr. Chandler turned to my mother, smiling so that she couldn't resist responding in kind. "Perhaps, Mrs. Chase, you wouldn't mind stopping the carriage. It is a fine clear day, and a walk after church is beneficial to reflection."

"But you don't know the way to the house," Tommy said. He signaled the driver, and the carriage pulled to one side. Mr. Chandler leapt out, and Tommy made as if to scramble out to follow him. "I'll go with you."

"No, Thomas, your wound still troubles you, no doubt," Mr. Chandler said. "But perhaps Miss Chase would be kind enough—"

"Of course she would!" My mother all but hauled me from my seat, all but shoved me out the door. I did not have time to protest—nor did I want to. "I'm sure she would love to discuss Reverend Grantley's sermon, a perennial favorite, with you. Go, Margaret, none of your puling! 'Tis but a short walk, and the cold air will whet your appetite."

I'm sure Mother, heartened by my lack of protest, wanted to give Mr. Chandler every opportunity to discover how sweet-spoken, demur, and well-bred I was.

As I exited the carriage, I thought I noticed a trace of sadness in Mr. Fairchild's eyes. I know that he had hoped I might consider him, when my "present melancholy" as my mother called it, had left me. I would have considered him, too, for he was a good friend and a true gentleman. If it had not been for Mr. Lamb's greed . . .

Mr. Chandler handed me out. As the door shut, Father leaned out, his eyes were bloodshot, red as holly berries.

"Chandler!"

"Mr. Chase?"

"I know exactly how long it takes to walk from here to the house," he said gruffly.

The carriage pulled away.

"Did you enjoy Christmas service, Mr. Chandler?" I took the arm he offered and we began to stroll.

"Luke is a pleasant and happy book to contemplate, but I find I am more interested in Swift."

My heart dropped. Was this some sort of blackmail? Perhaps he sought a kiss for a kept secret? Or was it worse than that, would he upbraid me for reading? Because, as everyone knows—or yet believes—a woman's wit is like a sharpened sword: Best hid away in the scabbard lest it do hurt to she who wields it and those around her.

"Mr. Chandler?" My voice was nearly steady, but I could only keep my eyes on the cobblestones on the ground ahead of me.

"Miss Chase, forgive my bluntness. I have been too long out of the company of society, and most times I find it a tedious necessity. If you have any thoughts on Jonathan Swift, I would be delighted to hear them. I would prefer that to a discussion of the holiday sermon, the weather, or any other nicety that I'm sure your mother has worked hard to instill in you."

We walked a few more paces, though I admit, my mind raced as my feet slowed.

"Miss Chase, I would delight to hear your thoughts. If not essays, then perhaps poetry? Are you familiar with Alexander Pope?"

Still, I could not speak. How could I, when I had been so long used to hiding my thoughts, stifling my tongue, curbing my mind in company? And yet, if ever I would speak my mind to him . . . I must do it soon, or lose the chance.

"If it helps . . . I know something of your history," he said, "and I have guessed at more. Forgive my impudence and familiarity, but . . . if I am correct—and I hope I am—I would . . . that is to say . . . I mean . . ."

"Presumably Tommy told you that I've recently come out of mourning for my fiancé," I blurted.

Mr. Chandler nodded, and I could not decide whether to kiss Tommy or strangle him.

"I was ill, a while back, and he was my constant visitor," Mr. Chandler said. "To divert me, he told me of your family."

"When he should have been at studies, I'm sure," I said. My life, a diversion! The hangman's scaffold for all men, Tommy and Chandler first in line at Tyburn!

"You misunderstand me. I wanted to hear about your family; Tommy's been a good friend to me." Mr. Chandler paused. "He mentioned your decline after your fiancé's death. And that your fiancé had died . . . badly."

Very badly, I thought. Richard had compounded the intemperance of two bottles of claret over cards with the foolishness of riding home late at night. His horse had been found riderless, grazing by a bridge the next day. Richard, his neck broken, was found in the stream below.

"Tommy also described your distress in discovering, after the fact, that your fiancé had done . . . things no gentleman would dream of."

It was true; after I'd learned what a polite monster I very nearly was wife to—a man who treated his parents' unwilling maidservants as his personal harem— I nearly despaired of a better fate. My discovery made me blush still: Not only had I perceived none of Richard's true character, but outside my family, it seemed the rest of the world knew, winked at his base behavior as a man's prerogative, and still thought him a fine match for me.

But being every bit as stubborn as my mother claims, I also determined never to be fooled again by pretty manners and a base heart. I sought to educate myself in the ways of the world beyond my safe home, listening as my brothers' tutors taught them, while I pretended to be wrapped up in some fancy needlework. I snuck books from the library. Tommy caught me reading once, but my admission and reasons baffled him, and what confuses Tommy is dismissed from his mind, often enough.

Or was it? I began to wonder.

"In my profession of the law, I am confronted by every degree of human failure and virtue," Mr. Chandler said, quickening his pace and glancing at me. "But I have rarely observed anything so admirable and courageous as your attempt to educate yourself, and by doing so, address the unfair and damaging constraints of polite society upon an individual."

"My brother is indiscreet," I said. Was it possible that Mr. Chandler understood?

He shook his head fervently. "Tommy never said, 'my sister, most unladylike and unnatural, reads that which should spoil a woman.' He merely noticed a volume on my shelf, and said 'ah, Mags would like that,' no more. He looked guilty, as if he'd betrayed a secret, and I pretended not to notice. But ever since then . . ."

Miracle of miracles, Mr. Chandler, so far from being appalled by my secret, had sought me out.

I decided then.

"I found Swift difficult, at first, and somewhat shocking," I began, cautiously, hesitantly. But surely, in the bustle of the street, people caroling, carriages rolling by, the sounds of happy Christmas greetings coming from every doorway, no one could hear me. No one but Mr. Matthew Chandler.

Nearly half an hour later, we arrived on the front steps, and when the door opened, the pleasant aromas of a feast assailed us. Mother fussed, but was so pleased that she beamed as she berated me for a slowcoach and meanderer. Dash dragged himself in, gave an aggrieved woof, and immediately departed for his basket. Father mumbled that the cold weather was too much for me and searched my face anxiously.

I could not help but smile.

As I entered the hall, it was as though I saw the house and its decorations anew. The holly and ivy garlands were a beautiful token of Christmastide, a reminder of our eternal life after death. They were also emblematic of man and woman united.

Shortly thereafter, Tommy led me into the dining room. "So, Mags. Did you like my Christmas present?"

I held out my wrist. "Yes, thank you, Tommy. As I mentioned this morning, the coral bracelet is very pretty."

"That wasn't what I was talking about," he said, pinching my arm. His glance darted over to where Mr. Chandler stood behind his chair, nearly obscured by the monstrous pyramid of fruit on the table. While the others exclaimed at the platters of turkey and beef that arrived, Mr. Chandler watched only me, and I fancy I saw a faint grin, confused and boyish, play across his lips.

"Just make sure that he can stay until our dance on Twelfth Night," I whispered, letting Tommy seat me.

The Ghost of Christmas Passed

Mary Daheim

Judith McMonigle Flynn tossed aside the photograph folders, chucked the phony holly, and rang the ancient farm bell.

"I found it!" she called to her husband, Joe. "The bell was in with some of the old stuff in the wrong box you brought from the basement."

"Then how can it be wrong?" Joe said in his musing, mellow voice. "It has the right bell."

Judith gripped the kitchen counter and pulled herself to her feet. "But it's labeled MISC.X," she said, pointing to the black marker letters on the carton. "The bell should be with the fireplace wreath and the Nativity set and the parlor candles." She gave the bell another shake. The sound was hollow, yet resonant. "This must be a hundred years old."

"Did your mother buy it when she was a teenager?" Joe asked with a mischievous glint in his green eyes.

Judith frowned at her husband. "Mother's not *that* old. Her family had it on the farm when they lived up toward the mountains."

"That property's a strip mall now," Joe said. "Bill and I drove by there last month when we went fishing."

Judith shook her head. "I know. I suppose it's been sold ten times over since Grandpa and Grandma Hoffman owned it."

Joe glanced up at the schoolhouse clock. "Speaking of family, what time does everybody arrive for the Christmas Eve festivities?"

"Around five," Judith replied, placing the bell next to the computer on the counter. "Renie's coming over early to help me get ready."

"When's Bill coming to help me?" Joe asked in a plaintive voice.

"Help you do what?" Judith responded. "All I need you for is to put up the draperies between the living room and the entry hall to cordon off the tree and the presents until Santa arrives. You and Bill can watch pro football the rest of the day. Husbands get in the way at holiday time. My cousin and I need to focus on the food."

Joe seemed dubious. "You sure?"

Judith nodded. "This year we have no B&B guests for the Christmas holiday. I've gotten too old to deal with outsiders while we entertain the family. The extra money's nice, but I prefer my sanity."

"Good plan," Joe said, removing the lid from a Christmas cookie tin. "Are these your spritz or Renie's?"

"Mine, of course," Judith replied. "Why?"

"Hers taste like plaster. I thought you two made the spritz together."

"We did," Judith said, watching Joe devour three cookies, all shaped like camels. "Hey, you ate breakfast less than an hour ago. You should watch your waistline, especially this time of year."

"I can't see my waistline," Joe said. "How can I watch it?"

"My point." The phone rang. "I don't want you turning out like Dan," she added, referring to her first husband who had weighed more than four hundred pounds when he died at the age of forty-nine. "Hello?"

"I'm ready," Renie announced in a foggy voice. "Shall I come over?"

"It's not ten yet," Judith said in surprise. "I thought you'd still be asleep."

"Not today." Renie definitely sounded only semiconscious. "It's Christmas Eve. Got to get ready for Santa. He's going to the German deli and can drop me off on his way."

Renie's husband, Bill Jones, had played Santa for years, taking up the mantle—or the sleigh—from Grandpa Grover. The tradition involved closing off the living room at the Grover family home, which Judith had converted into Hillside Manor Bed and Breakfast some sixteen years earlier. Every Christmas Eve, Santa stood in the dark and talked to all the relatives who were gathered in the dining room, entry hall, and the staircase. His arrival through the French doors was announced by the old farm bell. After Santa left, the tree lights were turned on and the draperies were removed. A glut of colorfully wrapped presents covered half of the floor and the Douglas fir stood shimmering in all its Christmas splendor. The tradition and the mystery delighted everyone, especially the children. For aging adults such as the cousins' generation, Christmas Eve was a nostalgic trip down memory lane.

"Come ahead," Judith said. "Say, maybe Joe can go with Bill to the deli. I've got a couple of things I need from there."

"Sure," Renie said. "I'll tell . . . Bill, right? Damn, it's early. G'bye."

Joe didn't have to be coaxed into making the trip to the south end of the city. He might be Irish, but he liked German delicacies, especially the various wursts and the tubes of raw meat for spreading on crisp sesame crackers.

While Joe got to work on the heavy dark blue drapes that served to hide the living room, Judith put back the items she'd found in the box where the bell had been misplaced. She should throw out the artificial holly; she hadn't used it in years. But Judith hated to get rid of things, no matter how old, how worn, or how useless. The holly went back into the carton, along with a defective string of Christmas bulbs, the faded red velveteen wreaths that had hung in the parlor windows when she was a child, and a half-dozen Christmas cards from years past and persons long dead.

The phone rang again. "Okay, twerp," Auntie Vance barked into the phone, "what shall I bring for tonight? And make it snappy. We'll have to wait forever to catch the ferry over to the mainland. We may not show up until New Year's."

Auntie Vance and Uncle Vince had retired to an island in the sound. They called it "The Rock" and pretended that they'd isolated themselves from the rest of the family. But despite Auntie Vance's rough tongue, she had the proverbial heart of gold—or, as Renie sometimes said, a lot of guilt. She and her husband visited frequently, usually bringing lunch or dinner for Judith's and Renie's invalid mothers.

"Shrimp macaroni salad," Judith said, glancing at

the list she'd made earlier in the week. "Your beef-noodle bake. And Grandma's sugar cookies."

"Forget the cookies," Vance snapped. "They taste like Grandma made them—before she died thirty years ago. Hey!" she shouted away from the phone. "Wake up, Vinster! Your head's in the soup kettle. Again."

Uncle Vince had a life-long habit of falling asleep—anytime, anywhere, under any circumstances, including at the wheel of his car. Some family members marveled that he hadn't gotten killed years ago. The rest of the relatives marveled that he hadn't killed Auntie Vance.

Renie and Bill arrived just as Auntie Vance hung up. Bill waited in the driveway for Joe who went out the back door as Renie came in.

"Good morning," Joe said to Renie.

"What's good about it?" Renie muttered, brushing past him. "It's not even ten-thirty yet. I should be eating Cheerios and reading the paper."

"I don't think Joe heard that last part," Judith chided as Renie staggered down the narrow hallway to the kitchen. "Gee, you look really awful this morning. Worse than usual."

Unfazed by the comment, Renie glanced down at her attire. Her blue jeans were spattered with mud and her frayed sweatshirt was emblazoned with JOYEUX NOEL, which lighted up. Apparently the battery was defective—or Renie was—since the only glowing letters read "Jo e No ."

"Now I see why Joe didn't stick around," Judith said. "You probably insulted him."

Renie was still studying her chest. "Oh—right. This

thing's really old. Bill bought it for me. He knows I don't do electrical. Anyway, if we're going to cook, I didn't want to ruin my clothes."

"Too late for that," Judith said dryly.

"Uh." Renie was unperturbed. "Who's the guy in the driveway?"

"What guy?"

"Tall, thirties, sharp overcoat, muffler." Renie frowned. "Maybe I imagined it. I dreamed I lost Bill in Brooks Brothers last night. He got scared by the price tags."

"I wouldn't doubt it," Judith said. "Bill's not a Brooks Brothers type. Have your kids all arrived in town?"

"All except Anne and Odo," Renie replied. "Their flight's due this afternoon. I was so afraid none of them would get here. It wouldn't be Christmas without them."

"Of course not," Judith agreed. "Mike and Kristin and the boys will be here around four. Assuming, of course, they don't have another rock slide on the pass." She frowned, thinking of all the times her son and his family had been prevented by bad weather from making the fifty-odd mile trip from their cozy cabin at the summit. But Mike loved his job as a forest ranger, and the Flynns were lucky that his current posting had been so close to the city. Renie and Bill weren't so lucky—all three of their children lived great distances away. Worse yet, none had produced children since they'd gotten married. "I was just going to start the potato salad," Judith said. "You can get out the paper plates and plastic tableware. It's all in the pantry."

Renie started to reverse her path, but stopped when she saw the carton on the counter by the computer. "What are these old pictures?" she asked.

Judith began removing potatoes from a bag by the sink. "I only looked at the one on top. It's from 1941— the Christmas after Pearl Harbor."

Renie opened the gray folder. "We've got one of these somewhere at home," she said. "My God, look how young everybody is!"

"Sixty-odd years makes a difference," Judith allowed, looking over Renie's shoulder. "Our parents were half our age. You're a toddler. I'm an infant, just two months old."

"I haven't looked at our copy in ages," Renie murmured. "Out of Grandma and Grandpa's six kids, only three were married by then—our dads and Aunt Ellen. Of course Uncle Al never has abandoned bachelorhood."

"Too busy gambling and running his tavern with the illegal off-track betting," Judith said with a smile. "But he's still got his girlfriend, Tess. She's coming tonight, too."

Renie tapped several family members who were all standing by a Christmas tree that looked almost exactly like the one in the same place where this year's evergreen dominated the big living room. Judith not only hated to throw things away, she didn't care much for change. Routine offered security; the unknown created dread.

Judith began putting names to the smiling faces: Grandma and Grandpa Grover; their eldest son, Cliff, married to Deb against whose knee Renie was resting; Donald, the second son, and his wife, Gertrude, who held Judith on her lap; Uncle Al; Auntie Vance; a pregnant Aunt Ellen and her husband, Win, visiting from their home in Nebraska; Uncle Corky, whose given name was Charles. They were all tall, as Judith herself had grown to be upon reaching her teens. Renie was the runt of the family, a skinny two-year-old in pigtails.

"A good-looking bunch," Judith declared, "and thank God all the men lived through the war."

"Our dads didn't fight," Renie recalled. "They were too old, but they served as air raid wardens."

"You remember the war," Judith said as Renie closed the photograph folder, "I don't."

"I can even remember that picture being taken," Renie said. "Your mother was holding a yellow squeaky toy to make you stop crying. They airbrushed it out of the photo. I thought that was dumb at the time. You were only a baby, for heaven's sake. Why shouldn't you cry?"

Judith smiled fondly at her cousin. Neither had ever had siblings, and they'd grown up like sisters. Judging from Renie's reaction as a toddler, the bond between them had already been forged.

"What's this one?" Renie asked, picking up another folder. "It looks really old." Judith watched while Renie opened the brown folder. "Your mother's First Communion," she said, answering her own question. "Did she ever look that sweet?"

"A fluke of the camera," Judith replied, taking in the white dress, veil, and pearl rosary beads. "Or Divine Intervention. Come on, we have to get to work."

"I have to wake up," Renie asserted. "Here, this big photo's even older." She opened a fraying black cover to reveal two middle-aged adults and five young people, all dressed in their finest World War One–era clothes. "Oh—your mother's family. Isn't she the only one who's still alive?"

Judith nodded. "Mother was the youngest. Uncle Ed died in his forties. Heart, I think, like my own father. Aunt Charlotte was fairly young, too. Cancer. Uncle Jack got hit by a bus. And Uncle Bart . . ." Judith stopped. "I never did know what happened to him. He must have been the black sheep of the family. Mother's hardly ever mentioned his name."

"Which one is he?" Renie asked.

Judith pointed to a strapping young man with dark hair. "He was a handsome guy, the second oldest, after Uncle Ed. I think there was at least ten years between Mother and her two older brothers."

Renie closed the folder and turned it over. "The family tree's on the back. It shows your grandmother and grandfather, and all the kids, but the only line that's continued is your mother's."

"That's because she put it together," Judith replied. "Come on, coz, get cracking. You *seem* awake."

"But whoever started the tree spelled Hoffman H-O-F-M-A-N-N. That's not the way Aunt Gert has always spelled her maiden name."

"It was probably some immigration clerk's mistake," Judith said impatiently. "Grandfather came to the United States from Germany before the turn of the century. There were lots of mix-ups with foreign names at Ellis Island in those days. Put a dozen eggs on to boil."

Reluctantly, Renie set the photos back into the carton. "I'll get the plates and stuff first."

"Fine. Just do *something*. Time's a-wasting, as Grandma Grover would say."

Renie went into the pantry and returned with two big shopping bags filled with disposable tableware. As she unwrapped plates, cups, and napkins, her eyes kept straying to the carton where she'd placed the photographs.

"Odd, isn't it?" she finally said. "We know so much about our fathers' Grover side of the family, but not about our maternal ancestors. Of course my mother was an only child. But you must have all sorts of cousins on the Hoffman side you've never met."

"Could be," Judith allowed, running water over the potatoes. "Mother's family didn't stay in the area. Uncle Ed and Uncle Jack moved to southern California and got into the oil business. Then they went to Venezuela—Maracaibo, I think. Aunt Charlotte married a Canadian and settled in Toronto. She and Mother kept in touch, but were never close. They visited once when I was about six with a couple of boys who were several years older than I was. Naturally, they kept their distance from a mere little girl like me."

Renie unfolded a large plastic tablecloth decorated with poinsettias, "And Uncle Bart?"

Judith shrugged. "He just sort of . . . faded away. I told you, Mother never talks about him. Goodness, she doesn't talk much about her other siblings, either. Once they left the area, she considered them deserters. All she could ever say about Uncle Ed and Uncle Jack was that they went to California to become big shots. She didn't approve of California—or big shots. And Charlotte was always that 'foreigner' after she moved to Canada."

"Odd," Renie remarked.

Judith turned away from the stove where she'd put the kettle of potatoes on the back burner. "What's odd?"

"Your mother was the only one to stay around here," Renie said.

"Nothing odd about it," Judith responded. "Where are those eggs?"

"I'm getting them," Renie said, opening the fridge. "Everybody else in her family seemed to have wanderlust."

Judith poured water into another kettle. "Put the eggs in here and salt them in case they crack. Mother was the youngest. She was eighteen when her own mother died, and her father lasted only another year or so. Mother was on her own, except for a maiden aunt who lived here on Heraldsgate Hill. That's when Mother moved into the city and went to secretarial school. She stayed with her mother's sister, Aunt Effie."

"Except for being raised on a farm, the movie people didn't use any of that in her life story," Renie pointed out.

"That was about the only fact they did use," Judith said, referring to *Gritty Gertie,* the film that had been based on Gertrude as a member of "The Greatest Generation." When a Hollywood producer and his entourage had stayed at Hillside Manor, the screenwriter had become intrigued with Gertrude's life story and talked her into using it as the basis for a movie about a so-called typical woman whose life had spanned most of the twentieth century. The end result was neither typical nor true, portraying the on-screen

Gertrude as brave but bawdy. "No wonder Mother hated watching it."

"The truth's often more interesting," Renie remarked.

"That's so." Judith turned down the burner underneath the potatoes, which had started to boil. "Speaking of Mother, I should bring her in here to help. She can cut up the onions. What's *your* mother doing today?"

"Worrying about me—as usual," Renie replied, "and entertaining her drop-in friends who'll bring her all sorts of stupid gifts she doesn't need, not to mention doughy banana bread and ugly refrigerator magnets. She'll be busy until it's time to pick her up to come over here."

"Aunt Deb loves company," Judith commented. "I'm going out to get Mother. Keep an eye on those eggs so they don't boil over."

Judith didn't bother with a jacket to walk the short distance between the back porch and the converted toolshed that served as her mother's apartment. It was cool and drizzly, a typical December day in the Pacific Northwest. Snow wasn't in the forecast, although Judith wouldn't have minded a slight dusting to enhance the season as long as it didn't impede driving on the city's steep hills.

She paused at the bottom of the back steps and then walked far enough to see the length of the driveway along the side of the house. There were several cars parked in the cul-de-sac, probably owned by family and friends of the other neighbors. If Renie had seen someone in the drive, it was probably a stray visitor who was unfamiliar with the area. It could, she reassured herself, even be someone scouting out the B&B for a future stay.

Judith opened the toolshed door and saw her mother sitting at her usual place behind a cluttered card table. "Want to help cook?" she asked.

Gertrude didn't answer. The old lady stared straight ahead, but appeared not to see her daughter.

"Mother?" Judith asked in sudden alarm. "Mother, what's wrong?"

Gertrude was very pale. Her arthritic hands clawed at the card table's edge. As Judith approached, the old lady swallowed hard and finally spoke. "Nothing," she said in a voice that was scarcely a whisper.

"You don't seem well," Judith said, putting a hand on her mother's forehead to check for fever. "You look like you've seen a ghost."

Gertrude grunted and pushed Judith's hand away. "I have," she said. "Go away."

Judith refused to budge. "Mother, you have to tell me what's wrong. Are you sick?"

"No." Gertrude shook her head. "Just let me be."

"I can't. It's Christmas Eve. If you're upset, I'm upset. At least tell me what's the matter." Judith quickly scanned the card table and the rest of the small sitting room. Nothing seemed unusual. Except, she noticed, a plaid muffler lying on the arm of the empty easy chair. "Where'd that come from?"

Gertrude turned to see what Judith was pointing at. "What?"

"That muffler, that scarf. It's not yours."

Gertrude let out a heavy sigh. "Somebody must have left it." She began fumbling with the candy wrappers, the jumble puzzles, and the playing cards on the table. "Get my heavy sweater. Your house is cold."

"You're coming?"

" 'Course I'm coming. It's Christmas Eve."

Judith decided not to press her mother for details. Every so often Gertrude suffered some kind of spell, even a faint. But for her advanced years, she was in good health. Crippled, unable to walk on her own, occasionally forgetful, and a bit deaf, but otherwise the old lady was usually able to cope, despite her protestations to the contrary. She was, as Judith sometimes put it, too ornery to die.

"Renie's here," Judith said, helping Gertrude get ready to go outside in the motorized wheelchair that made life much easier for both mother and daughter. "I found the old farm bell, by the way."

"Good," Gertrude said. "Where was it?"

"Joe had put it in the wrong box," Judith said as she let her mother go through the door first. "You know how I hate to go up and down the basement stairs since I've had my artificial hip. That means I have to trust Joe to organize everything we store downstairs."

"Lunkhead couldn't organize his clothes," Gertrude snarled. "It's a wonder he doesn't wear his pants on his head."

"Now, Mother . . ." Judith began, but stopped. She was too relieved that Gertrude seemed to have reverted to her usual caustic form.

Renie greeted her aunt with a hug and a kiss on the cheek. "What's with you?" Gertrude demanded. "Your bosom glows in the dark."

Renie looked down at her sweatshirt. "I'm festive."

"You're festiferous," Gertrude snapped.

"That's not a word, Aunt Gert," Renie countered.

"It is, too. I made it up years ago. And it suits you. It means you're as welcome as a boil." The old lady revved up her wheelchair and sped past her niece.

Gertrude began peeling onions; Renie started making salmon pâté; Judith mixed the ingredients for artichoke-crab dip. The CD player on the counter played Christmas carols, and Sweetums the cat roamed around the kitchen, apparently hoping for a taste of the seafood. Tempting aromas wafted through the air, Bing Crosby crooned as if it were 1944, and harmony reigned among the three women. Or at least as much harmony as the cousins could expect with Gertrude telling them at five-minute intervals what they were doing wrong.

"Nobody ate artichokes in my day," she asserted, glaring at her daughter. "You should have boiled the potatoes with the skins on. Your generation's too lazy to peel them after they're cooked. You have to do it the easy way. Serena," she rasped, eyeing her niece, "why are you putting that salmon in the blender thingamabob? Do it by hand. How can you tell if it's smooth, if you aren't mixing it yourself?"

"I could put my hand in the blender to check," Renie said.

Gertrude's chin jutted. "Do it while it's still running."

By noon, Judith was beginning to feel as if the buffet supper preparations were coming together. She'd almost forgotten about her mother's unsettling behavior earlier in the day. She had, in fact, forgotten about the unfamiliar muffler left on the easy chair. It was, after all, Christmas Eve.

* * *

"Let's take a break," Judith said. "I'll make some lunch. What would you like, Mother?"

"Ham sandwich," Gertrude replied. "I saw that ham in the refrigerator. Cut me a big slice. White bread. I don't like that dark stuff with seeds. They get stuck in my dentures."

She turned to Renie. "Coz?"

"Sounds good," Renie said, "but I like the seven-grain bread. Got any Swiss cheese?"

"Not yet," Judith said. "Isn't Bill buying cheeses at the German deli?"

"You're right," Renie agreed. "I'll wait. The guys should be back any time." She gazed at Gertrude, who was taunting the cat with a sliver of Dungeness crabmeat. "Say, how about a hot buttered rum?"

Judith frowned. "We have to stay focused."

Renie looked exasperated. "A mug of hot buttered rum isn't going to make us tipsy. It's Christmas."

Judith gave in. A little pick-me-up wouldn't do any harm. "I'll make the sandwiches, you do the toddies. The batter's on the second shelf in the fridge."

Gertrude finally permitted Sweetums to eat the crab. He showed no sign of gratitude, narrowing his eyes at the old lady, lapping up the crab in a single gulp, and licking his whiskers as if to say, "I am Cat. I win again, Stupid Human."

Judith made ham sandwiches for her mother and herself. Renie prepared the hot buttered rum and poured the steaming liquid into coffee mugs decorated with holly decals.

"Bottoms up," she said, toasting Gertrude and Judith.

Gertrude took a swig and coughed. "Ack! This is strong!"

"No, it's not," Renie said. "Honest, Aunt Gert, I'm not trying to get you drunk."

"Hunh." Gertrude gave her niece the evil eye before she took another, slower sip. "It *is* tasty, though."

Judith sampled her own toddy. "Renie's right, Mother. I can barely taste the rum in my mug."

Gertrude looked skeptical, but kept on sipping.

"Hey," Renie said to her aunt, perching on the edge of the kitchen table, "Judith found some of those old family pictures this morning. Want a peek?"

"What pictures?" Gertrude asked, looking downright suspicious. "The ones of me in my Flapper days? I looked like Joan Crawford, didn't I? Why didn't they get her to play me in that dopey movie?"

"Communication problems," Renie replied. "Joan was hard to reach. St. Peter's cell phone battery went out."

"Your battery went out a long time ago, nitwit." Gertrude took another swig of her drink. "Still, I like what your bosom says. JOE NO. Sounds good to me." She chuckled richly at her own skewed humor.

"Mother . . ." Judith sighed. She didn't want to get into an argument, not on Christmas Eve.

Renie hopped off of the table and went over to the carton to get the photographs. She handed the 1941 picture to Gertrude first. "Remember this?"

The old lady's wrinkled face softened. "Oh, yes. Yes, I sure do. See? Don't I look like Joan Crawford?"

"Remarkable," Renie murmured.

"It's your mouth," Judith put in. "And the hair style." In fact, Gertrude *had* resembled the late film star in both of their primes.

"Look at your father," Gertrude said to Judith. "Isn't

he handsome? He never did have much hair, though. And what's Cliff doing to Vance? It looks like he's pulling bugs out of her hair."

Renie's father was turned slightly away from the camera, plucking at Auntie Vance's curly blond bob. "I think," Renie said, "knowing my dad, he was probably trying to get a rise out of her. Dad enjoyed teasing his sisters-in-law, especially Auntie Vance because she always gave as good as she got."

"We had fun," Gertrude declared. "We always had a good time." She shuddered slightly. "Look at Al and Corky and Ellen's hubby, Win. We didn't know then if they'd ever come back from the war in one piece. Or at all. Scary times. Those boys really were the greatest generation."

After refilling Gertrude's mug, Renie slid the older photo onto Gertrude's lap. "How about this one?"

Opening the folder, Gertrude frowned. "My folks," she said softly. "I haven't seen this in years." With a hand that shook a little, she sipped more rum toddy. "Oh, my!"

Judith tried to catch Renie's eye and give her cousin a warning to back off. Renie ignored her. "Good-looking people," she said. "I'm sorry I never knew any of them—except you."

"Don't be," Gertrude snapped. She ran her hand over the picture as if she could feel her family's presence in the room. "Oh, they were all right. Nobody's perfect." She bent her head closer to the photo. "They look fuzzy. Where's my magnifier?"

With a distrustful glance at Renie, Judith picked up her mother's mug and took a small taste. "My," she said pointedly to her cousin, "Mother's drink seems to be unusually powerful."

Renie feigned innocence. "Oh?"

Gertrude looked up. "What're you talking about?"

Judith switched her mug for her mother's. "I think I have the wrong drink," she said. "Let's get back to work. You still have to make the liver pâté, coz."

"Hold on," Renie said, with a scowl for Judith. "Tell me about your family, Aunt Gert. What happened to all those handsome brothers?"

"They croaked," Gertrude replied, closing the folder. "So did my sister, the Canadian turncoat."

"You seem to be the youngest," Renie noted. "Did those handsome big brothers spoil their baby sister?"

"Coz!" Judith barked, waving a cooking fork at Renie. "Knock it off! We've got tasks to do."

Renie, however, was looking mulish, a not uncommon expression for a woman who would rather get her own way than win the lottery. "Shut up," she snapped. "Where's your famous curiosity?"

"This isn't the time for it," Judith shot back. "It's after one o'clock. Our husbands are here with the rest of the food."

Joe and Bill trooped in through the back door, each carrying several large white paper bags and singing "O Tannenbaum" in very bad German.

Judith noticed that Gertrude's expression showed a rare sense of relief at seeing her son-in-law and her nephew by marriage. "Hullo, boys," she said, raising the mug that Judith had been using. "Have a tooty. I mean, *toddy*."

Joe shot Gertrude a wary glance; Bill made a noise

that sounded like "Brmph." The two men set all their purchases on the counter and left the kitchen via the backstairs.

"I bet they're going to the family quarters to watch football," Renie murmured, "or basketball. Even hockey, if they can avoid being asked to do anything else today."

Judith shrugged. "It's better if they're not in the way." She glanced at Gertrude, who was humming "Adestes Fideles" in an off-key accompaniment to Frank Sinatra. The old lady had tears running down her cheeks.

"Mother," Judith said, "what's wrong now?"

"I miss your father," Gertrude said softly. "I miss my folks. I miss everybody."

"Oh, Mother!" Judith put her arm around Gertrude's sloping shoulders. "Of course you do! Christmas can be a sad as well as a joyous time. We all have memories of lost loved ones."

"Not like mine," Gertrude declared, trying to wipe away the tears.

"You mean your brothers and your sister moving away?" Judith said. "Renie and Bill's kids live far from here. They're lucky if they see them once or twice a year."

"It's not the same," Gertrude asserted.

"That's true," Renie put in. "There's e-mail and phone calls and even cameras on the computer that can . . ."

Gertrude emphatically shook her head. "I'm not talking about modern doodads." She sniffled and cleared her throat. "I mean the ones who just . . . go."

Judith studied her mother's face. Gertrude was a

little glassy-eyed. Perhaps the heavy dose of rum had made her maudlin.

Judith pulled a chair up beside her mother and sat down. "I'm not sure what you mean. Go where? To heaven?"

"Hell's more like it," Gertrude muttered, her tears no longer falling. She looked angry—and then bewildered. "No—I don't mean that."

Gertrude looked not at Judith but at Renie. "You're the one asking all the questions. It's usually my dopey daughter who has to find out everything. Some sleuth! She doesn't even know a criminal when he's staring her in the face."

"Hey, Aunt Gert," Renie began. "I didn't intend to upset—"

"Be quiet!" Gertrude snarled. Calmly, she folded her hands in her lap. "It's time to tell you anyway," she went on, looking at Judith, who had edged away in the chair. "I don't think it's smart to take this kind of stuff to the grave."

Judith started to protest. "Mother—"

"You, too," Gertrude rasped. "Keep your trap closed! And listen."

Judith leaned forward in her chair; Renie hopped back on the table. Neither spoke, but waited for the older woman to continue.

"My folks were good people, but strict," Gertrude began. "Papa and Mama were born in Germany. We all were. But Papa came to this country first, to take a job on his cousin's apple orchard east of the mountains. He sent for us a year later. I was just a baby."

Judith nodded. She knew this part of the story.

"Cousin Josef—Joe, they called him." Gertrude

grimaced at the name. "I remember him—he wasn't a bit like Lunkhead, despite the name. He knew how to make money, and the orchard was a big success."

Judith wanted to interrupt and defend her husband, who, unlike his predecessor, Dan, was a good provider. But she thought it best not to derail her mother.

"Papa didn't like the weather on the other side of the mountains," Gertrude said, looking straight ahead in the direction of the kitchen cabinets. "Too cold in the winter, too hot in the summer. When I was four, he moved us all over the mountain pass where we settled on a farm he bought with his savings. It wasn't an orchard—a couple of apple and cherry trees. But we had chickens and cows and a swaybacked horse and a big vegetable garden, enough food to feed ourselves, but Papa had to take a job in one of the mills a few miles down the road." She paused to sip from her toddy. "The horse's name was George, and that animal was the cause of it all, I'm sure of that." Gertrude nodded twice. "George was an ornery critter. Stubborn as any mule—Mama always said George was part mule, but he wasn't. Anyway, he kicked Bart in the head one day. My brother was never the same after that. He got ornery and moody. He didn't want to live on the farm any more. A year or so later—he was twenty-five—he went off to the city to find a job. He got on with the city clerk's office and fell in love with a girl who was engaged to one of the city attorneys."

Gertrude seemed to be running out of breath. She took a wrinkled handkerchief out of her housecoat pocket and blew her nose.

"Can I get you anything, Mother?" Judith asked.

Gertrude shook her head. "Let me finish. Bart was crazy about her, and maybe she led him on, I don't know. Anyway, he thought she liked him and intended to break off her engagement. The problem was, and this is what I figured out years later, being too young at the time to know what goes on in people's heads— that the girl was one of those softhearted, or soft-headed, people who can never hurt anybody's feelings, even when it's the thing to do. I've never had that problem."

"Very true," Judith put in, aware that her artificial hip was beginning to ache. She was past due for her six-hour dose of Percocet, but didn't want to distract her mother. "You always are . . . direct."

"Honesty's the best policy," Gertrude declared. "So this girl—I don't remember her name, don't want to, really—told Bart that her fiancé was the jealous type and if he ever caught her even talking to another fellow, he'd do something awful, so she'd have to stop seeing Bart even on a casual basis. My brother was heartbroken. The next morning, he left the rooming house where he lived up the hill from city hall and came downtown. He waited in a doorway, and when this attorney fellow got off the streetcar, Bart shot and killed him."

Judith was so stunned that she lurched sideways in the chair. Renie let out a gasp and pressed a hand to her lips. Gertrude sat rigid in her wheelchair, still staring straight ahead.

"He was arrested right away," the old lady went on. "He was tried and convicted, but was found insane. Bart was sent to an asylum. Within six months, he escaped. Nobody ever heard from him again."

"My God!" Judith exclaimed in a shaken voice. "How did your parents stand it?"

"They didn't," Gertrude said, finally turning toward her daughter. "They were both dead within a few years. Disgrace, sorrow, worry—you name it. They changed the spelling of our last name—as if they could wipe out Bart's crime. It was really because of their shame over what he did. Guilt, too. My folks suffered, right into the grave."

Renie had slid off of the kitchen table. "Did they think your brother was insane because of the head injury by that horse?"

Gertrude shrugged. "I suppose. I always figured that."

"He could've gone anywhere," Judith murmured, more to herself than to her mother or Renie.

But Gertrude, despite her alleged deafness, caught the words. "Or nowhere. At least not very far. I thought he probably tried to run away on a train. The asylum wasn't far from the railroad line. He may have been hit by the locomotive or killed by some hobo. I couldn't imagine him not contacting the family somehow, just to let us know he was alive."

A barrage of thoughts flew through Judith's mind. She'd always known that her paternal grandparents had died fairly young and left Gertrude an orphan in her late teens. She'd been aware that her mother's siblings hadn't kept close ties. It was understandable that Gertrude had developed an inner toughness that sharpened her tongue and sometimes soured her disposition. And later in life, Judith's father had passed away in his prime from a heart condition.

But life, Judith knew from her own experience, was

rugged. No one got through it unscathed. She'd had her own dark secrets, especially when she'd married Dan after Joe had eloped with another woman. Judith was carrying Joe's child. Thirty-odd years ago, things were different. Unmarried mothers bore a social stigma, especially in the generation that had spawned Gertrude. Judith needed a husband and a father. And Dan needed her, if only as a source of steady income.

But murder was far worse than bearing a baby out of wedlock. And when Gertrude was young, insanity was another taboo, no matter what the cause. Judith's heart welled up with a newly kindled sympathy for her mother.

"I wish," she said, "you'd told me this years ago. It would've been easier on you. You know I'd never have reacted with anything but understanding."

"Me, neither, Aunt Gert," Renie asserted. "Frankly, it makes a good story."

Gertrude gave her niece a dark look. "Don't try to be a smart-mouth," she warned. "There's nothing good about it."

For an instant, Renie looked embarrassed. But humility had never been her strong suit. "Okay, so why are you telling us this now?"

Gertrude started to pick up her toddy mug from the small tray on her wheelchair, but apparently thought better of it and put her hands back in her lap. "Because," she said, her voice lower and more raspy than ever, "Bart came to see me today."

Judith was too alarmed to say anything. Her mother became confused occasionally—or pretended that she was—but she'd never shown signs of being delusional.

Renie simply looked curious. Gertrude kept her eyes on her lap.

"How do you mean?" Judith finally asked.

Gertrude didn't answer. The portable CD player had gone silent after a choral rendition of "I Saw Three Ships."

"Mother?" Judith put a hand on the old lady's arm. "Tell us. Were you dozing? Was it like a dream?"

Gertrude kept her eyes lowered. "I want to go back to my box," she said, with her usual contempt for the converted toolshed.

"Not yet," Judith said. She thought about her options. Call the doctor? Have her mother lie down? Wait until she was completely sober from the rum toddy? "Let's finish up in the kitchen. I still have to put some presents under the tree. Then I'll get Baby Jesus out of the Nativity box so we can put him in the crèche this evening."

"That's not Baby Jesus," Gertrude mumbled.

Judith frowned. "What?"

"Baby Jesus got busted." Gertrude still didn't look at Judith. "The one you've got is a fake."

Judith and Renie exchanged curious glances. The Nativity set had been made in Germany and handed down to Gertrude and then to Judith. The figures weren't elegant like the Holy Family trio Judith had bought in Italy when she and Renie had traveled there forty years earlier. The older set had probably been cheap, but was no less loved for its dime-store price.

"You mean," Judith said slowly to her mother, "the figure we've always used isn't the original."

Gertrude twisted her hands in an agitated manner, but her gaze remained fixed. "Yes. It's a fake," she repeated.

Judith looked again at Renie, who was finally showing signs of remorse.

"Damn," Renie said under her breath. "Why didn't I leave well enough alone?"

Judith frowned at her cousin, but said, "Let's do the liver pâté. Maybe I should make a Jell-O mold. That's always refreshing with so much rich food."

She went to the fridge and got out the chicken livers, the mushrooms, and the scallions. "Here, coz, get the pâté started. The butter's in the dish on the counter."

"Okay." An unusually docile Renie took the ingredients from Judith. "You want to cut up the mushrooms, Aunt Gert?"

"What?" The old lady seemed lost in reverie. "Mushrooms? Oh—sure. Give me a paring knife. I can cut them on my tray."

Judith slipped another CD into the player. The Three Tenors burst forth with their own heavily accented version of "White Christmas."

"Can't those guys speak English?" Gertrude demanded.

"Of course," Judith replied. "But English isn't their first language."

"Sounds to me like it's about in ninth place," Gertrude grumbled, attacking the mushrooms as if they might be trying to escape.

Relieved that her mother seemed more like herself, Judith smiled. "They sing beautifully, though."

"I like Bing better," Gertrude said. "His English is fine. He grew up around here."

A few minutes later, Joe showed up in the kitchen, seeking snacks. "Is that salmon pâté ready?" he asked.

"No," Renie said. "It has to set in the fridge for at

least a couple of hours. Why don't you and Bill eat some of the Katzenjammer Kids' deli food? You've got enough to feed another German army marching on Stalingrad."

"Good thinking," Joe said, opening the fridge. "What would Bill like?"

"All of it," Renie replied, "plus some weird pop. Got any Perky Papaya or Tantalizing Tangerine?"

"We don't buy that offbeat brand," Joe said. "Diet 7-UP will have to do."

"How about strychnine?" Gertrude suggested.

Joe paused with his hands full of paper plates piled high with cheese, bread, sliced meat, and pickles. "How would you like it?"

"Up your you-know-what," Gertrude retorted.

Joe grinned. "Merry Christmas to you, too," he said, and headed for the backstairs.

Renie turned to the stove where she was melting a half pound of butter for the liver pâté. She gave a start when the phone rang. "Maybe that's Anne, calling from the airport."

Judith picked up the receiver. It wasn't Renie's daughter. It was Cousin Sue, calling from east of the lake.

"We may not get to your house until six," she said. "Our bartender, Emil, was just arrested."

Sue and her husband, Ken, had taken over Uncle Al's restaurant years ago, complete with the responsibility of running his illegal poker room and bookie operation.

"What happened?" Judith asked, trying to ignore curious looks from Renie and Gertrude.

"Oh—nothing too serious," Sue said in her customary imperturbable manner. "Emil's been talking to another restaurant owner about a job, but Ken and I thought it was just a ploy to keep us from complaining about him dipping into the till. He *is* a good bartender, you know. But it turns out he was serious and this other owner—his name is Nick—Nick the Norwegian, he's known as—wants to take over the card-room operation, so he got Emil to put a bomb in our car last night, but it didn't go off because our battery died, and AAA found it when Ken called to get a jump start. We didn't want to call the police, but the man from AAA insisted—he hates car bombs—so we had to have Emil arrested because he confessed right away. He feels terrible, and we feel bad, because it's Christmas Eve. Anyway, we're not closing until four, so we may be late. See you." Sue hung up.

"What was that all about?" Renie asked.

Feeling dazed, Judith rubbed at her temples. "I need my Percocet," she murmured. "That was Cousin Sue."

"Oh," Renie said. "What now?"

"Do you really want to know?" Judith asked.

"No," Renie said. "I assume it's the usual disastrous consequence of leading a life of crime. Is she making her taco salad?"

"I didn't get a chance to find out," Judith admitted.

"She'd better," Gertrude muttered. "The cat likes it a lot."

The cat had exited the kitchen somewhere between Bart's homicidal assault and his escape from the asylum. Judith swallowed her pain pill with a glass of water.

Gertrude gave the mushrooms a final whack. "No wonder Sue always has problems. Ellen should never have moved to Nebraska. All that flat land gives people peculiar notions. Win should've moved here. Then Sue would've been raised right. At least she had the good sense to settle back here after she was grown."

"She moved here," Renie put in, "because Uncle Al gave them the restaurant. Sue and Ken couldn't make a go of their corn-kernel jewelry store in Nebraska. If you can't peddle that stuff in the Cornhusker State, where can you make a living off of it?"

"Uncle Al never should have turned that restaurant over to them," Judith declared. "He knew everybody in the area and whose palms to grease. But Sue and Ken came as outsiders. It's a wonder they haven't been . . ." She stopped short of saying "arrested." It didn't seem like a tactful subject to bring up after Gertrude's revelations about Uncle Bart. ". . . staying in worse places than campsites," Judith amended.

"Ellen's cheap," Gertrude declared. "She was always cheap, but she got worse in Nebraska. Who goes camping in December?"

"Aunt Ellen and Uncle Win," Renie stated. "They camp when they drive here from Nebraska because Aunt Ellen won't pay more than five dollars a night for a motel."

Judith agreed. "Aunt Ellen called this morning. They spent the night in Oregon and should arrive around three. I told them they could stay here at the B&B because I'm not taking guests until the twenty-seventh, but she wouldn't hear of it. They're staying a whole week, and Aunt Ellen refused a free room, saying that it wasn't right to take money out of our pockets, and they were perfectly willing to put their tent up at the nearest campsite, which, I might add, is forty miles away."

Renie shook her head. "Relatives. Who has crazier ones than we do?"

"What's that?" Gertrude glared at her niece. "I don't want any talk about craziness. Not today."

"Sorry, Aunt Gert," Renie apologized. She removed the liver pâté from the burner. "Coz, let me help you put the rest of the presents under the tree. The pâté has to cool before I mix it in the blender."

Judith had stashed the presents on the second floor where the guests usually stayed. She'd made a half-dozen trips to bring them from the third-floor quarters earlier in the day, and had forgotten to ask Joe to bring them the rest of the way to the main floor.

"What did you think of Mother's so-called visit from her brother Bart?" Judith asked after the cousins reached the top of the backstairs.

"She dreamed it," Renie replied. "What else? If Bart really was still alive, he'd be about a hundred and ten."

"Yes." Judith led the way to the settee in the hallway where she'd put the gifts. "I agree. But there was one strange thing I noticed when I went out to get Mother. There was a muffler I didn't recognize on the easy chair."

Renie grimaced. "Green plaid?"

Judith nodded.

"That's what the guy I saw in the driveway was wearing," Renie said. "But he was young. Maybe he stopped to ask directions."

"Why not come to the house?" Judith frowned.

"He might have, of course, while Joe and I were getting things from the third floor and the basement. We wouldn't have heard him ring the bell. Mother may have talked to him and become confused." She shook herself. "I can't fret about that now. Here," she said, handing presents to Renie. "Be careful of the bows."

"Do you think your mother's story is true?" Renie asked, steadying the pile of presents with her chin as she started down the main stairway.

Judith was right behind Renie, clasping three medium-sized gift boxes to her bosom. "You mean Bart shooting that attorney and being sent to the asylum? Well—that'd explain why Mother never spoke of him."

Pushing the draperies aside, the cousins entered the big living room. The Christmas tree stood near the far end of the room, in front of the baby grand piano and in back of the matching sofas that flanked the fireplace. Evergreen garlands hung from the plate rails that ran along two walls. The mantel was festooned with various candles, music boxes, and the Holy Family from Italy. The full Nativity set was on the buffet, except for the Christ Child. "Fake" or not, He wouldn't be put in the crib until later that evening.

"Gorgeous," Renie asserted, eyes wide as she saw the pile of gifts that stretched a full four feet around the tree, "even when the lights aren't turned on. But my gosh, what a glut! Did you sell your soul to buy all this stuff?"

Judith shook her head. "It's not just from Joe and me. Mike brought their presents for the kids day before yesterday. He was tired of the boys tearing up their place to find the packages. Plus, some of the other relatives had their presents shipped directly to Hillside Manor."

"We've got quite a load ourselves," Renie said, "even without—sniff, sniff—grandchildren. Maybe Bill should go get our share now."

"Wait until you make your formal entrance," Judith advised. "You know how the kids love to hear rustling noises coming from the living room when it's shrouded in darkness."

Renie looked at her watch. "It's almost three. I should check to see if Anne and Odo's plane landed. They might have called our house and one of the other kids didn't bother to let me know."

"Typical," Judith remarked as Renie went to the phone on the cherrywood table and dialed her home number.

"Tony?" Renie said. "Oh, Tom—sorry, I see so little of you two boys that I forget which is which . . . No, it's not a guilt trip. It's a simple truth . . . What? . . . Tell Nana I'll call her back when I get home . . . Yes, I'm dressed warmly and Bill drove safely for that whole mile from our house to Judith and Joe's. Let Nana know that if she calls again . . ."

Renie was grinding her teeth between sentences. Obviously, Aunt Deb had been on her daughter's trail again, fretting over her health and well-being.

"No," Renie all but shouted, "you don't have to tell her you *are* worrying about her when she tells you not to . . . Never mind, just answer a question—have you heard from your sister and your brother-in-law?"

Renie put a hand to her head. Apparently, Tom didn't know the answer and was asking the other family houseguests.

"Cathleen says what?" Renie finally exploded. "Okay, okay. Fine, when they get out of the shower, tell them . . . never mind, I'll tell them myself. Your father and I will be home shortly." She hung up and shook her head. "Our children and their spouses are idiots. Maybe it's a good thing we don't have grandchildren. The gene pool has been drained. The flight got in early, but nobody seemed to notice that Anne and Odo arrived at the house. Or if they did, they forgot."

Judith refrained from saying that the three Jones offspring were spoiled. She didn't dare: The dozens of presents under the tree for Mike, Kristin, and the two grandchildren were ample evidence that she'd done her own share of indulging the younger generations.

"I'm going to see how Mother's doing," Judith said, heading back to the kitchen.

"I'd better head home and greet the latest arrivals." Renie stopped in the entry hall and went upstairs to get Bill.

Gertrude was flipping through Judith's recipe file. "Got oranges? Got cranberries?"

"Yes. Why?"

"I found Grandma Grover's recipe for a molded Jell-O salad. You need whipped topping, too. And cloves."

"Okay." Judith heard Renie and Bill coming down the backstairs. They called out goodbye and left.

Mother and daughter prepared the Jell-O salad. Judith avoided any mention of the disturbing conversation about Bart. Gertrude seemed a bit subdued, even preoccupied, but didn't bring up the subject again. Joe finally sauntered into the kitchen, asking if he could help.

Judith shook her head. "I think we have everything under control. Both pâtés are finished, the Jell-O salad is setting, and the ham is in the oven. It's too soon to put out any of the food. I'm going to take Mother to her apartment so she can change and then I'll get dressed."

Joe nodded. "I'll get the serving dishes ready."

"Good." Judith beckoned to Gertrude. "Let's go, Mother. You have to make yourself beautiful."

"Oh, yeah?" Gertrude retorted. "What time does the fairy show up with her magic wand?"

"Right before she shows up to help me," Judith replied, walking ahead of Gertrude to open the back door.

The rain had stopped and the air had turned much colder. Looking into the darkening sky, Judith noticed that the clouds were slowly moving and a crescent moon was rising in the east. There might be frost by morning and perhaps the sky would clear later in the evening. That, Judith thought, would be a perfect December night.

As usual, the heat in the toolshed was turned up to almost eighty degrees. Gertrude needed the extra warmth to help her circulation. Judith usually didn't mind the near-tropical temperature, but she'd been working even harder than usual and had broken into a sweat.

"Anything you need?" she asked hurriedly.

"Where do I start?" Gertrude responded in an exasperated voice.

"I'll come to get you just before five," Judith said. She stopped, unable to see the muffler that had been left on the easy chair. It was nowhere in sight. "Who did that plaid muffler belong to?"

Her mother scowled at her. "What plaid muffler?"

"The one I saw on the chair when I came to get you earlier."

Gertrude looked at the chair. "You're drunk. You drank the rest of my toddy, remember?"

"Yes, but I'm quite sober. There wasn't much left in your mug."

"Then beat it and let me make *my* mug pretty for the company. Shoo!"

Judith couldn't take time to argue, but she did glance into the small bedroom, the tiny bathroom, and the kitchenette. No muffler. Maybe whoever left it had come back. During the day, the toolshed door was always unlocked, as were the doors to the main house. It was a low-crime area—except, of course, for the homicide cases Judith herself seemed to attract.

By ten to five, she was ready. No one had yet arrived, not even Mike and his family. Traffic was probably exceptionally heavy on the pass and all the way through the dense suburbs that led into the city. Checking the full-length mirror in the third-floor master bedroom, Judith gave a semi-enthusiastic nod of approval: she wore a long black taffeta skirt, red scoop-necked sweater, and a gold pendant that had been a gift from a B&B guest who did business in Dubai.

"Hey," Joe said, coming out of the bathroom, "does my wife know you're here? I told you never to make house calls."

"The motels are full because of the holiday," Judith deadpanned. "We'll have to settle for this crummy B&B."

"Mmm," Joe murmured as he kissed Judith's throat. "You smell good, too."

Judith smiled. "You look quite dapper yourself." Indeed, Joe had always had good taste in clothes. Balding he might be and a paunch had been added, but the round face with its magical green eyes still drew Judith like a magnet. Forty years had passed since they first met. They had both changed inside and out, but the emotions were still there, undimmed by time and distance and even by blessed familiarity.

"We'd better go downstairs," she said as Joe continued to nuzzle.

"Uh-huh." He didn't stop.

"Joe!" Judith giggled and pulled away. "Come on! It's Christmas Eve."

Joe sighed. "Yes, it is. Damn."

Aunt Ellen and Uncle Win arrived just as Judith and Joe descended the stairs to the main floor. Hugs and kisses ensued.

"I'll take over the kitchen," Aunt Ellen announced in her no-nonsense manner, "and if Vance tries to tell me what to do, I'll have to hurt her."

"Go for it," Judith said, deferring to her incredibly efficient aunt who was already ordering Win to go get Gertrude.

Two minutes later, Auntie Vance and Uncle Vince entered the house. "Where's that rotten sister of mine?" Vance snarled. "I saw that crappy old car of theirs with the Nebraska license plates out front. Vinster, wake up! We're here. You can sleep while you're driving home."

Uncle Vince, who was leaning against the wall, gave a start. "What? Sure, Little Girl, I'll do it. But it's looking kind of rough out there." It was Vince's standard answer when Vance asked him to take the boat out to check the crab pots—no matter how calm the waters might be. He gave Judith and Joe a half-smile as his wife tromped out into the kitchen.

Judith smiled back at Uncle Vince. "If you want a nap, you can go into the front parlor. We'll let you know when the food is ready."

"Okay." Vince leaned back against the wall and closed his eyes.

Joe volunteered to haul the presents from the aunts and uncles into the living room. Auntie Vance had wrapped hers in traditional Christmas paper; Aunt Ellen had used the *Beatrice Daily Sun*.

Judith started toward the kitchen, but the noise had suddenly become deafening. Vance and Ellen were arguing, as usual, and Gertrude was telling them both to shut up or she'd make the cat puke on their shoes. Uncle Win was fixing himself a drink. Two drinks, in fact.

"For Vince," he said, pointing to the second glass as Judith sidled into the kitchen. "I think I'll join him. Wherever he may be sleeping."

"Try the hall," Judith suggested.

Uncle Corky and his clan had arrived. On their heels came Sue and Ken's two sons, their wives, and five children. The crowd of newcomers chattered and squawked in a whirl of motion.

"Hey!" Corky shouted to Vince. "Wake up, man! Old Blood and Guts has got us heading for Sicily! We're going to take Messina and Palermo and keep going all the way to freaking Berlin!"

Uncle Vince gave another start, blinked his eyes, and saluted. "Yessir! On the double, sir! Right here, General Patton!"

Judith helped divest the younger clan members of coats and hats. Uncle Al and his girlfriend, the elegant Tess, entered just as the latest arrivals were being ushered into the dining room and the parlor and anywhere else that kept them out of the living room.

Tess, who was the heiress to a large timber company, handed a small box wrapped in gold foil to Judith. "My hostess gift," she said in her genteel voice. "I thought it was something you could use. Tuck it away until later."

"Thanks," Judith said, in awe as always at Tess's refined beauty even in advanced age. As far as Judith was concerned, Uncle Al's greatest luck had been in finding Tess.

Tess, however, was watching the rambunctious children racing through the entry hall and up and down the main staircase. "Goodness," she murmured. "Maybe you should open it now. For safekeeping."

Judith backed up into the corner between the door to the downstairs parlor and the credenza that sat by the stairs. Tess held her ground, despite the efforts of Andy and Marie to use the garland on the stairway to lasso her.

"Stop that!" Judith called to the children, who were her great-nieces or something like that. Because she saw most of the children only once a year, she wasn't always sure who belonged to whom. She wasn't even sure they were Andy and Marie.

Trying to hurry, Judith dropped the gold organza ruffle bow. Gracefully, Tess bent down to pick it up.

Judith was embarrassed. "Thanks. It's hard for me to . . ."

"I know. Your poor hip," Tess finished for her. "You must be worn out with all these preparations."

"Well . . ." Judith shrugged and lifted the small box's lid. Inside was an envelope with her name on it. And inside the envelope were three crisp one hundred dollar bills.

"So expensive," Tess said softly, "to put on such a holiday extravaganza. Since I didn't bring any food, I thought that might help defray the cost."

Judith hugged Tess. "Thank you so much!" Over Tess's shoulder, she saw Renie, Bill, and the six other Joneses come through the door. All of them were carrying cartons, shopping bags, and boxes filled high with presents. Aunt Deb, in her own motorized wheelchair, brought up the rear. "Don't worry about me," she said to no one in particular. "I'm coming as fast as I can."

"Hi, everybody!" Renie shouted, eliciting a minimal response from anybody under ten. Bill nodded vaguely, set down his carton, and removed his tan all-weather jacket with its two-dozen pockets and fourteen secret compartments. Or so Renie claimed.

"Anne and Cathy and Heather will put the presents in the living room," Renie informed Judith. "Got a flashlight?"

"Tell them it's on the buffet," Judith said, slipping the hundred dollar bills into the pocket of her skirt. "I've got a votive candle burning there so they can see it."

Tess had moved on, greeting Aunt Deb and solicitously inquiring about her health. Uncle Al was in the doorway of the dining room making quarters disappear to the wonderment of a couple of kids who weren't Andy and Marie. Or maybe they were, Judith thought, her head a-spin.

"Where's the Green Goddess salad dressing?" Joe asked as he came out from the kitchen.

"Do you have white-wine glasses?" Aunt Toadie inquired. "I found the Burgundy ones, but I can't . . ."

"Use coffee cups," Aunt Ellen interrupted. "What difference does it make? Back in Beatrice, we drink wine out of a box."

"Move it, lard ass," Auntie Vance said to Joe, despite the fact that her backside was much wider than his. "What are those kids doing on the stairs? Hey, Monsters—get the hell down here! Go in the basement and inhale some gas fumes from the furnace!"

Renie grabbed Judith's hand and bodily pulled her into the first floor bathroom.

"Holy Mother," Renie gasped, "I can't hear myself think! How do you stand it?"

Judith shuddered. "I'm postponing my nervous breakdown until the day after Christmas."

"I'd forgotten how loud this family can be," Renie said, leaning against the sink.

"But under it all, they get along," Judith pointed out.

"Yes, in their own weird way. And," she added wistfully, "they're all so *big*. Except me."

"Runt," Judith said with a smile. "Isn't that what Uncle Al called you as a kid?"

Renie nodded. "A throwback. But that's why we're here. I assume that being small, I'm the one who crawls in through the French doors to turn on the Christmas lights after Bill does his Santa bit. Where's the flashlight, then? Or do I feel my way around the floor to find the switch?"

"I'll get you another flashlight," Judith said. "Heaven only knows where your daughter and your daughters-in-law will put the one I had on the buffet. Besides, Mike and his gang still aren't here, and neither are Sue and Ken."

"That's right." Renie peered at her watch. "It's five-thirty. We've got to get this show on the road."

"Ha." Judith grimaced. "That's up to Aunt Ellen. We're probably ready to eat. The dining room table is loaded with food."

"Good," Renie said, moving to the door. "Anything new on the Bart incident?"

"No," Judith said with a frown, "except that when I took Mother back to the toolshed, that muffler was gone."

"Really?" Renie looked perturbed. "By the way, who else was in the living room when Anne put the last of our presents around the tree?"

Judith frowned. "Uncle Al?"

"Anne said he'd come and gone. But she heard a noise, not right by the tree," Renie explained, "but closer to the French doors."

"Maybe it was outside," Judith suggested, "though none of the family would come in that way. It could've been Sweetums."

Renie looked doubtful. "Anne didn't make it sound like a cat."

"We can't worry about that now," Judith said. "What do you suppose is holding up Mike and Kristin?"

"Traffic," Renie said, opening the bathroom door. "What else? It was even slow on top of Heraldsgate Hill when we came over here just now. You can imagine what the freeway is like."

Judith could. Bumper to bumper, and all sorts of idiots with fender-benders and flat tires and running out of gas.

The cousins emerged from the small bathroom. Aunt Ellen pounced. "What are you girls doing in there? Smoking?"

"No," Renie replied, "but you are." She pointed to her aunt's cigarette. "I remember when all the aunts used to go upstairs to smoke so Grandma Grover wouldn't know."

Aunt Ellen merely puffed at her cigarette, laughed, and rushed away, no doubt to organize the line that was forming at the dining table.

"Talk about General Patton," Judith said to Renie, "Aunt Ellen could have organized the military in both Asia and Europe during World War Two."

"I thought she did," Renie responded. "Her gig with the Red Cross in Calcutta was just a ruse, right?"

"Probably," Judith said vaguely. She watched the guests move smartly through the supper line. The Grover clan rarely hesitated making decisions about food. They wanted all of it.

"At least," Renie said as she stepped behind Uncle Win, "our mothers haven't started their dueling wheelchair act."

"Don't even think about it," Judith said, recalling an occasion when the two old girls had gone at it and almost wrecked a hotel room.

Renie beckoned to her cousin. "Come on. Aren't you eating?"

"Not until Mike and his family get here," Judith said. "I'm worried."

Somehow, over the din of voices and plates and

serving spoons, she heard the phone ring. The quietest place to answer it was in the living room. Hurrying as fast as her artificial hip could take her, she ducked behind the draperies and felt her way to the cherrywood table.

"Hello?" she said into the receiver.

"Mom?" Mike said. "It's me. We've got a problem."

Judith felt her heart start to race. "What kind? Where are you? What's wrong?"

"We stopped to get the boys some burgers and fries," Mike replied. "It took longer than we thought and when we came out of the café, our SUV was gone."

Judith was both relieved and upset at the same time. "You mean stolen?"

"No. Towed. I guess I parked in a No Parking zone. Can somebody come and get us?"

"Where are you?"

"In North Boone," Mike said. "At the Hat Trick Café."

Calculating quickly, Judith realized that her son and his family were over thirty miles away. "I don't know . . ." She hesitated. Who in this group would want to make a sixty-odd mile round-trip drive on Christmas Eve? A sudden thought occurred to her. "Where did they tow it?"

"Not far," Mike said. "There's a towing yard about a mile from here. Trouble is, we have to pay three hundred bucks to get it out, and I don't get paid until the day after New Year's. We're a little short this month, what with Christmas and all."

Judith put her hand on the pocket of her skirt. Easy come, easy go, she thought. What else is new? "I'll pay for it," she said. "Can somebody at the café give you a ride to the towing site?"

"I'll see," Mike said, sounding uncertain. "They're about to close."

"Be here as soon as you can," Judith said, suddenly distracted by a creaking noise at the far end of the room. Hanging up, she ventured past the bay window and the bookcases. Unable to see where she was going in the dark, she stubbed her toe on a large present and would've fallen if she hadn't braced herself on the piano bench.

The sound grew fainter. Judith didn't dare turn on a light for fear that some of the children would see it and think Santa had already arrived. Nor did she risk venturing any closer to the French doors where she thought the noise had emanated. A serious fall—and a possible trip to the emergency room—would ruin everybody's Christmas Eve.

She waited for at least a full minute, but there was no sound outside, only the buzz of excitement and clatter of dishes inside the house. As Judith came out of the living room, Joe was heading for the front parlor with a plate full of food. She dismissed the odd noise and swiftly relayed Mike's message.

"Dumb stunt," Joe muttered. "Should I drive up there?"

"No," Judith said. "At least not until we find out if they're truly stranded. If Mike can get the SUV out of hock, they should be here a little after six. Traffic always slows down on Christmas Eve about this time of the day."

"I'd better tell Bill," Joe said. "He'll want to know that his Santa act isn't going off until six-thirty."

Even though the line at the buffet table was only three deep, Judith had lost her appetite.

"Where's Ma and Pa?" Jeffrey Dalton asked her as he came away from the table.

Jeffrey was the elder son of Sue and Ken. "They told me they'd be late," Judith replied, deciding not to go into details.

"Oh—yeah. That bomb thing." Jeffrey shrugged and headed for the kitchen. Jeffrey and his brother, Murray, obviously were accustomed to the hazards of their parents' business.

Aunt Ellen and a toddler were the only ones still dishing up. "Is our daughter in another jam?" Ellen inquired.

"Nothing new," Judith hedged, wondering who had put a Ping-Pong ball in the potato salad.

"Oh." Aunt Ellen also seemed undisturbed. "The bomb scare happened while we were having breakfast at their restaurant this morning. I insisted that Sue and Ken let us pay for our meal, but she made a fuss. Those two don't have very sound business heads. If they'd let me tell them how to . . ."

The phone was ringing again. Judith excused herself and went into the noisy kitchen. About a dozen family members were sitting at the table, on the counters, and even the floor, happily stuffing their faces. Judith could hear the phone but couldn't see it anywhere. The ring seemed to be emanating from Cousin Marty, who had put his well-padded rear end on top of the dishwasher.

"Marty?" Judith said with a feeble smile.

"Huh?" Marty shoved a cracker covered in salmon pâté into his mouth.

"You're sitting on the phone."

"Ah!" Marty jumped up and looked around. "You're right," he said with his mouth full. "I just thought my hemorrhoids were acting up again. Never had 'em ring like that before, though."

Judith grabbed the phone and went into the hallway where it was quieter. Mike's cell phone number showed up on the caller ID. "Mike?"

"Hey," he said, sounding more cheerful. "We got a ride to the towing place. Guess who? Cousin Sue and Ken happened to come by. Well, not exactly 'happened'—they had to ID the Hat Trick Café owner as the guy who tried to blow them up this morning. The FBI are on the way. We'll be at your house in half an hour, with Cousin Sue and Ken right behind us. Unless they have to go into the witness protection program or something. Ha ha!"

Shaking her head, Judith decided to put the receiver in the other pocket of her skirt. Who knew, she thought as she went back through the kitchen, what the next call might bring? It was a typical family gathering, with the usual mayhem and madness that beset the Grover clan.

Madness. Why had that word popped into her mind? Because Uncle Bart had gone crazy after getting kicked by a horse? That didn't qualify as the kind of insanity that was inherited. Judith tried to put the thought out of her mind.

After all, it was Christmas Eve.

"Where's Baby Jesus?" Renie asked. "Some of the little ones want to know."

"I'm not sure I want to know *why* they want to

know," Judith said, watching Uncle Corky's grandson, Bingo, use the discarded organza ribbon from Tess's hostess gift to tie up a wriggling toddler. "Baby Jesus is in the freezer where He stays until after we open the gifts."

"Oh—that's right. I forgot," Renie said. "At our house, we put Him in the manger before we come here. Premature delivery, I guess."

"How's Mother doing?" Judith asked, finally serving herself some ham-and-macaroni salad and a bit of the Jell-O mold.

"Fine. She's only gotten into it twice with Auntie Vance and once with Aunt Ellen. Oh—she ran over Aunt Toadie's foot with her wheelchair—on purpose, I think. Toadie was trying to catch one of her kids who wasn't wearing any pants."

"Which one?" Judith asked.

"Marty," Renie replied. "You'd think now that he's hit fifty, he'd act more grown up."

"Maybe it's his hemorrhoids," Judith murmured as she carried her plate to the dining room window and leaned against the antique washstand she used for the guest bar. "Gosh—it's relatively quiet in here."

"That's because everybody's full and half asleep—except," Renie added, "for Uncle Vince, who's been asleep ever since he got here."

"And before that," Judith noted. "It's his way of coping with Auntie Vance's big mouth. Of course he wouldn't ever do anything if she didn't nag. Where are all the kids?"

"Tom and Tony, and our son-in-law, Odo, took them outside, believe it or not," Renie said. "Don't worry—they'll herd them up in time for Santa Bill."

Judith looked at her watch. "It's almost six-thirty. Mike and his family and Sue and Ken should be here any minute. I don't know why Mike and Kristin had to feed the kids on their way to our place. They knew there'd be plenty of food."

"The younger generation," Renie remarked, "is different."

"It always is. Four generations under this roof tonight," Judith said in a musing tone. "That picture from 1941—think how many people have been added since that Christmas. And how many are gone."

Renie nodded. "We were younger then than most of these kids are now. We're about the same age as our grandparents were in that photo. Where did all the time go?"

"It went in school and marriage and birth and death. It went with war and peace and laughter and tears." Judith suddenly felt foolish. "I'm getting maudlin."

Renie, however, put a hand on Judith's shoulder. "Not really, coz. We're getting old . . . er. You just described Life."

"Yes." Judith nibbled at her food. She still had little appetite. Too much turmoil, too much noise, too many people—and at the back of her mind, wondering if her mother was losing her grip on reality.

Raucous sounds erupted from the back of the house. Judith immediately recognized the shouts and laughter of her grandsons, Mac and Joe-Joe. She set her plate down on the washstand and hurried into the kitchen with Renie right behind her.

And right behind the boys and Mike and Kristin came Sue and Ken, looking, as usual, utterly laid-back.

Also as usual, Ken was carrying his portable bar—which was one of the reasons he and Sue were always so relaxed.

The grandsons were in high gear. At seven and five, they not only still believed in Santa Claus, but that the whole world belonged to them. Judith hugged both boys tight.

"I'll alert Bill and make sure the rest of the kids are back inside," Renie whispered to Judith.

"The bell's on the back porch by the French doors," Judith informed Renie. "I'll round up everybody."

Five minutes later, the entire group was jammed into the areas where they could hear Santa speaking from behind the draperies. Judith was standing in the entry hall by Mac and Joe-Joe. They fidgeted and exchanged a couple of punches.

"Don't," Judith whispered. "Santa will bring you coal."

"What's coal?" Joe-Joe asked.

"I know what coal is," Mac said with disdain for his younger brother. "You don't know anything."

"Hush!" Judith ordered.

"How about a knuckle sandwich?" Uncle Al asked, holding out his fist with the big signet ring that had been given to him by the old-timer who owned the local racetrack. "Smell this!"

The boys giggled, knowing that Uncle Al liked to tease.

Nervous laughter, shuffling feet, and snatches of whispered conversation were the only sounds in the house. The creatures were stirring, but not breaking ranks.

Suddenly there was the sound of the old farm bell,

ringing in the distance. Judith heard the French doors open. Silence fell over the Grover clan.

"Ho-ho-ho!" said Santa. "Is everybody here?"

Judith looked at Renie, who was positioned near the door to the dining room so that she could make her escape through the back when Bill was finished. Renie nodded, the signal that Bill was disguising his voice enough to fool the kids, if not the grown-ups—except maybe Marty, who wasn't too bright.

The questioning began, not only for the children, but the adults as well.

"I hear you've been making snow angels, Mac. Why did you put horns on them? Santa doesn't like little devils. Ho-ho-ho!"

"I didn't, Santa, honest!" Mac cried.

"Well, that's not what Santa heard," said Bill. "Joe-Joe, where's your mother's pie plate? Is it true you stuck it in your pants because your dad threatened to spank you?"

"Yes, Santa. I mean . . . I forget."

And so it went, with denials, confessions, repentance, and plenty of laughter. Finally, Santa announced that it was time to move on to his next stop—Saks Fifth Avenue, where he had to pick up a little something for his extravagant wife. "I'm getting her a designer muzzle—size extra large," he said. "Ha-ha-ha! Ho-ho-ho! Merry Christmas!"

The bell rang again; the French doors closed.

Judith turned around. Renie was gone, on her way to hit the lights before the draperies could come down. The children had broken out into squeals and shouts, waiting to burst into the living room.

Judith had moved closer to Joe. "Aren't the boys

cute?" she whispered. "They're practically hyperventilating."

Joe turned to look at his boisterous grandsons. "They'd be cuter if they piped down. I may have to arrest them for disturbing the peace." Suddenly, he reached down and grabbed Bingo, who was trying to crawl under the drapery. "Whoa! You can't go in there without an escort."

Bingo scrambled to his feet and shot Joe a dirty look. "Are you a cop?"

"Yes," Joe answered. "I'm also your . . ." He looked at Judith. "What am I to this kid? Who is he?"

"Just call yourself uncle. 'Aunt' works for me," Judith replied. "He belongs to one of Cheryl's twin girls. I think."

"Bingo sounds like an alias," Joe remarked.

"It is. His real name is Blaine. I think," Judith repeated. "What's taking Renie so long? Can't she find the switch? Can you see her moving with the flashlight in there?"

Joe shook his head. "I can't see her at this angle. The switch is at the far end of the room. Should I check from the parlor? I can see the whole thing from there."

"Well . . . no," Judith said with a frown. "Wait a couple of minutes. Renie's not terribly good at complicated mechanical tasks—like flipping a switch."

At least two minutes passed before the Christmas lights suddenly glowed from the garlands, the wreaths, and the tree. A huge gasp went up from the assembly. As Joe removed the drapery, the children rushed forward.

And stopped.

The room should have been empty. Renie always went out the same way she'd come in, joining Bill and returning to the house via the back door. It wasn't Renie or Bill who stood near the lighted Christmas tree, but a tall young man Judith had never seen before in her life.

Except that he did look vaguely familiar and was wearing a green plaid muffler over his camelhair topcoat.

"Bart!" Gertrude gasped from her wheelchair, which she'd propelled forward in the wake of the children. "Bart!"

Judith hurried to her mother's side. "It can't be," she said earnestly. "It's got to be . . . someone else." Or a ghost, Judith thought.

"It *is* Bart," Gertrude rasped. "He told me so himself when he came calling today."

Joe, who had no idea what was going on, walked up to the handsome young man. "Are you a relative I don't recognize?" he asked.

The young man nodded. "A relative of your wife's—and your mother-in-law. My name is Bart Hofmann. A couple I ran into outside let me in. Apparently, the front doorbell doesn't work." He put out his hand.

Puzzled, Joe shook the other man's hand. "We probably couldn't hear it over the din of the children," he said. "Uh . . . would you like something to eat?"

Gertrude rolled up next to Joe. "Tell 'em I'm not crazy, Bart. I'm just . . . surprised."

Bart bent closer to Gertrude. "You're not crazy, Aunt Gertrude. I'd have come to see you sooner, but I found out that the spelling of the family name had been changed. You were hard to track down."

"Let's get out of the way," Joe suggested. The new arrival's appearance meant little or nothing to any of the children and had only evoked mild curiosity out of the adults—except Aunt Ellen.

"What's going on here?" she demanded. "You look like somebody I know. My brother, Al? Or Corky? Well?"

Judith found her voice, which had been shocked into silence by Bart's presence. "Let's go into the front parlor. It should be empty."

It was, except for Uncle Vince, who was dozing by the fire.

"I can't stay long," Bart said, standing by the hearth while the others sat and Vince slept. "I have a flight back home to Chicago at eleven. I've been trying to trace my ancestry for several years, ever since my father died when I was in college."

"He was Great-Uncle Bart's son?" Judith asked.

"Yes. His name was Arthur. He had a bad heart and died fairly young."

Judith nodded once. Maybe bad hearts, instead of insanity, ran in the family. Her father, Donald, had also died young from heart trouble.

"Anyway," Bart went on, "I've been traveling on business—computer software. I was in Salt Lake City a few weeks ago, so I spent my spare time using the Mormon genealogy resources. I finally managed to find you, Aunt Gertrude, and made up my mind to visit when I came here next." He smiled, a very warm and charming smile. "I went to the front door of the house when I arrived late this morning, but nobody responded."

"My husband and I must have been out of hearing range," Judith suggested. "We were all over the place, organizing for tonight."

"So I went around back and saw that smaller building," Bart explained. "And then," he added with another big smile for Gertrude, "I found you."

Aunt Ellen had been listening with her usual rapt attention. "Aha. You found more than my sister, young man. You happened to come upon the whole clan. We came all the way from Beatrice, Nebraska, for Christmas. You could have stayed with us in our tent."

"Um . . . thank you," Bart said, "but my company pays for lodging."

Judith posed another question. "Did you know your grandfather—your namesake?"

Bart shook his head. "He was in his forties before he married my grandmother. He died before I was born. I understand he also was . . . a bit eccentric. But I really don't know much about him except that he . . . how can I put this? Maybe he suffered from depression. They didn't know how to treat it in those days, of course. But I heard he talked to himself a lot, as if he were addressing people that nobody else could see. I'll try to track down the Canadian branch when I go to Toronto in March." He looked at his watch. "I should call a cab. Sorry for the intrusion, but my time here is very limited. My fiancée will kill me if I miss that flight."

"She mustn't do that," Gertrude murmured, her expression serious.

"Oh, I'm kidding," Bart said, patting the old lady's shoulder. "I'll write when I get home. On the next trip here I'll come at a more convenient time than

Christmas Eve. Then I could meet all the other relatives. That should be fun."

"Yes," Judith said, "please do that."

"I'll see you out," Joe offered.

"Thank you," Bart said. "Oh!" He looked embarrassed, as he reached into his overcoat's inside pocket. "I almost forgot! I wanted to give you this. My father told me that his father carved it himself. My mother found it among Grandfather's possessions with your name on the box. That's how I knew your name." He handed Gertrude a tiny cardboard box and bent down to kiss her cheek. "I'm sorry." Straightening up, he spoke to Judith. "I should've called before I came by."

"No problem," Judith said. "I see you retrieved your muffler."

"Yes." Bart shook Judith's hand. "You don't lock your doors around here, do you?"

"Not during the day," Judith said.

Bart smiled again, and followed Joe out of the parlor.

"Well!" Aunt Ellen shook her head. "That was fascinating. I did Win's family tree with help from his aunt who was a member of Nebraska's historical society. Now I'd better start on my own ancestry. Right, Gert?"

"Don't bother," Gertrude mumbled, still holding the box in her hand.

"Now Gert . . . " Aunt Ellen began.

But Gertrude turned the wheelchair on and raced at full speed out of the parlor. Judith hurried after her.

"Mother," she said, managing to catch up in the living room by the buffet, "wasn't it nice of your great-nephew to stop by?"

Gertrude didn't answer. She stared ahead with

unseeing eyes, oblivious to the gift-giving mayhem that was taking place all over the living room. Renie, as usual, was doling out the gifts with the help of her three children. Bows, ribbons, and wraps sailed through the air as lids were lifted and packaging was undone. Shouts of "Thank you, Vance and Vince!", "How did you know I wanted this, Uncle Corky?" and "Oh, dear, you shouldn't have spent so much on a poor old coot like me," from Aunt Deb.

Tony Jones brought Judith and Gertrude a couple of presents. "You're getting behind," he said. "We've got quite a pile for you guys by the window seat."

"Sorry," Judith said in a distracted manner.

As Tony rushed off, Judith pointed to the unopened box from Bart. "Don't you want to know what's in there?"

Gertrude looked up at her daughter. "Do I?"

"Shall I open it?"

"No!" Gertrude glared at Judith. "I will." Her arthritic fingers fumbled with the lid, but she finally removed it from the box to reveal tissue paper that was so old it had turned yellow. Poking a finger inside, she felt something and shook the item free.

It was a hand-carved figure of Baby Jesus. Gertrude bit her lip. "Bart broke the real one." Her voice shook along with her hands. "Temper. Just before . . . he moved from the farm." She sucked in her breath and clutched the figure tight. "I expect he carved this in the booby hatch," she said in her more normal voice. "Why did he wait so long to give it to me?"

"Well . . ." Judith began, "he never really had a chance, did he?"

"Not until today." Her gaze was far off, perhaps ninety years distant. "Let's put Jesus where He belongs," she finally said.

The last of the presents were being opened—save for Judith's and Gertrude's. The timing was perfect. Judith asked Joe to call for silence. Renie, on cue, struggled to her feet from her place by the tree and turned on the CD player. A chorus began to sing "It Came Upon a Midnight Clear."

Miraculously, the revelers went silent. Even the children stopped squealing and shrieking. Judith moved to the buffet and held her hand out to her mother.

"No," Gertrude said. "Let me."

"Go ahead."

Gertrude's hand still shook as she held the Infant. "Bart said he was sorry. I forgive him." She placed the Babe in the crib.

Judith opened her mouth to say that Gertrude mustn't confuse the great-nephew with the brother. Suddenly she realized that maybe her mother wasn't confused—and that in any event, it didn't matter.

The music played on:

"And ye, beneath life's crushing load,
Whose forms are bending low,
Who toil along the climbing way
With painful steps and slow,
Look now! For glad and golden hours
Come swiftly on the wing.
O rest beside the weary road,
And hear the angels sing!
"Peace on earth, good will to men,

From heaven's all gracious King."
The world in solemn stillness lay,
To hear the angels sing.

"Amen," said Gertrude.

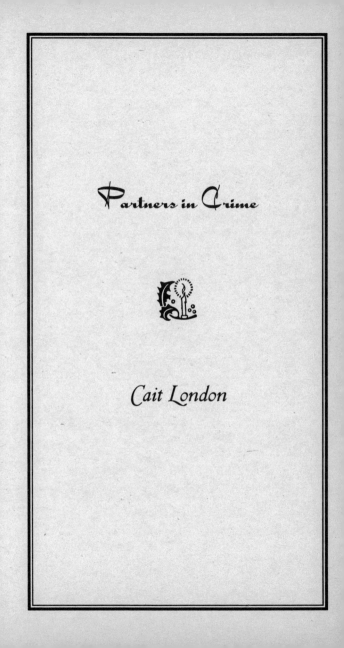

Partners in Crime

Cait London

If she weren't so terrified of the three men circling her, she'd be really angry right now.

Wearing dirty tattered clothing and ragged knit caps and jackets, the three men surrounding Cecilia Lattimer also needed shaves and haircuts. The wind sweeping snowflakes down the dark alley carried their odor.

These men looked like they wanted to do more than a little misbehaving.

But then, she believed that she was on someone's hit list, her home entered and de-organized, and now her car wouldn't start—just after a tune-up. Cecilia should have expected trouble.

As a professional organizer, she really resented the systematic destruction of her office, closets, shelves—and the telephone hang-ups. Nothing was simply shoved to the floor or scattered about; files had been misplaced, her kitchen pot lids weren't hanging in order, the bedding sets in her linen closet had been mixed, and her closets no longer were bunched in blouses, jackets, and slacks. Nor were they separated by color. Her dress shoes had been mixed with her joggers and summer sandals.

The sound of the town's snowplow bounced off the alley's brick walls as it passed by. At six-thirty in the evening, the small Missouri town of Dewdrop had settled in for the night—except for the state patrol and the town's deputies who were probably holed up at Lori's Café, just a block from where Cecilia was cornered. She imagined the lawmen sitting around the café, shooting the bull, soaking up free coffee and dining on the special—while she needed them.

"I'm on my way to a meeting" she said to the men circling her. "I'm the president of our local Christmas Cheer Club and tonight we're wrapping gifts— Christmas is just a week away, you know . . . and we're very busy. I'm bringing the cookies, and I'm certain you don't want me to be late—they'll miss me," she added for effect and hoped that the men didn't notice the fear in her voice.

Because these men might be involved with the recent thefts in Dewdrop, and she did not want to antagonize them, she didn't add that the club's last meeting was really important. The club was faced with their usual tasks of delivering cheer and gifts to those who seemed in the dumps *and* replacing the gifts that had been stolen from beneath Christmas trees.

Cecilia looked at the man who had just entered the alley. He was big. He was dirty and he was hairy. His eyes glistened dangerously in the shadows.

"Hello, boys." Seemingly at ease, he leaned against the opposite brick wall of the alley, his hands in his army surplus jacket, the ear flaps of his cap disappearing somewhere into the mass of his hair and beard.

The men turned to him, but backed closer to Cecilia. One said, "No one invited you."

That was good, Cecilia thought as she remembered television scenarios where the gangs battled among themselves. Her view was blocked by the men's backs, but she heard the swish of something cold and deadly—like a knife being pulled from its sheath.

There was silence and then the three men looked at each other. Apparently in silent agreement, they hurried off into the snowy night. Cecilia didn't question their departure, but that left the big man standing on the opposite side of the alley. He watched the men disappear and then his eyes pinned her. He had that wolfish hunter look, and her skin prickled and tightened.

Cecilia held the cookie container closer to her. They reminded her of the warm safety of her home, but it really wasn't safe anymore, was it? The gingerspice scent floated momentarily around her and she heard the pounding, fearful beat of her heart.

"Rather dumb to be out on a night like this, isn't it?" he said quietly as the snowplow passed and the light flashed on the pinpoints of his eyes. Then as though doomed, he said, "Let's get going. Wherever you're going."

Somehow, through her tightened throat, Cecilia managed to repeat her mission. But because she resented the "dumb" remark, honor forced her to add, "My car wouldn't start, or I would have driven to my meeting."

His snort seemed disbelieving and filled with ex-haulted male competence. He stepped out onto the street, and did the left-right scouting thing. Then the sweep of his hand indicated that it was safe to move to the sidewalk.

"It's damn cold out here. Let's move it," he said impatiently when she stood still, considering the danger of moving too close to him. Her head only reached his shoulder, and he could easily— Cecilia held her breath and forced herself to move by him. She had no idea why the three men had left her alone with him—but then, she suspected that thugs had their own pecking order. Strange—to think that the lawless were somewhat organized. But then, wolves had alpha males, didn't they?—the rest of the pack wary of them.

Cecilia shivered inside her long cherry-red berber coat and drew the hood over her gaily knitted Scandinavian cap. The man's eyes narrowed and slowly moved down her coat to her red snowboots. His nostrils flared, but then most men's did when catching the scent of her gingersnaps. When he looked at her face again, he seemed to be enjoying a private joke. Now that was irritating.

"Going to Grandma's house?" he asked.

"No, I'm going to my meeting. Thank you for your help. I'm late and I have to hurry," Cecilia stated as she hurried away from him.

The firm grip at her winter coat's collar halted her. "They're still out there. I'll walk you to the police station, where you can file a report. But it's a really dumb thing to do, lady—out in a snowstorm by yourself."

"You're telling me," she muttered. *She couldn't file a report. Not when the police chief is probably at the bottom of her recent problems.*

"What's that?"

"I'm not reporting *anything*."

" 'Anything?' What else has happened?" Those wolfish pinpoints of his eyes locked onto her. When she refused to answer, he nodded and walked silently beside her.

Despite her long coat, her knit cap, and insulated snowboots, her body was still bone-chilled. Fear had a way of doing that and she'd had a lot of fear lately—especially since she'd learned that the so-called upstanding police chief would do anything to protect himself from the one person who knew that he had a mistress and who could expose him—one Cecilia Lattimer.

Cecilia had no doubt that her messed home and the three men were Police Chief Monroe Ringer's way of getting his Shut-up or Die message across to her.

She braced herself and turned to the stranger, who towered over her. Snow drifted down between them, settling on his cap and broad shoulders as he hunched beneath his coat. She had to get rid of him. "Thank you for helping me, but I can manage just fine now."

"Why aren't you reporting this? I'd say it was a little dangerous back there, for a woman who's not smart enough to stay in where it's safe."

Assaults on her intelligence were not necessary; she'd already had enough of that from her ex-husband and her ex-fiancé. She began walking away. "I'd rather just go to my meeting. I can manage now."

"Oh, yeah. The Christmas Cheer Club," he repeated

softly at her side, as if making a mental note to himself.

The blizzard's freezing wind whipped at her, as if reminding her that she needed to repay him, before getting rid of him. As they were walking, Cecilia handed him the cookie container. "Hold this."

She dug into her pocket and pulled out her wallet, extracting a twenty from it. She held it out to him. "Thanks. We're coming to a café where *you* can go in and get a hot meal. The food is good."

The stranger looked at the collection of police cars parked in front and shook his head. He handed the container and the bill back to her. "I'll stick with you."

Men did not stick with Cecilia; they feared she would try to organize them and they usually ran for cover.

As they came closer to the café, Cecilia wondered if she should make a break for it and run into the café. Then she saw her ex-fiancé exit the building and stop on the front steps. Edward Regan immediately spotted her and started walking toward her. "Dumb thing to be out on a night like this, Cecilia. You should have better sense. But then, you were never one to make sense, were you? What the hell are you doing walking in a blizzard?"

As the town's biggest attorney, high on the social ladder, Edward wasn't making her night any better. A fresh gust of wind hit her, and she turned to where the stranger had been standing. Only the snow flurries remained, the streetlights pooling into the swirling mist. She glanced at the café's windows to find the police chief and his deputies staring out at them, no doubt waiting for the usual fiery confrontation.

Edward's gloved hands wrapped around her upper

arms. To the people inside, it may have looked like a pleasant greeting; it wasn't. He leaned down to her, all clean and shaven and handsome—and extremely furious, his ice blue eyes flashing at her, the line of his mouth cruel and hard. While Edward was the darling of his mother's social set, he was also a bully, which was why Cecilia couldn't marry him. "Let me go, Edward."

"Tonight just proves how incompetent you are in decision making. You should have married me a year ago. Now you'll have to apologize and crawl before I'd have you again. You need help, Cecilia—a man to make your decisions for you."

"I've made one decision right now. If you don't let me go, I'm going to kick you. Remember the last time you tried to muscle me?"

Edward visibly shrank back, apparently struck by that painful memory. But still furious, he leaned down to her. "I'll make good my promise to ruin you, you know. No woman ever humiliates Edward Regan."

"No, you do that nicely by yourself." Cecilia pushed on through the snowstorm, warm now with righteous anger.

The tall, hairy stranger swung in beside her and Cecilia ignored him. "I don't have time for you."

"You have a problem with that guy?"

He was a stranger in Dewdrop. He'd be moving on, a ship in the night. She could tell him anything—almost. "That's my ex-fiancé. He has a little problem with me. I said 'no' at the altar."

She thought she heard a chuckle as she walked down the street layered with impressive homes. Somehow John Lattimer's former mistress and now second wife, Tracy, had managed to have the most important meeting of the whole year at her home. It was festive, of course, decorated to the hilt, which was good advertising for Tracy's gift shop, Fancy Stuff.

Cecilia stared at the Lattimer plaque on the walkway. She shivered at the memory of how her ex-husband, John, had told her he really loved Tracy and would be marrying her as soon as possible.

"We're here. Thanks for the company. Have a good night, and the shelter here in Dewdrop really is very good."

The stranger was looking at the bedecked house, studying it closely. Cecilia wondered if he could be part of the ring that had burglarized Dewdrop. He turned to study the other homes on the street, all massive, two-story, and loaded with Christmas presents beneath the trees.

"Don't even think about it," Cecilia ordered quietly.

"Huh?" He was still studying the layout of the upscale homes. Cecilia thought of the home she had shared with John—modest, warm and— She inhaled suddenly, John knew exactly how well she loved order in her life; he would know to put the files beginning with KL in front of the KE files. He would know to put the smaller pot lid between the two larger ones. He would know how small differences, like turning the china cup handles in opposite directions would upset her.

Engrossed in her John-as-a-suspect thoughts, Cecilia had no time to deal with this stranger. "Look. I know what you look like. If I have to, I'll report you as a suspicious character, and I really wouldn't want to do that."

She wasn't prepared for his "Why not?"

"It's the Christmas season, that's why." Balancing fear, anger, and holiday cheer was a regular emotional teeter-totter.

And in a few moments she would be facing her ex-husband's new wife. Tracy would be in form, dropping careful little snippets about how she made John sexually happy—and what John had said about his lacking ex-wife.

The big stranger looked down at the cookie tin marked LATTIMER, and then to the bronze marker of her ex-husband's home, clearly matching them. Whoever he was, this man was noting everything. Pride demanded that Cecilia make a distinct difference between her home and John's new one—with Tracy. "This isn't my home. I have to go. Thank you," Cecilia said as she hurried to the house.

When Tracy answered the doorbell, she stuck out a Santa Claus cap. "Put it on. Where have you been? We've been waiting forever for you. Jayne's already been into the punch."

"Car problems." Cecilia removed her winter cap and coat, aware that Tracy had noted the cheaper brand names with a superior sniff. And had overdecorated as usual, her home alight and atumble with expensive Christmas decorations, all sold at Fancy Stuff.

"John is working in his office. You know how he is, a man holed up with his work," Tracy said in her usual taunting tone that said she was the woman who got the prize that Cecilia still longed to reclaim. "Everyone else is here. Their husbands dropped them off, so they wouldn't have to walk in the blizzard. You can sit on the hallway stool to remove your snowboots."

Cecilia ignored Tracy's last dig and smiled at her friends, all five sitting on the floor, amid a storm of wrapping paper and ribbon. "Hiya, Cecilia," Jayne called warmly, and Mary hurried to make a place for Cecilia on the floor. "Tracy thought we should go ahead and work on our list of people who needed Christmas cheer, because you were late."

Lists were usually Cecilia's task, because she was very efficient and organized.

Her mind still on the disarrangement of her home, her stalled car, the three men, her ex-fiancé, and the alpha male stranger, Cecilia settled into the clutter of paper rolls, ribbon, and tape. She automatically placed all the tape within a small basket, where they could be easily found. She neatened the paper rolls and lined them on the carpet, placing the ribbons in an empty box, separating them by color. All of that busy work brought her mind back to Dewdrop's police chief and how just yesterday she had accidentally dialed his private number.

"Hold on," Monroe Ringer had simply said and as she waited, he'd gone on with his conversation on another telephone line. She wanted to wait and apologize for misdialing. After all, it would be rude to just hang up.

Without putting her on hold, Monroe spoke to someone else, "I don't care how you do it, just clean up this mess. I don't want any problems. Don't tell my wife anything. She doesn't need to know. Hell, yes, I'll pay the tab somehow. Just get Cecilia Lattimer."

"Get Cecilia" had caused her to shiver. Because she knew exactly why: Monroe was new in town, an upscale city cop who wanted to move to a small town. His wife was evidently classy and very pregnant. And it wasn't his wife in his arms, snuggled up to him in that police car when Cecilia drove by. The girl was young, gorgeous, and her arms were around his neck. From the backseat, Monroe had glowered at Cecilia, and since then his suspicious looks had raised the hair on her nape.

Monroe could not afford gossip or upsetting his wealthy, pregnant wife—and Cecilia was now on his hit list. And running wasn't an option because she had clients and contracts. Mistress-adultery-exposure without actual proof wasn't an option either. Cecilia had kept her uneasy silence, and therefore safety, until "Get Cecilia."

"I don't know how thieves can steal presents from under the tree. It's just horrible," Amy was saying. "Cecilia, you've just put a purple bow on that blue package. Is something wrong? Is something bothering you?"

Cecilia stared at her work. She wished she'd never seen Monroe and the girl snuggled together in the backseat of that police car; she wished she'd gone to Florida to visit her brother and parents. Just tonight, her fear factor had escalated and she had to do something to protect herself.

Instead, she said, "We're going to have to start thinking about fund raisers for next year. We're over budget because of trying to replace the stolen presents."

After the meeting, Cecilia dreaded walking out into the night. But the roads were hazardous and she didn't want to endanger her friends—and she would not accept Tracy's too generous offer of staying the night. She would be more alert this time and walk—or run—home.

Cecilia hurried down the street and the big stranger appeared at her side. She didn't look at him, but lifted her cookie tin. "Here, you can have what's left."

"Thanks."

"It isn't nice to hurt someone who feeds you." What a thing to say to a potential hit man! But then, having just seen Tracy wrap her arms around John, lifting her leg to circle his—humiliation and anger were back. If anyone wanted to hurt Cecilia now, she'd mow them down.

The stranger moved silently beside her, blocking the icy wind and snow. The scent of her gingersnaps and his "Mmm. Good" was vaguely comforting. Then he asked, "You're really steamed. Why?"

"I've got a lot on my mind." *Like Tracy making out with John in front of me . . . how rude!* "What's your name anyway?" *Just in case I have to write it in the snow with my own blood.*

"Berenger."

That would be a long name to write as she lay dying. Cecilia hurried on, braced against the wind. Then her house appeared at the end of the block—small, formerly safe, with a home office and an attached garage. On the street in front of her house, she stopped so suddenly that the stranger's body hit hers, almost knocking her into the snowbank that blocked her driveway. She stood looking at her house, dreading entering it. Her anger had slid away, replaced by fear. If Monroe wanted to intimidate her, he was doing a good job of it.

"Problem?" Berenger asked softly beside her.

"Of course not."

"It's your house, isn't it? It has C. Lattimer on the door, just like the name on your cookie tin here." He handed the tin to her. "Not very smart, putting your name out there where anyone can find you. Bet you have a personalized license plate, too. You probably list your name in the residential section of the telephone book? Don't you know how dumb that is, to put your name and address out there?"

Her anger stirred, warming her. Of course, she did all three. But it was a small town. Hiding was really not an option. "Maybe. Look, I'm just considering my options and how to get rid of you. And I'd feel better if you just—" Cecilia stared after the man walking up to her front porch. "Hey, get away from my house!"

"If they're in there, you might need me," Berenger stated too quietly, and she knew who "they" were. She remembered the men's looks, as if they were stripping her clothes away.

"I'm okay. Please leave." Cecilia shivered and hurried to her front porch. She dug into her bag and foraged for her house keys.

He took them from her, unlocked the door and moved inside.

"This is unnecessary," she said, following him.

When he stopped and seemed to listen, she ran into his back. His arm went out, nudging her against the entrance wall. He moved down the hallway. "Stay put. Do you usually leave windows open in winter?"

"No, I—" Then she noticed how cold her snug home was, despite the furnace blowing warm air against her boots. A chilly breeze swept down the hallway, then it stopped. Berenger appeared, almost filling her hallway. He moved silently through the house, and into the garage.

Someone had been in her house—again. She'd barely gotten her office back in shape and had just started reordering her bedroom closet and now . . . Cecilia hurried to her formerly organized home office and stood, frozen between fear and anger. Not a good place. Her shelves of supplies and books had been reordered; she didn't want to think about her filing system.

Berenger appeared at her office door. "Someone messed with your car. It's okay now, but your bedroom is in a real mess. They left the window open—clothes everywhere. Looks like they were picking out outfits—jackets in one place, coats in another."

"I wasn't finished yet. I was rearranging my closet."

He pushed back the hood of her coat and scanned her face. "You look—I can't tell. Either you're real mad, or you're real scared."

"Don't mess with me," she managed between her teeth. Monroe really better not try to take this intimidation any further, or she'd make certain he paid dearly.

"Are you threatening me?" Berenger leaned closer, peering at her as she took off her cap and mittens and started to unbutton her coat.

Cecilia decided to leave it on, just in case he had ideas like the three men in the alley. "If he messed up my CD collection, I'll kill him," she muttered.

"Lady, you could be in danger and you're worried about *that*?"

"It takes hours to redo a closet properly, the files and shelves in this office, and my CD collection— If he took out the CDs and put them in the wrong cases, I will—"

Clearly confused, Berenger shook his head. His expression said he worried about being too close to her, that he could get caught in the explosion. "I think your home is safe now," he stated cautiously.

"Great. Just great. Look, if I give you some food, will you get out of here?"

"I might," he answered, evidently still cautious. "But I think I should hang around until morning—or you call the police."

"I told you, no police. Follow me."

In the kitchen, Berenger watched Cecilia warm the lasagna. "Aren't you going to take your coat off? You're starting to sweat."

She worked furiously, packed the lasagna into a thermal bag, added a plate and fork and another batch of cookies, and handed them to him. "You'll like the shelter. Thanks. Good bye."

He looked at her closely, and in that moment, Cecilia's fear and logic returned: She was alone in her home. No one would know if she were attacked now— She should have gone to Florida for the holidays. Damn her honorable traits and devotion to duty, to the club and to those who really needed their gifts replaced. "Please go," she whispered unevenly.

"Okay. Thanks. Just lock your door and think about calling the police." Then he was gone. Too quickly. Perhaps to return when she was sleeping and— Cecilia watched him through the window, a big man disappearing into the snowy night. She hurried to her Christmas tree, stripped the bells from it, and hurried to place them around her windows as warnings—just in case.

· **2** ·

In the morning Joe Berenger emerged from his camper, which was parked in Cecilia Lattimer's driveway. He yawned and stretched and noted her neighbors checking him out from behind their window blinds; he wanted everyone who might be interested in harming Ms. Cecilia Lattimer to know that she was now under his protection. Playing bodyguard to her wasn't what he had planned for his holiday vacation away from the St. Louis undercover division, but since Monroe had asked for his help with the thefts occurring in Dewdrop, Berenger had complied.

The cousins had grown up together, and Joe had unexpectedly found the person Monroe thought had the most access to what happened in town, Cecilia. She'd grown up there, married and divorced there, and from what Joe had already learned, Cecilia was appreciated, loved, but according to Monroe she could be a real pain in the butt when she started organizing. As a professional, she had access to homes, offices, and stores and the flow of Dewdrop's hot gossip.

Berenger leaned against the camper, hitched up his collar against the wind's chill, and adjusted his sunglasses against the blinding glare of the snow and thought about Cecilia. She just reached his shoulder, had big green eyes that were either filled with fear—or flashed with anger. A few strands of reddish hair had escaped her knitted cap, and the rest of her had been too bundled in that coat to judge her figure.

In his experience, a woman who could bake and cook like Cecilia probably was curved. Berenger's curiosity deepened; he really wanted to see her out of that coat.

She was complex—more than the female-usual—a woman who preferred sweltering beneath a winter coat rather than removing it. And she hadn't reported the break-ins. Why?

Like others in town, Cecilia's presents had been taken. Someone was out to get Cecilia, and they knew exactly how to unnerve her—that said, it was someone familiar with her; someone with a grudge that ran deep and personal. Joe had checked beneath her car's hood and noted the pulled wires; someone had wanted her to be walking last night and they knew the route she was apt to take. And for some reason, Cecilia did not want to report her encounter with the three men, the theft of her presents, or the entry into her home.

Apparently, Cecilia knew everyone in town, and she hadn't used the three men's names. Berenger had decided to let them go; he was after whoever had the brains to put together that potentially dangerous incident.

Monroe had said she'd been acting "spooky" lately; she virtually ran when she saw him coming. Oh, yes, Cecilia definitely knew something, and Berenger was going to stick close to her.

At her house window, she was furiously motioning for him to go away. Berenger reached inside his camper, retrieved her thermal bag and dishes, and walked to her house. She answered the front door on his third try, jerked it open and scowled up to him. She had covered her snowflake decorated pajamas with her long coat, and her bunny slippers had plastic eyes that stared up at him. He wondered what her toes would look like, probably little and naked and sexy; Cecilia didn't seem like a woman who used polish or wiles. She looked like a lady.

"Here's your dishes," he said as he noted how cute she looked, all cuddly and warm—okay, that flush was probably due to anger, because her eyes were doing that flashing-anger thing again. The boyish cut of that reddish brown hair emphasized her eyes and exposed those cute little ears.

She grabbed the sack. "Thanks. Now get your camper and pickup out of my driveway."

"Can't. I'm out of gas."

"I've got things to do. Some of us work for a living, you know. And I've got to go shopping . . . my car won't start, and if it did, you'd be in my way."

"My mama always told me to work for my keep. I'm not much for handouts. Maybe I could shovel your walkway and help out—"

"Please remove your camper and truck from my driveway," she repeated, clearly digging in to evict him. Berenger couldn't let her do that. He studied her carefully. "Not going to report the break-in last night, too, huh?"

"It won't happen again."

Despite her firm tone, that quick shadow over her expression told him that she was really scared and had not a clue about how to proceed. Berenger was set to stick close and protect her. "If you're going shopping, maybe I could carry things for you."

"No." She closed the door, then opened it again, considering him with those green eyes. Berenger noted how the sunlight danced across the fringes of her eyelashes, how it gleamed on her soft mouth as she licked her tongue. "Well, okay. I'll be just a minute. By the way, why do you think those three men left last night? I mean, there's only one of you," she said finally.

"Not a clue." *Or maybe they didn't like the .38 he was holding. . . .* "I'll wait in my camper."

Minutes later, Berenger answered the rap on his door and Monroe entered the camper, closing the door behind him. "How's it going?"

"She's plenty scared and someone is making a point with her. She was cornered in the alley last night—three men—here's their descriptions." Berenger handed his notes to his cousin. "What's she done anyway?"

"Nothing. People generally like her. But she likes to move into their lives and organize, which really irritates the hell out of people, because they can never find their stuff after she's done her thing. I once lost a whole set of files down at the department, and she was just there a minute. Women seem to like her closet arrangements, though, space making and all that. Keeps the town handymen busy—unless she does their workshops and tools. She almost married the town's biggest lawyer, but jilted him."

"He's sworn to ruin her. Maybe—" Berenger answered another knock on the camper.

Cecilia peered up at him. She glanced past Berenger to Monroe. "There's a police car parked by my mailbox," she stated too firmly.

Berenger sensed that Cecilia had come to defend him from the authorities and he ran with that idea. "The chief here wants me to move on or he's going to haul me into jail. Since I'm out of gas and broke, I guess—"

Cecilia didn't miss a beat; she owed Berenger a favor and she repaid it with: "He's just fine where he is. He's my guest. You may leave, Chief."

She held the door while Monroe exited. The men shared a look, and then Cecilia stepped into the camper. She stood in the center, studying the sagging couch-bed with his sleeping bag still opened, the magazines and books Berenger intended to read on his vacation, the clutter around his stove, the heap of dirty and clean clothing on the floor. "You actually live in this mess?" she asked incredulously.

He'd taken months planning this trip and stocking his camper. It contained everything he wanted—just the way he wanted. It was a work of macho art. Then he remembered Monroe's warning about Cecilia's potential danger, and Berenger didn't want one thing changed. He started nudging her back toward the door and when she was standing in the snow, trying to peer around him and into the camper, Berenger stepped outside and locked the door. "Let's go."

"But I . . . that place really needs organization. It's tiny, but you could have a lot more room if you'd—"

He used his body to keep nudging her away from his camper. He blocked her view, because she was still turning around to look at the camper as they walked toward the house. "It's fine the way it is."

"You could sort that clothing, fold it, and place it in an overhead rack. You could—"

"Please don't waste any time or energy on me.

Thanks for keeping me out of jail, by the way. It sounded like you didn't like the chief."

"I don't."

"Any specific reason why?"

Her lips closed tightly and Berenger made a mental note to ask his cousin why he was in disfavor with Cecilia.

On the snowy street in front of the house, a woman was passing and waving at her. Cecilia smiled briefly; apparently friends, they exchanged Christmas cheer. Another woman came up the drive and hugged Cecilia; she cuddled a toddler. Then Cecilia turned to Berenger. "Have you eaten this morning? A good breakfast always starts a person out right. Let's eat, shop, I'll make a business call or two, and then this afternoon, I'll help arrange your camper. It could do with some good organization, and then we'll work on you—on your goals and—"

She was looking at him critically, as if she were dissecting him. He saw her mouth move, but whatever else she was saying was lost in the fear tumbling through Berenger's brain. A slight chill ran up his back. He began to see why someone who knew Cecilia well, and whose life she had rearranged, might want revenge.

But cornered in an alley by three men was a little more dangerous than messing up a CD collection and file cabinets.

"You need a shave and a bath," she was saying when his mind cleared.

"Huh?"

Cecilia was already moving up her walkway; she turned to him. "My brother's stuff is in my bathroom.

You can use that. I try to keep the guest bathroom stocked. And you—well, cleaning up will do wonders for your self-esteem. It could start you off on a whole new direction."

Usually well shaven, Berenger scratched the beard he was thoroughly enjoying. He wanted more insights into the reason someone might be trying to unbalance this woman, and moving around her home would give him that. He watched the heavy coat sway in the area of her hips as she walked into the house, and remembered that he still hadn't seen her without padding.

She stopped at the front door, stared at him. "Well, come along. I'm already off schedule and I've got that shopping to do."

· 3 ·

Cecilia tried to concentrate on the café's floor layout: The nonsmoking section tables were placed erratically, which, if placed in a neat line, the waitresses would move easily through them.

Smoky, the cook and owner, was glaring at her as she stood with Berenger behind her. With him at her back she now felt very safe—if only she hadn't seen that big gun holstered across his chest. She'd noticed it wasn't new. At the house, he only reluctantly removed it when she had pointed and started to stammer fearfully. "Are you wanted for any crime?"

"Not that I know of."

"Why do you need it? I mean, is the mob after you? Are you on the run?"

"Not now. I guess I just feel naked without it."

"But you were in the mob," she had pressed fearfully. "Ah . . . were you ever a hit man?"

"Never. But I've been in some tough places. Soup kitchens and shelters aren't always sweet, you know."

His slow firm answer had had the ring of truth. In her brother's clothes, Berenger looked big and hard; his expression amused as she studied his shaven face, the hard cut of his jaw, that firm mouth, those black eyes. Somehow, she'd ended up trimming his hair, and he'd held very still as she moved around him.

Okay, she had motives for taking a stranger under her wing; she was devious. And scared, uncertain of what she should do, but she definitely wasn't reporting anything to the police chief. Cleaned up, Berenger looked quite nice, she'd thought, in a woodsy outdoorsman sort of way. Despite his gun, he looked capable, and appearances counted. Just maybe she could turn his life around.

Smoky the cook eyed Berenger. "He with you?"

Smoky's tone inferred that after an ex-husband and an ex-fiancé that no man would be interested in Cecilia. Her evil side perked up to defend her maligned man-catching ability. She hoped that gossip would carry that man-in-hand tidbit back to Tracy and John. "Very much so. We'll want breakfast."

The owner's hands were planted on his hips as he blocked her way to the nonsmoking section; he spoke over her head to Berenger. "You can't rearrange anything here. We like it how it is."

"But I drew out a floor plan, free of charge. I can come down after hours and—" Cecilia found her elbow taken and Berenger's tall body nudging her along to the line of booths. He seemed to like nudging her along, seating her in the booth, and then using his body to push her, making room for himself. She felt safe, despite the warning tingling of her senses.

"Tell me about your ex-fiancé," Berenger was saying as he dug into the café's super big breakfast, "and your ex-husband."

Cecilia reached into her large shoulder bag and extracted her PDA. She ignored him and worked feverishly over her schedule.

"Someone has it in for you. If I'm in this act, supposedly involved with you, I want to know right now why you're not reporting your break-ins."

"There have been burglaries all over town. I'm not the only one. And they only took things the first time."

He sat back to stare at her as if he wanted to see into her bones, to dig out the truth. She felt as if she were being interrogated, which was ridiculous. "You're sweating," he noted in an I've-got-you, amused tone.

She had to confess and whispered, "I think the police chief is having an affair. I saw him, and I think he's after me, trying to intimidate me."

Berenger seemed amused. "Is that right?"

She leaned close to whisper and when he turned, their faces were very close. "Your eyes are very expressive," he whispered.

He smelled great—soap and man—and it had been such a long time. . . . Cecilia took a heartbeat to recover. "I am a witness to his infidelity. He has a lot to protect— his position in town, and his wife is pregnant and she's wealthy. They've only been here a year and I didn't know who his mistress was, but she's young and not from around here. I grew up here. I know everyone."

"I'll just bet you do."

Cecilia dug out her business cards and placed one on the table; Smoky might have a change of mind. "Let's go. We'll have to go to Tracy's gift shop."

"Problem?" His tone was back to the crisp, just-the-basics, his expression closed and piercing.

"My ex-husband's new wife owns it."

His quiet "Oh" said he understood everything; there was one place in town to purchase last-minute gifts, and it was from "the replacement," and the terms weren't friendly.

Inside Fancy Stuff, Berenger took in Cecilia's determination as she wandered around the counters and shelves layered with everything overpriced and unnecessary. Crowded with last-minute shoppers, it was small, cluttered, and presented a potential disaster zone for a large man. Berenger stood still, sizing up the people who seemed distracted but friendly toward Cecilia.

Tracy took in his appearance immediately. Berenger sized her up: Tracy was cold, fake and she definitely had a grudge, weighing in with a snooty, "So this is your new one. I hear he has a—well, let's just say it isn't new—camper and pickup parked in your driveway."

Cecilia skipped right over any inference of involvement and said crisply, "He's . . . a friend, and just passing through. He's having car trouble. It will be moved soon."

In a matter of less than a block, from the café to the shop, Berenger had gone from an intimate relationship with Cecilia, back to the needy guy. The girl had her defenses up.

Tracy eyed Cecilia's credit card. "I hope this is good."

"Would l be using it, if it weren't?" Cecilia bristled.

Tracy shrugged and smiled, catlike, and stuffed the gifts into a sack. Cecilia handed it to Berenger on her way out of the store. "Happy Holidays," Tracy singsonged behind them.

Outside the shop, Berenger toted Cecilia's sacks. "You don't like her, do you?"

"I wouldn't have gone in there, but it's the only gift store in town. And I have to go to her house to collect the gifts and deliver them to the families." Cecilia steamed along beside him and muttered, as if to herself, "Thank God, I already sent my family's presents to Florida. The charges on my credit card are going to take years to pay off. I'd better do some more advertising and take my business cards around, do some free consulting to stir up more work."

Berenger needed to know if John, Cecilia's ex, could have it in for her. "That's rough. You could have cut the atmosphere with a knife. Did you try to give her some tips on her place? The café guy didn't like it at all."

"I don't want to talk about it anymore. You were helpful last night, and I just feel obligated to let you know the layout of whatever is happening in my life . . . since you seem to momentarily be in it anyway. But you'll be gone—preferably this afternoon—because we're going to put some gas in that truck and you can be on your way."

Berenger wasn't above playing his aces. Monroe would need time to work on the three men's description and Berenger wasn't leaving Cecilia undefended. "I sure wish I had somewhere special to go for Christmas," he said wistfully.

Cecilia was trudging along beside him, apparently still locked in whatever was going on between her and the second Mrs. Lattimer. She glanced at him as though just remembering his presence. "You *must* change your lifestyle. I saw your scars when you were trying on my brother's shirts."

Ms. Lattimer knew how to look at a man, the down-up kind of personal that made him feel prime. "Nothing important . . . a couple of bullet holes and there was that knifing."

Cecilia stopped and stared at him, her mouth opened. He couldn't resist raising a finger beneath her chin, lifting it to close those soft lips. "Do you have any more shopping to do?"

He could have fallen into those wide green eyes, wrapped himself up on that curvy body and in her gingerbread scents, and—

"You really should leave," Cecilia said as she took back her sacks and started to hurry away.

He walked beside her. "Your car didn't start because someone jerked the wires in it . . . right in your garage. They wanted you to be walking that night, and they knew the route you would take."

She turned and stopped so fast that his arms went up around her as they collided. Against her cute little ear, he whispered, "Lady, I'm big and I'm mean, and you need me—until whoever broke into your house is caught." More than anything, he wanted to keep Cecilia safe.

Wrapped in his arms, she shivered delicately. "My heating bill is going to be enormous."

Berenger noticed his own rising heat and nudged his nose a little beneath her knitted cap, where her hair smelled like flowers and gingersnaps. "It could happen again. Those guys mean business. You're pretty visible. They could visit your house—while you're there."

"Visit my house? With me in it?" Cecilia's voice was high and tight with fear. She held very still, those green eyes wide upon him as a little quiver ran through her body. He really liked that little quiver, because it wasn't from fear. And he liked the slight huskiness of her voice. "So you'd be like a . . . a bodyguard?"

"Something like that. I could run errands for you, pick up the presents at Tracy's house for you."

"I really do not want to go there. She makes such a big deal out of— You're holding me too tight."

"Yeah, I guess I am. I don't want anything bad to happen to you. Not every woman makes great gingersnaps. Which is what I'd want—maybe some lasagna, too—for payment, and enough money to head out after this thing is over, of course."

He released her slowly and she considered his offer. "I guess—I guess you could help deliver the Christmas Club's presents to those who really need cheering up. I need some house fix-it stuff done. Do you know anything about cars?"

"I get by. Will work for food," he stated firmly. "But then, a single woman with a new man in her life might stir up gossip."

He watched that tidbit sink into Cecilia. According to Monroe, she was on the hit list of the town's biggest attorney, a man who had sworn to ruin her and was definitely a bully. And Monroe had said that everyone knew that Cecilia had been shattered by the breakup of their marriage and that John Lattimer was open about "trading up." An ex-husband would know about her little quirks, what would unnerve her that no one else would know, like a messed CD collection.

Cecilia was apparently considering him. "You do need help. Your life, I mean. That awful camper. And there are things littered over your pickup's dashboard—cups, maps, sunglasses."

That uneasy little chill went up Berenger's spine; danger came in all sorts of cute little packages. "Hands off."

· **4** ·

"You were walking all over town today with that guy this morning. No one knows him, or anything about him. Tell him to get that truck and camper out of the driveway. It just doesn't look good for a single woman to have a man move in with her that way," John ordered on the telephone as Cecilia worked on her floor plan for a new real estate office.

"You're not my husband anymore, John. And this isn't your home any longer, so you do not have anything to say about my life—or my property. . . . I bought you out, remember?"

"It doesn't look good, Cecilia. I have a certain reputation to maintain. You've got to stop going into Tracy's shop and upsetting her."

Cecilia took a calming breath; it didn't work. "I was shopping for presents, John, and it wasn't nice to tell Tracy our bedroom secrets, that I liked to plan our romantic nights, John. She just happens to spread that stuff all around town."

"Is that what this is about? Getting back at me? Everyone knows that you just took Edward's proposal because you were on the rebound and that you still love me. You're going to have to let go. I'm not coming back. I'm calling Monroe and having him check out that guy. He's probably wanted somewhere for something."

"I wouldn't have you back on a platter, and Monroe has already been here and talked with him." Cecilia remembered Berenger's broad shoulders and muscled body and the way he held her close and tight, his cheek warm against hers, his deep voice rumbling intimately around her. John was probably right—Berenger was definitely the kind of man that women would want—for something.

"There's been break-ins all over town. He's probably involved," John was saying.

Cecilia held her breath. John could be right. The three men were new in town or she would have recognized them, and then Berenger had turned up. Clearly, he and Monroe had an association, and one they didn't want known. But then, Cecilia had grown suspicious of associations, after missing her ex's with Tracy during their marriage.

And clearly involved in an affair, Monroe had plenty to lose—his reputation, his job, and maybe career; also his pregnant, wealthy wife.

Cecilia ended the call firmly, then stood in front of her window, studying the battered camper and truck in her driveway. *Was it possible that Monroe had hired Berenger? A man working in the law would know*

*those outside it, wouldn't he? He'd know their spe-
cialties, like murder?*

Berenger had been gone since early afternoon, probably chatting with his boss and getting orders on how
to make her death look like an accident. Dying at
Christmastime wasn't her preference. Cecilia wondered how many times he'd used that big revolver in
that worn harness.

Edward's black Lincoln slid slowly by her driveway. His phone call followed within seconds, his
anger snapping over the line. "What the hell are you
doing with that vagrant's camper parked in your driveway? What the hell are you doing walking all over
town with him? Don't you have any sense at all?
You've really done it this time, Cecilia."

Edward's dark side was something that he hid very
well, but in private, his anger could be explosive. "I
know what I'm doing at all times," Cecilia stated quietly.

"There's been robberies all over town and he's
probably in on it."

"I don't think so, Edward." *I really think he's here
to silence me and I can't tell the police chief that I'm
on to him.*

"You've finally sunk to what you can get," Edward stated arrogantly. "I cannot take you back after
this."

"Yeah, sure, yada yada. Good bye."

Cecilia studied that camper. It was disgusting,
layered with men's stuff. On the other hand, maybe
beneath that stuff, in the cabinets, maybe there was
something she could use to prove that Berenger was
Monroe's hit man.

Or, if he was involved with the burglaries, maybe the camper and truck held some of his loot.

Minutes later, Edward called again. "There's something funny about this. Monroe isn't being helpful at all. But I'll find out who this guy is and what he's up to—why he's in town."

Of course, Monroe wasn't fingering his hit man.

Cecilia studied that camper. At any rate, she was going in. . . .

· 5 ·

Berenger hitched up his collar against the wind chill and the mist that could turn to snow. Monroe had the three men under surveillance in a nearby town. All three were small-time hoods, without enough brains between them to plan and coordinate the Dewdrop burglaries—and they would have taken jewelry and other valuables, not just the wrapped presents.

In the distance, he saw Cecilia's twinkling Christmas tree lights, and pictured her cooking and wrapping presents; it was a sweet little image. Maybe he'd get to see her without her coat; he'd turn up the furnace if he had to.

Berenger stopped walking; the twinkling lights were actually in her driveway—around his camper. He hurried to the lighted camper, listened to the faint sounds within, the Christmas carols, the woman singing along with them, then jerked open the door.

Cecilia was without her coat, dressed in a red sweater and jeans that hugged her bottom, and she was holding a box. She thrust it at him. "Trash. Put it in the can in my garage."

While he stood in the snow, holding the box and staring at her, trying to adjust to her invasion, Cecilia thrust another box at him. "Recyclables. You'll have to sort into the bins in my garage."

"What the hell have you done?" Berenger realized that he'd just bellowed.

"Here's my garage door opener. Close it when you're done. Is that 'What the hell' line the only one men have in their vocabulary today?" she asked airily as she closed the door in his face.

Berenger stood there holding the two boxes, trash and recyclables. The Christmas lights circling his camper twinkled hypnotically. He began to blink in sync with them, wavering between evicting Cecilia's busybody self and the curvy image of her body. He decided to think about how to do both as he went to the garage and began sorting recyclables and depositing trash. Finished, he returned to the camper, stopped to glare at the twinkling lights, noted the extension cord running from her garage to his camper, and stepped inside. "You've ruined my camper," he stated, just to start things off.

Apparently used to such confrontations, Cecilia placed a big red candle on the table where he preferred to lay his magazines. She watched Berenger take in the new order in the camper, the overly neat collection of his favorite magazines, the television hidden away from easy couch-viewing, the usual spices on the counter had vanished.

"Make that your pickup, too. Everything will be a lot neater if you use that organizer box I put in it."

The encounter was too much. Berenger took off his coat, sat down on his newly cleaned couch-bed, the sleeping bag neatly rolled beneath his pillow, and held his head. He felt weak and confused. Cecilia patted his shoulder and took his coat, placing it away in a closet. She lit the candle and placed a plate of gingersnaps beside it. "A lot of men have that same reaction. Women accept, men take a while to adjust."

"I could kill you," he said, looking up at her as his hand circled her wrist.

"I know, but could you please wait until the holiday season is over?" she whispered unevenly.

"I'm not going to kill you," he corrected warily.

"People shouldn't say things they don't mean."

"I bet a lot of people do that around you."

She considered past conversations. "Maybe."

Cecilia looked down to where his hand circled her wrist, his thumb stroking that smooth skin. He had big hard hands; his touch was gentle and warm. The twinkling light from outside lit his face to the rhythmic heavy beat of her heart. "I think the smell of those cookies is getting to me," he whispered as he stood. "I'll walk you back to your house."

"You're evicting me."

"Something like that."

Berenger entered the house first. Cecilia had accepted this as bodyguard procedure. He moved through the rooms, and came back to stand beside her. His look down at her was long and searching, and Cecilia fought blushing.

"He was an SOB, wasn't he? Your ex-husband?"

"We weren't on the same wavelength."

"My ex-wife and I weren't either."

"Ohh, and losing her threw you into this life? You shouldn't be afraid of committing again. Things will work out."

Berenger's lips seemed to be forcing back a smile. To his credit, he didn't remind her that her engagement to Edward hadn't worked out. "Yeah. Maybe."

Then he kissed her. Hard and long and soft and sweet and then, pretty darn hot, like he was gathering her all into him, to keep forever, all snug and safe and—hot. She hadn't realized that he'd picked her up until her feet slowly touched the floor. "Mistletoe—on the decoration above us," he explained rather hoarsely, his arms still around her.

"Uh-huh." Her fists were still locked to his shirt. The flannel was old and soft and comfortable. *She could wear it as she cooked breakfast. . . .*

"Look, I should tell you that—"

She didn't want his confession, that Monroe had hired him to silence her. "I need to wrap presents. Good night."

Berenger seemed to hover there, reluctant to leave. Then he nodded and closed the door behind him. Cecilia stood still and savored that warm, well-kissed feeling. The door jerked open. Berenger had on his coat and he looked fierce—and puzzled. "How did you open my truck and camper?"

"I picked the locks. I'm really good with hairpins."

He stared at her blankly, then turned and walked toward the police car that was waiting for him on the street.

They probably had plans to make, didn't they? The cover-up of her murder would take some doing, made much easier with the help of the local law. Her own plans concerned wrapping gifts and finishing Christmas delivery to those who needed it.

Cecilia looked at the mistletoe ball above her doorway and sighed. Good kissers were hard to find, ones good enough to make her feel safe when she wasn't. She would hopefully finish Christmas, then resolve what to do about Monroe's mistress.

· 6 ·

"My mistress? Your sister, who's dying of her latest heartbreak?" Monroe chuckled, then settled into the facts of the new burglary; he turned up the police car heater. "Another one. Same M.O. In and out . . . knew just what they wanted. No valuables or anything else taken. Family was at the local church program. Surveillance for those three men said they haven't left the house of one of their sisters, except to carry out garbage and make snowmen."

"It's someone here, then. Someone who knows the town and what's going on." Berenger drank coffee and settled in to eat Monroe's wife's german chocolate cake, but his mind was on Cecilia's safety. Edward and John, her exes, had queried Monroe about the "vagrant parked in Cecilia's driveway." Apparently both males felt they still had propietary rights, and Berenger could see why the men wanted her: Cecilia's kiss said that beneath her ladylike demeanor, she was a very hot, spicy package.

"Got any ideas?" Monroe was asking as he dug into the cake.

"Someone has a thing against Christmas or they'd

be taking valuables. It's someone who wants to make a point. Anyone match that profile? And was anyone else's home messed up like Cecilia's, or their cars tampered with?"

"No. I'd say this might be payback from her ex. She told me that after she found out John had been seeing Tracy, Cecilia picked the lock to his office and walked in on them. Likewise, Edward and his secretary. Then Cecilia rearranged all their files." Monroe's grin said he approved.

The next afternoon, Berenger collected the club's gifts from Tracy Lattimer. Tracy wasn't exactly a warm hostess, making him wait outside while she collected the bags. "So nice of Cecilia to send you. I really shouldn't give these to you, but she called, okaying it. You're walking?"

"My truck is—" Decorated with twinkle lights? "Out of commission."

"Just don't drop anything, or take it for yourself," she ordered and closed the door in his face.

Berenger hitched up the red bags containing the presents, slung them over his back, and started walking toward Cecilia's. Accompanying her on the deliveries would give Berenger a good view of anyone wanting to dampen the holiday mood.

He wasn't expecting the Santa Claus suit she'd whipped up for him.

Her car was waiting on the street; the tire tracks in the snow said she'd backed out and around his pickup and camper. Dressed as Santa, Berenger crunched his six-foot-four body into the compact car's passenger seat and held on to the dashboard as Cecilia sailed around Dewdrop's streets. Between spreading cheer and gifts, she seemed oddly quiet and distracted. The families whose gifts had been stolen were overjoyed; the grumpy bah-humbug people were friendly to Cecilia, joining in the Christmas carols. Children sat on his lap and some of their mothers, too. No one suspicious appeared in their route, and arriving back at Cecilia's, Berenger held his breath as she drove around his camper and back into her garage. He was invited in for stew, freshly baked bread, and a recap of how everyone enjoyed the gifts. In a holiday mood himself, Berenger couldn't resist tugging her onto his Santa Claus lap and asking her, "And what do you want for Christmas, little girl?"

"I've got a big problem," she said quietly. "And I don't know what to do about it."

"Try me. And I do not think that the chief—or anyone else—has hired anyone to kill you."

"This is something else. I think I know who is behind these burglaries, and there's only one way to find out."

· 7 ·

Not every man would think "she just might have a good idea," and agree to be her partner in crime.

But then, Berenger seemed to know underworld tricks very well, using them as they B-and-E'd into Tracy and John's home.

"I just had to finish up a little shopping and stopped in to get one of those snow balls, you know, the little clear glass thingies that you turn and the snow inside stirs up and drifts down—"

"Just the facts," Berenger ordered as he made his

way down the Lattimer hallway with Cecilia behind him.

"It was just there—" Cecilia bumped into his back when he stopped to open a door leading to the attic.

"What was?" Berenger wasn't a talking man—when on a mission. His tone sounded like business. But then, maybe breaking and entering was his business.

"It was a little ceramic house that lights up and you can put a whole bunch of them together like a town. This one was unique, with a little kitty in the window, one of a kind, handpainted. Emma Schwartz showed it to me when she bought it at a craft show last summer. . . . I don't know anything about you—and I'm with you, breaking into Tracy and John's house."

"If the stolen goods lead to Tracy, she might be involved. She could have gotten sloppy, and this is your idea." He started up the steps, his tiny flashlight picking out the way ahead.

"Yes, I know. But I needed help. I've never been involved in a crime before."

"Always a first time."

"Never again."

"They all say that." His tone sounded distracted and Cecilia needed to make her point. "How would it sound if I made accusations that were really unfounded? Like I'm still the disgruntled, ugly, unappealing—"

"You've got plenty of appeal. Your ex-husband is a dope."

"That's unfounded. You don't really know him."

"I know you. Any guy who would mess around with a good thing like you deserves what he gets. Look at that, will you?" Berenger's tiny flashlight pinpointed to boxes of—

Cecilia kneeled to examine the contents. "Loot. That's the burglary loot. I'd know it anywhere. Toys from the Marshall family, that little town for their boy, that doll for their girl—"

"You can identify the gifts?"

She looked up at him, her face stark and pale in the dim light. "This is awful."

"Makes sense. Tracy is recycling the gifts in her store, which means she's also probably selling the more identifiable ones elsewhere."

Berenger was fishing out his cell phone. He looked at Cecilia as he spoke quietly. "Monroe, I'm at the John Lattimer house. Cecilia is with me. Looks like the stuff from the B and Es is in the Lattimer attic."

· 8 ·

"You're the police chief's cousin? And that was your sister he was holding? She'd just broken up with her boyfriend and he was comforting her?" were Cecilia's last words to Berenger through the search of the Lattimer home and Tracy and John's arrest. At the police station, she sat pale and tense through the argument between her ex and his present wife, Tracy.

John Lattimer was rigid and clearly not involved in his wife's crimes. "How could you? It's Christmas, Tracy. Cecilia always works very hard to make Dewdrop's Christmases good for everyone."

"That's just the point, John. Cecilia this, and Cecilia that. I had to do something, John," Tracy argued fiercely. "Sales were slipping. I could have lost the shop. You're always telling me how organized Cecilia is, how much of a success she is because she's just . . . so . . . perfect. I hate her. I couldn't let my business go down when she's doing well. Don't you understand? She won everything in high school, the president of the student body, the first chair clarinet, the cheerleader captain, and everything I wanted, she got—including you. I did it for you, John. You wouldn't want a failure for a wife, would you?"

Berenger looked up from writing his report. "If you were hosting the club that night, how did you manage to break into Cecilia's house the second time?"

Tracy's voice filled with disdain. "I'm in shape, that's how . . . I can run to her house in five minutes, even in the snow. I was in the moment she left the house. I knew she'd probably stop to chat with everyone—they all like her. I just told the ladies that I forgot to lock my shop's back door and I was back before they missed me."

"The other thefts. Did you have accomplices?"

"No. Do I look like I need help?" Tracy countered angrily, her neck vein throbbing.

"I'm going home now," Cecilia stated quietly. "And no, John, I don't want you back."

Berenger started after her, but her look froze him in place.

Later, in his camper, Berenger brooded about how to approach her.

As he sat in the dark, the pickup's motor suddenly roared and the camper was in motion, backing out onto the street. Berenger struggled for footing and fell onto the couch. He was just picking himself up again when the truck roared again, the gears grinding, and the camper lurched forward. As he held on and the contents of the camper tumbled around him, Berenger prayed that it wouldn't roll over, though he was certain that only one tire was on the ground, the other in the air.

Finally, after a few minutes, the pickup collided with something and stopped abruptly. Shaken, Berenger tore the wreath that had been on the door from his head. He listened as gears ground, the camper rocked, and he decided it was stuck—permanently. He jerked open the door, noted the campground, and Cecilia tromping off toward the highway. She turned to yell at him, "This is where campers go, in a campground, not in my driveway. There's a right place for everything, and it's not you—in my life."

Berenger struggled for reality, and balance. He was a little dizzy from the ride. "I don't know where the hell we are, but it's freezing. You are *not* walking back into town."

"Oh, I'm not, am I, Mr. Police Man on vacation? Cousin to the police chief? Undercover Cop-Man?"

"Get back in here. I'll call for a ride. Be sensible."

Cecilia lifted her head at that and faced him as he approached her. Her teeth chattered as she stated haughtily, "I . . . am . . . always sensible."

"You're scaring me. It must be ten below and a wind chill of way less than that. I'll take you back to town. You can have the pickup to go back by yourself if you want. Here, I'll unhitch the camper and I'll stay here."

"It's stuck."

Then Cecilia began to cry, the soft sort of a wounded cry that could javelin right into a man's heart. Berenger didn't know what to do, but he had to get her back into that camper and get her warm. He stripped off his quilted flannel shirt and put her into it. She was shaking badly and the tears on her face could freeze. He rubbed her arms. "Look, honey. You'll freeze out here. It's not much, but the camper is warm, especially stuck against those trees like it is."

Hit by the camper, a tree had fallen, covering it with snow. Steam was coming out from beneath the pickup hood, and a woman Berenger wanted very much was sobbing quietly.

Cecilia sniffed and wiped the long sleeve of his shirt across her nose. "I was going to give you a new life, a second chance. How can I do that when you—?"

He was clearly a real dog; the woman knew how to raise his guilt factor. Berenger moved in to block the wind from her body; he noted the snow falling heavily. A new terror spread through him: What if she caught pneumonia? "Let's just get you warm and I'll call to have someone come and get you. This probably isn't the time, but I'd really like to see you—maybe a date or something, maybe a regular relationship—when you get back to maybe trusting me. So if anything happened to you, say pneumonia, I'd feel really bad."

"Yeah. That makes sense," she said dully.

Inside the camper, Berenger wrapped her in his blankets and coats and hurried to heat cocoa. He glanced at her and found color returning. She stared at him, silently laying on the guilt. "I'm sorry, really," he said.

"Yeah. Sure." Her tone disbelieved as she studied the foam on the cup of cocoa. "If I were home, I'd have marshmellows on this. I really want to be home—

what's your name anyway? Joe? From the report, it said Joe Berenger."

"That's me—Joe." Uneasy with what Cecilia would do next, and fearing that at any moment she would decide to run off into the snowstorm rather than be trapped one more minute with him, he sat looking out of the window. If he looked at Cecilia, she'd know how much he wanted her, and that might frighten her even more.

"This is awful. The weather radio said a blizzard is coming, road advisories and all that."

"Uh-huh. But I'll get you home tomorrow, Cecilia. I just don't think it wise to leave now. Tomorrow, I'll get help." Then his next thought turned him to her. "How did you get my pickup started? I have the key."

She delicately sipped her cocoa. "Hot-wired it."

He stared at her blankly. "You are a woman of many talents."

"True." Cecilia placed her cup on a magazine and stared at it. "You need coasters. And what was that you said about dating me?"

"I regret springing it on you that way. I should have worked out this thing, explained it, and come at you in a different way. I intended to. Then you saw that thingie at Tracy's shop and we moved in on her—you looked real cute in that Ninja outfit you wore to her house. You'd be great undercover—I mean, working as an undercover cop," Berenger hesitated because Cecilia was staring intently at him. She probably didn't believe anything he said; he didn't blame her. To conceal his nervousness, he stood. "I'm going outside. You probably want some time alone, to settle down. I'll see if there is anything I can do about the pickup."

"This place is a mess," she said and stood, facing him.

He realized her need to neaten and order her emotions at the same time, the organizing kind of a woman she was. He wished he could give her more, in the middle of nowhere, with a blizzard coming. He wanted to say how she filled his heart, how just looking at her made him warm. But right now, things were looking sad to unlikely. "Look, I—" he began and decided against more, closing the door behind him.

Cecilia straightened the camper and put the events of the evening in order with her thoughts about Berenger—Joe, the undercover cop, the cousin of the police chief. Putting the facts she knew aside, Cecilia itemized her emotions as she lit the candle and snuggled down inside the shirt scented of him. She was warm, snug and safe, and Berenger had just said he wanted a date and "maybe" a relationship. None of those were bad things.

The good thing was how she felt when he kissed her—she felt like a hottie and a woman ready for a deeper relationship with a really good, safe man. He was uneasy now, fearing that he'd mispoken. But he hadn't, not really, he'd said what was in his heart, and his heart was good. She'd seen how as Santa Claus he'd handled the children and talked with the elderly, reassuring them that someone still cared. She'd seen so many of Berenger—Joe's—good points and, yes, it was true, he lit a spark that needed kindling and organizing and growing. . . .

She smiled at the knock on the door, because a really thoughtful man would do just that, and wait for a reply, though the temperatures were freezing. When she opened the door, he was standing and holding a small pine tree. "It's not much, but I thought—"

Berenger-Joe must have seen something in her face, something that she couldn't hide, because he stepped into the camper with the tree. He stood there, big and powerful and sweet, holding the tree tightly as he waited for her to speak. Then he held it out to her and said, "For you. A present."

"It's lovely, thank you. Our first Christmas tree." She held it, just as she would a bouquet of roses. "You need me, Berenger-Joe. Don't you?"

He leveled one of those dark intent looks at her, the kind that brought a flush to her cheeks—it was sweet and a bit devilish, and very hot. "Yes, ma'am. I truly do."

"There's just one thing: I truly do not like that thing men do, the 'What the hell have you done now' thing."

"I'll rephrase. What about: Would you please keep your fingers off my stuff, honey?"

She smoothed a snowflake from his hair, already feeling in charge and possessive. This one wasn't getting away; he was a keeper. "First, my friends, a little get-together at my house—and your cousin and wife. Then we have to fly to Florida to meet my family, then yours—I understand it's extensive . . . I'll pack for you. I'm good at organizing, you know. . . ."

She watched him carefully place the tree aside and turn to her. He brought her into his arms with a gentleness and warmth that she wasn't letting go. Then his searing kiss stopped her priority list of to-dos.

"You're not predictable at all, are you?" she asked much later in a breathless tone. "We'll have to work on that."

Holly Go Lightly

Suzanne Macpherson

"Fa-la-la-la LA, la-la-la laaaa," Nick Fredricks boomed through his third Christmas carol and wondered what had possessed him to sing a medley of holiday tunes in the shower, particularly "Jingle Bell Rock," Holly Townsend's favorite song.

Holly—the ultimate Christmas girl. His holidays had never been the same since she'd touched his life with her special magic.

Nick turned off the water, stepped out of the shower and felt for a towel. She had certainly been in his thoughts lately. Perhaps it was the time of year. He could swear he even smelled her perfume in the air: Obsession. Perfect for Holly. She was obsessed with Christmas and all things wild and crazy.

Perhaps this was all about his recent engagement to Gwen. Memories of the past and all that. After all, he'd planned on proposing to Holly that fateful Christmas Eve two years ago. If only she hadn't decided to go so over the top that day. Why did she always have to push things to the edge of respectability?

Whatever it was making him so nostalgic, he had

places to go and people to see, so he better snap out of it. Where was that damned towel?

Holly reached her hand toward him, but it passed like fog through his arm. Oh, how she would love to touch him again. She floated toward the ceiling and watched him in all his dripping nakedness. He had beautiful strong legs and an athlete's body she remembered so *very* well.

Nick still made her heart stand still. Being dead, her heart standing still wasn't much of a problem these days. Holly giggled into the steamy bathroom air and noticed it made a nice tinkling sound like delicate brass wind chimes in a summer breeze. Surprisingly, Nick seemed to *hear* that sound!

She wondered what else she could do. She'd tried thunking him on the head and talking in his ear, but so far she'd only managed to create a silvery chime sound when she laughed and to make him sing her favorite Christmas carols.

Holly slid down like a melted chocolate until her ethereal body was as close as a whisper to Nick's warm living body. Not that she could feel cold or heat, but a sharp memory of his touch struck her and vibrated through her soul. *Oh, Nick, you silly, sexy man.*

But she had more important things to do than cause him to get all hot and bothered, as fun as it was. She had to catch Nick by the short hairs of his inner soul and lead him into the light. It was vitally important, and she had to work quickly. She only had tonight.

* * *

Now why the hell had he gotten a hard-on? It wasn't like he was thinking of Gwen. It wasn't even her weekend to sleep over. Nick finished drying off and rubbed a spot of clarity in the fogged-up bathroom mirror.

He knew what it was. It was Holly that had caused his temporary arousal. It was Christmas carols and the memory of making love to her in this shower, and that funny tinkling, musical sound that must be some wind chime she'd hung up outside he'd forgotten about, and it was this odd sense of her that surrounded him today.

Well heck, they'd broken up on a Christmas Eve much like this one, and it'd been about a year ago he'd gotten the odd note from her friend telling him Holly had been killed in an automobile accident down in Carmel, California.

He couldn't believe she'd been so foolish as to drive that damned vintage VW bug of hers around some foggy curvy highway in the middle of the night anyway. No airbags, no protection at all. He felt a terrible sadness for her loss sweep over him. He'd been such an idiot cutting her out of his life. Two years without Holly and his holidays had never been the same.

But now he had Gwen. Good old Gwen, she'd be a very suitable wife. *She'd* never wear tinsel in her hair.

Nick finished drying off and slid into his knit boxers and gray flannel pants. This dinner with his parents to tell them about the engagement was an important evening for him and Gwen.

He stepped out of his walk-in closet as he buttoned his white shirt and looked around his bare but well-appointed flat. Would Gwen put a woman's touch on it and decorate it for the holidays? He remembered how Holly had gone hog wild and dragged a full-sized tree into his small living room, or more accurately, made *him* drag it in.

He'd truly never seen anyone as creative as Holly. She'd used every odd thing imaginable to decorate that tree; a tinfoil star, tiny birds she folded out of colored paper, snowflakes she cut out herself, cookies she baked herself. She'd made him buy scads of twinkling white lights and strung them all around the entire flat. Then she'd turned all the house lights down and slowly unzipped her red velvet dress and made him understand what made the holidays jolly.

Jingles, the cat she'd left behind, startled and patched out like a demon possessed when Nick came into the living room. A stack of unopened Christmas cards scattered every which way as Jingles streaked over the coffee table to the piano, then back to the sofa. Then Jingles twisted his ears back like a madman, eyes blazing like hot coals, and shot into the open kitchen, his claws clicking against the tile floor.

"What the hell is the matter with you, cat?" Nick rounded the kitchen counter and looked down at Jingles, who was now licking his paw in a very nonchalant manner.

"I suppose it's all about food, isn't it buddy?"

Nick didn't have the heart to tell Jingles his days in this house were numbered. Gwen wasn't too keen on having the cat of an old girlfriend around. Besides, she had allergies. It didn't help that Jingles tended to climb all over her, then go in for a sharp bite every time Gwen visited.

He put extra kibble in Jingles's bowl. "I'll be back later, bud. Don't do anything crazy. No parties." Nick scratched the top of Jingles's head. He really hated to part with him.

Nick went over to the side table in the living room and gathered Christmas cards off the floor. One had really taken a claw-full. Jingles had practically shredded the envelope. Impulsively, Nick opened it. It was a beautiful card, hand-painted and hand-lettered. The picture was a watercolor of a mother and her child. The mother held a star ornament in her hand and the child reached for it with a smile. Very heartwarming.

He tipped his head and stared at the picture. There was something so familiar about them. He opened the card and read, "May the Joy of Christmas Keep Your Spirit Bright. Best Wishes, Carol and Joy Chandler."

Carol Chandler. He flipped the clawed-up envelope over and saw the address was Carmel, California. Now, why would Holly's friend from Carmel send him a Christmas card?

On the back of the card she'd signed Carol Chandler, *artist*. He looked long and hard at the painting again. She was a very talented woman. She had a lovely smile, or at least she painted herself that way.

Nick set the card up on the piano and checked his watch. He better get going. Gwen wouldn't appreciate him being late tonight, of all nights.

His new blue blazer had a strange blotch on it. Damn it, the cleaners must have screwed it up. He rehung it neatly on its wooden hanger and thumbed to the back of the closet until he found his old blue blazer. It was still fine and would have to do. After all, he had his gray slacks on already. He heard the tinkling chimes again. He'd have to get outside when the rain let up this weekend and take those things down.

* * *

Good old Jingles. Score one for the cat.

Holly had been listening to what was rolling around Nick's head. He certainly hadn't forgotten what a great time they had together, and she was quite pleased to hear that he regretted their terrible breakup.

Who dumps their lover on Christmas Eve? And for what? His inability to accept her outfit? His stick-up-his-butt attitude about their dinner with his parents? Like the Fredericks cared if she wore a battery-operated Christmas tree sweater that twinkled in the dark or tinsel in her hair. It was all about appearances for Nick.

He was even planning to dump the cat they rescued together so that this Gwen person could keep her black, scary power suits cat-hair free. I mean, *really*.

And marry Gwen? That was just completely wrong. She knew this for a cosmic, written in the stars, fact. If Nick married Gwen he would be one miserable, lonely man for the rest of his earthly life. She couldn't let him be such a dope *again*!

Holly noticed her burst of anger made the candle Nick had on the glass dining table burn brighter. Interesting. His mother had put that fat red candle with fake holly circling it there, she just knew it. It was the only holiday decoration in the entire place.

Nick had a neat and tidy collection of rooms with their gray and beige and putty color schemes safely in place. Silly man. Where was a burst of red when you needed it? Where was his *tree*? The fake ficus didn't count.

She darted around the apartment remembering their time together. Remembering that she had forgiven him for being a foolish, frightened mortal of a man and breaking her heart on Christmas Eve two years ago. She also remembered she was on a mission. She had to get Nick down to Carmel to her beloved friend Carol. And to Joy. So very much depended upon that.

Jingles, her cat, looked up at her and meowed. Holly had heard from others that sometimes animals could see you and even feel your touch. Now what other naughty but necessary things could Jingles help her do? Of course getting a cat to help you was about as easy as trying to get *her* to behave when she was mortal. She'd been a high-spirited, headstrong girl, for sure. Poor Nick.

The honest truth was she'd been a foolish mortal herself, and now she had to make up for it. Driving her old VW Bug that foggy night had been the death of her. The only blessing was that she'd been completely alone in that car. Sure she'd had last-minute Christmas shopping to do, and well, she was a girl that took her holiday seriously, but she should have never taken such a risk when there were others depending on her.

That's why she needed to send Nick down to Carmel. Nick could fix the mess she'd made. He was the *only* one who could put things right. Underneath that gray-flannel, blue-blazered exterior, Nick had an amazingly loving heart.

Holly had promises to keep—*and to break*—before she could travel on.

• 2 •

Carol Chandler struggled not to cough and wake little Joy. It was bad enough she'd come down with this never-ending cold; she certainly didn't want Joy to catch it.

She set down *The Night Before Christmas* storybook and tucked the sleeping child into her crib under the antique quilts she and Holly had found in Carmel's Seaside Antiques. At least Joy would be warm. Carol just couldn't shake the chill she'd developed.

The single bed beside the crib beckoned her to crawl under the covers and sleep. But first she had to make some magic for Joy. Tomorrow was Christmas Day. Their last Christmas in this little house. It was sad, but maybe she'd find a nice warm apartment with modern plumbing and wiring. That's if she could save up the first and last month's rent to move. Well, she just had to, because old Mr. Meanypants the landlord had given her an eviction notice for Christmas. Out by New Year's Day.

The two-foot-high Charlie Brown tree she'd basically stolen from the side of the highway looked pretty pathetic, even with Holly's collection of crazy, clanking Christmas junk, as they used to call it. But Joy didn't seem to mind. The twinkling lights and pipe-cleaner snowflakes fascinated her.

God, how she missed her best friend, Holly. How she wished Holly were here to put the magic back in this season. They'd helped each other out in so many ways.

It was the best of days when Holly had come to find her in Carmel. The bond they'd formed in high school had lasted a lifetime.

She'd known the minute Holly strung a garland of firecrackers and paper dragons across the top of the front window at the Carmel Espresso and Art Gallery for Chinese New Year, she was still a special soul.

Both of them had been dumped by their long-time boyfriends, both of them without family, they'd found strength in each other. Two creative spirits serving up lattes in the morning and painting at night. How she wished Holly was here now to give her that strength back. She needed strength.

Thank God for the woodstove. Honestly, the frame wood, meant for stretching and mounting canvas for her paintings, made a pretty cheery fire. Carol pulled on a second pair of sweatpants, a second sweater, an old stocking cap, and the fingerless gloves she used to paint in when the weather turned cold. She wrapped a muffler around her neck and looked in the mirror.

Her eyes were blurry, but she could see a very padded Carol Chandler looking back at her. What a mess she was with her fever-induced rosy cheeks and chapped lips. Wisps of stringy blonde hair stuck out from under her red stocking cap. Carol set the kettle on to make herself a cup of tea later. Maybe it would help her brighten up.

She slid on her boots to go out to the shed. She needed to play Santa's helper for just a little while longer. She'd found a used toy kitchen for Joy and it just needed a few more repairs.

The kitchen was a little old for her, but Joy loved pretending to cook, and Carol just loved the thing, period. Joy loved to sit beside Carol in the real kitchen, stirring her pretend oatmeal in an old pot with a spoon while Carol made the real stuff. She'd probably be cooking for both of them by the time she was seven.

Carol knew she should have finished this sooner, of course, but she just hadn't had the energy. At least she'd sold enough hand-painted Christmas cards to add a new set of play pots and pans and a great bag of fake plastic food to the under-tree pile. Holly would have loved it.

She stepped outside to the back shed and uncovered the little kitchen. It sure felt heavier than she remembered. The effort of trying to pick it up made her coughing start up again. She felt a flush of heat rush over her. At least she was warmer. But then the evening chill sent a bone-cold wind through her that made her teeth rattle. Hot, cold, could she just pick one?

Somehow she managed to drag the toy kitchen inside. Holly had shown her just how strong and resourceful single women could be, and she drew on that strength now. She always wished she felt as confident as Holly had. Things just hadn't gone very well since Holly died.

If she could only sell a few more paintings and get the landlord off her back. Maybe when the weather got better and the ocean settled down a bit, she would feel better and start painting again.

She'd paint Holly's seashell garden when the spring grape hyacinth and daffodils bloomed between the drifts of sand and shells that Holly had created in their front yard. She'd paint beautiful red-haired Joy sitting on her tiny blue chair in the sunlight.

Carol got to her knees and worked on the toy with stiff, cold fingers. She fastened the little red gingham curtain she'd made over the pretend window with its cheerful scene of birds and spring flowers. She'd repainted them a bit brighter. Boy, she could use a little spring right now.

The kettle finally hissed at her from its perch on the woodstove. She rose to get it, but a wave of dizziness knocked her back to the floor. Crouching on her knees, she waited for it to pass. Slowly, she reached the counter above her and pulled herself upright.

She must be sicker than she thought.

It wouldn't do for her to pass out and have Joy wake up and be frightened if she couldn't get to her. No, it wouldn't do at all. She steeled herself as she sat down hard on the old white painted kitchen chair. What was she going to do? She sure as hell wasn't going to call her nasty landlord next door.

She pulled down the receiver from the kitchen phone and stretched the coiled cord down. Maybe Sylvia Belltower was home. After all, it was Christmas Eve. Surely she was home. She always closed up the gallery early on Christmas Eve. Unless she went to her daughter's for the night.

Jingles was a good bad cat. After Nick had rushed out the door to his Gwen, Holly had coaxed Jingles into all sorts of mischief with promises of the butter Nick left out and a catnip mouse stuck under the couch long forgotten. Jingles was amazed and purred when Holly stroked him with her invisible, wispy hands.

He seemed to understand her much more clearly than when she was alive, or maybe he just liked to *pretend* he didn't understand her when she was alive, the big orange-striped tabby devil.

She looked into his eyes and he meowed at her. She was tickled pink with his kitty idea. What a twisted plan! They seemed to be able to communicate on a deeply feline/female cat-to-ghost kind of way, and Jingles understood what she needed to accomplish in a very cat kind of way.

An open closet here, a box of decorations dumped out there, strands of lights all over the place, and in the blink of an eye Jingles had made a very creative holiday mess. He'd also batted quite a few glass balls around the room. All that was left was a kitty concerto when Nick returned to get her point across.

Jingles was reunited with his catnip mouse and directed toward the cube of butter Nick had neatly placed in the butter dish but forgotten to put the lid on. Bon appétit, Jingles!

It served Nick right for thinking of parting with Jingles, who was now sitting on the counter making kitty tongue marks across the butter's top. Nick would freak and throw the whole thing out. She would have just scraped off the top and smiled.

Holly closed her eyes and thought of Nick. In a quick flash of spirit-speed she found herself hovering over his parents' long formal dining room table. The room was aglow with candles and silvery holiday decorations with pale mint green accents and white berries sprinkled among the frosted blue spruce and pine. It was so upscale and elegant. Nick's mother was a whiz at decorating.

There was Gwen, tightly bunned brown hair, a black suit as usual, with a white high-necked blouse. This is what you wear to your Christmas Eve engagement party with the folks? Oh please, a nice red silk flouncy thing or maybe a full Scottish Highland tartan skirt with a black velvet weskit. Not bank teller wear.

Okay, it was no good giving fashion advice to Gwen from the afterlife. Gwen was hopeless, on many levels. She was a selfish, uptight woman who was deceiving Nick. It was about time he figured that out.

Holly floated above the silver candelabras and got a feel for what was on everyone's mind. In her own mind she felt an anxiety pluck at her. She was running out of time.

She blew a kiss to Nick, mingled with love and forgiveness and a nagging sort of pinch. He sniffed the air as if he'd been touched by her breath. What these people needed was a bit of truth mixed in with their cranberry-and-pineapple compote. Or better yet, in their champagne.

Holly dipped her finger in each glass of champagne as the Fredericks' faithful butler poured one after the other. Porter had always liked her. He looked up in the air and winked, the old devil. Maybe he could feel her somehow. Maybe the two of them could mingle up some magic. Holly stirred some cosmic truth serum into each and every glass of bubbly. Each glowed pink for a moment then paled down to champagne with a steady stream of bubbles.

Nick was practically overwhelmed with the scent of Holly's perfume again. "Good grief, Mother, are you wearing Obsession? I can smell it from here."

"Why no, son, I'm not. I prefer not to mingle my scents. It's prime rib and champagne for me tonight." His mother looked at him oddly. Then she looked at Gwen. "You look a bit warm, dear. Would you like Porter to take your jacket?"

Gwen took the glass of champagne off the table and took a sizeable gulp. "I guess so." Gwen pulled her jacket off and handed it to Porter, who nodded without smiling.

Nick wondered why Gwen was so nervous. He sipped his own champagne and smiled at her.

Gwen hiccupped. Nick thought she looked like she'd swallowed a bug. She'd been extremely uptight all night and he'd hoped a little champagne would loosen her up. He hoped she wasn't still dwelling on that offer her father had made him. Nick was no stockbroker. He was a teacher.

"Are you all right, dear?" Nick asked.

Gwen gave him an odd smile. Then in a rather loud voice, she addressed the family. "Has Nick told you about the offer my father made him? He'd be a fool not to take it. He can't languish in the economics department of Seattle State forever. He doesn't really have what it takes to cut it as a stockbroker, but Daddy is willing to give him a chance, for my sake."

Nick's neck actually snapped as he twisted to face her. "What the . . . ? I thought you were fine with my being a professor. I thought you liked the faculty parties. You fit in so nicely. We discussed this offer of your father's last week, and I told you very clearly I wasn't interested." Nick looked at his parents and felt a rush of embarrassment. "This isn't really the time to bring it up, Gwen, after all."

"Well, why not? Maybe your parents can talk some sense into you. *After all,* it's not like I want to lower myself into the leather-elbow-patch-on-the-tweed-jacket set at my age. What are you thinking, that I'd live in a little cottage near campus with you and have three or four kids? I'm a career woman. I have goals. I have no intention of ruining my life with a pack of snot-nosed brats." Gwen paused. "Oh my gosh, Nick, I didn't mean to say all that. I must be drunk. What's in this champagne anyway?" She sipped it again then put her champagne glass down. Porter, standing behind her, calmly refilled the glass.

"So, when you said you'd marry me the other day, you lied about wanting kids?" He stared at her and couldn't believe what she'd blurted out at the dinner table, and with his parents yet!

"I thought I'd talk you out of it later when you saw how much fun it was to travel and be rich and not have those kinds of responsibilities."

That was enough to make Nick feel slightly ill. "We'll discuss this later, Gwen."

"Fine. Pass the champagne, Porter, and keep it coming," Gwen snapped. "But don't think we won't."

Porter rolled his eyes.

So much for the warm and lovely toast announcing their engagement. Nick took a swig of his own champagne. The cranberry floating in it got stuck in his throat. He gagged and coughed. Through his watery eyes he watched his parents pass knowing looks between them and clink their own glasses together, sipping at their champagne.

Porter made a round and refilled everyone, then disappeared through the swinging door to the kitchen.

"Isn't it time for the salad, Mother?" Nick struggled with his napkin, dropping it on the floor. He didn't want to have a scene in front of his parents. It was Christmas Eve, for heaven sakes.

"Something must be holding it up. No matter, we still have our cranberry-pineapple tropical delight here." She stabbed a chunk of pineapple and smiled at him.

His mother looked drunk.

"Remember when Holly came to dinner wearing

tinsel in her hair and a light-up Christmas sweater? She just lit the entire room up, didn't she?" His mother waved her fruit fork in the air, pineapple chunk and all.

Now Nick *knew* she must have hit the sherry before dinner. But instead of giving her a scowl, he laughed, suddenly remembering that night vividly. "Good grief, I was mortified. That was the night we split up, you know. What a stupid idiot I was to care about what she wore."

"You certainly *were* a stupid idiot, son. You've never had a girlfriend since that could hold a candle to her," his father blurted out. Nick stared at his father, who seemed as surprised as the rest of them at saying such a terrible thing in front of Gwen.

The white candles all along the dining table flared up and sparked. Everyone jumped, then laughed, except Gwen, who was tapping her fork on the table, glaring at Nick.

Nick felt strangely compelled to tell his parents what had happened to him today. Then it just sort of rolled out of his mouth before he could stop to think. "I know this is going to sound crazy, but all day long I've felt like Holly has been around. I keep smelling her perfume, and well, the cat sort of picked out this Christmas card and made sure I read it. It was from her friend in Carmel that wrote me about Holly's death last year.

"Do you think Holly is trying to tell me something? Or is she just going to be the girlfriend of Christmas past forever?" Nick asked.

His mother raised her champagne glass in a toast. "Here's to the ghost of Holly. Honestly, son, you should have married her and had beautiful little curly-headed children together. Gwen here certainly has no intention of bearing your offspring." His mother actually had the grace to put her hand over her mouth and looked shocked at what she'd said. Her cornflower blue eyes went from complete surprise to complete amusement, much to Nick's chagrin.

"Mother!" Nick laughed. He didn't *mean* to laugh, it just popped out like a champagne bubble.

With that, Gwen's hand slammed on the table. Her fork sprang up, did an odd triple salchow and toppled into her fruit-cocktail dish. The contents of that dish catapulted straight onto Gwen's white blouse. Red cranberries and yellow pineapple wedges flew everywhere. She gasped and stood up quickly, batting at pieces of fruit.

"Oh, gosh, Gwen. Let me help you." Nick stood up and reached in his pocket for the handkerchief he kept in all his jackets. Better that than his mother's vintage white linen napkins. But what he pulled out wasn't white, and it wasn't a handkerchief. It was a pair of red lace thong underwear. He recognized them immediately after he held it out for careful examination. Holly's.

Gwen screamed.

"Gwen, this isn't what it looks like. I can explain. This is a very old jacket, and these were Holly's. She was a very, very sexy woman." Why the *hell* couldn't he stop saying things like that? He heard tinkling wind chimes again and this time he knew perfectly well they weren't hanging outside the window.

Gwen let the pineapple and cranberries fall on the floor. "You people are really something. Obviously we've made a huge mistake, Nick. We're lucky to find out in time."

"Obviously." Nick shook his head and thudded into his chair, still staring at the red lace thong. Where the *hell* did those come from?

"Consider this night, and this engagement, over, Nick Fredericks. Porter, *Porter,*" Gwen screamed. "Get me my coat and call me a cab."

Porter came through a different door, the open pocket doors that led to the entry hall. In his arms he held her jacket and her black overcoat. He held her jacket out neatly for her to back into.

"You're a cab," Porter said.

"What did you say?" Gwen twisted around.

"Your cab, miss . . ." he said with a small gesture toward the outside, "is already here."

"Goodbye, Nick." Gwen glared at him.

Nick stood by his chair and waved. "Goodbye, Gwen. My apologies about your blouse. Have it cleaned and send me the bill." He wondered how the cab had gotten here so fast. But then Porter was always a step ahead of the family. He also wondered how he'd been such an idiot as to not see what Gwen had up her sleeve. Stockbroker indeed. And no children? He *wanted* children! *Several* of them even.

Gwen paused, then twisted at her finger, pulled off her engagement ring, and threw it at Nick. Oddly, the ring traveled through the air so neatly he just reached out and caught it in his hand.

When he looked back at the doorway, she was gone.

"Good riddance," his mother said cheerily.

"Mom, Dad, what the hell is going on?"

"Looks like you narrowly escaped a bad marital choice, son," his dad replied in his matter-of-fact tone.

"What is this thing with me breaking up with women on Christmas Eve? That's just got to stop." Nick shook his head.

Porter had swiftly, quietly cleaned up after Gwen's unfortunate incident and set the salad course out for everyone. He poured a dark red wine and removed the offending champagne glasses.

"Oh, Nicky, isn't it obvious that Holly was trying to save you from a bad choice?" his mother said. "It is rather amusing that Holly picked Christmas Eve to enlighten you. Apparently ghosts have a sense of humor. Harold, isn't it thrilling to have our own Christmas ghost?" She leaned over and touched her husband's arm affectionately.

"I've seen your great-grandfather in the upstairs study several times. He's rather possessive of the mahogany desk." Harold Fredericks always kept a calm tone no matter how strange things got.

"Well, maybe now that I've become unengaged, she'll leave me in peace." Nick stuffed the red thong back in his pocket and resumed eating dinner. For some reason he didn't feel the least bit disturbed that his fiancée had just unengaged herself from him.

He did, after all, want children quite badly. He wanted to keep this wonderful family of his going. His parents would be terrific grandparents, and he didn't blame them for being impatient with him for taking such a long time to find a suitable wife. Or maybe what Holly had in mind was a *less* suitable wife: a wife that would fill his life with laughter and love. A strange image came to his mind. The painting of the woman and her child he'd left on his piano.

"I hope Holly has someone else in mind for me. I'm fresh out of prospects. I've dated the entire English department and half the art department.

"There is someone out there for you, dear, I just know it. There's always the social science department. Maybe a nice psychologist," his mother rambled.

"Because I must be crazy to believe the ghost of my old girlfriend is messing with my love life?" Nick added.

At that comment the candles flickered and flared again, and the chandelier above them gave a gentle shake and tinkled in the breeze, like music. Except there was no breeze.

"No dear, not crazy at all," his mother answered.

When Nick unlocked the door to his apartment he did all his usual things, coat off, gloves in the hall basket, keys on their hook. But just over the partition wall he caught a sparkle of twinkling lights out of the corner of his eye. Had he left the stove light on? Was something on fire? He sniffed the air.

Nothing. Nothing but a huge whiff of Holly's perfume so strong it gave him a chill down his spine. He coughed. He wasn't meant for supernatural moments like these. He was a realist.

Two steps into his living room and he realized that he'd have to change the way he thought about the supernatural.

Although truly deranged, his living room had been given a Christmas trimming. The decoration box formerly in his hall closet had mysteriously spilled its contents and it looked as if Jingles had rolled himself in a light strand and gone berserk. There were bright red and green glass balls littering the floor, lights wrapped around the glass coffee table, and a crazy never-ending strand of silver tinsel garland around almost everything.

The cat lay calmly on the sofa licking his paw. He could almost explain this, except for the part where the lights were on—but *not plugged in*.

He sat down on his piano bench and stared at the festive mess around him.

"What is it you want from me, Holly?" he whispered.

Without so much as his elbow to blame, the piano played a few high, lovely notes. Nick jumped out of his skin and turned to stare at the black and white keys.

There on the piano was the Christmas card he'd received from that friend of Holly's in Carmel. Carol Chandler.

He picked it up and stared at the hand-painted image again. The envelope fluttered to the floor. Jingles took this moment to leap from the sofa to the piano and walk across the keys. The weird part was it sounded a whole lot like "Silent Night."

"Well if I'm supposed to be a wise man I guess I'd better get myself down to Carmel. Can it wait till after Christmas?" he asked out loud.

As if to answer him, the entire room went pitch-black, including the magical lights. The cat hissed and jumped off the piano.

Nick sighed. "The red-eye it is. That's going to cost me a fortune, you know."

The darkness became illuminated by the tangle of miniature Christmas lights that ran the length of the living room, one by one slowly re-igniting until they crackled like fire crackers.

"No one will ever believe this," he mumbled. But he went to his computer on the side desk and booted it to life. The screen glowed blue in the dark room. When he opened up his browser screen the Alaska Airlines site stared back at him. How nice of his ghostly travel agent.

Ten P.M. flight. He could just make that. He better call his parents and let them know he was going on an insane wild-goose chase at the hands of a deceased and determined spirit.

"Can I please have some lights back so I can find the phone?" he said.

The lights surged to life. Nick shuddered. It was a trip to Carmel or be haunted by his crazy girlfriend for the rest of his life. He had no idea where he was going, or why. All he had was the address of Carol Chandler to guide him. And Holly, his friendly neighborhood ghost.

· **3** ·

Carol was cold, so cold. She pulled the quilts around her and tucked them in until she was a sausage of quilts. It had taken every ounce of her strength to finish up Joy's gifts and set them out for their little Christmas morning. Sometimes living in a Carmel beach cottage wasn't the best thing for staying warm and dry.

She lay on the single bed next to Joy's crib and listened to the wind howl through the uninsulated walls and floor. A cough broke free even though Carol tried to suppress it. So much for all that over-the-counter voodoo she'd swallowed. She covered her mouth with her pillow and rolled into a ball, coughing until her ribs ached. A strange swirling dizziness overtook her and for a minute she imagined Holly standing over her.

"Holly," she rasped. But then Holly was gone.

Carol knew she just needed to sleep. Sleep would help. She'd be better in the morning.

Nick wondered if Holly the obsessed ghost knew what a pain in the ass it was to get to Carmel from Seattle. First he flew into San Francisco then boarded a highly unstable shuttle flight, which took him to a miniature airport in Monterey, then he had to hunt up his rental car in the middle of the night on Christmas Eve. It was like the twilight zone. Not a creature was stirring, not even a Zappo's Rent a Wreck agent. He found the keys duct-taped to the window with a note saying, "Merry F**king Christmas, if this car is stolen it's going on your credit card."

Whatever. He had a car. He had a map. He sped down the curved highways toward his destination. Carol Chandler was getting a surprise visitor for Christmas and it wasn't Santa Claus.

The fog crept in on little cat feet in the damp dawn of the earliest hours of Christmas Day. When he came to the turn-off road for the Carmel Cottages a strange glow illuminated the sign.

Hell, his entire life was a strange glow. He thought of what his blank page of a future looked like. He was no longer seeing a life with Gwen, not that their picture had ever been that clear. He had no idea what was in store for him. He was nowhere man.

He turned the corner and searched for Beachcomber Way, and then number seven. There were no Christmas lights up on the tiny house, which he found very odd considering this holiday adventure.

But just what had he been expecting? He was flying blind here. Nick got out of the rental car and walked through a very interesting driftwood, beach glass, and shell garden. It was so Holly, he knew he was in the right place. He pulled his jacket around his ears and shivered. Who knew what await him.

His knocks on the door brought no reply, so he peered in the paned windows. The cottage was dark inside.

He didn't want to scare this woman to death, but he had flown down here to talk to her. He walked around the perimeter of the house hoping to see a glimmer of life.

They were all probably snug in their beds with visions of sugarplums dancing in their heads. Like he should be, back in Seattle.

He could go have coffee and come back in a few hours, then try again. *"Hello there, Ms. Chandler, I've been sent here by my former girlfriend, who by the way is deceased, to stop her from haunting my every waking moment. Merry Christmas."*

Hell, he could have at least brought the woman a present. Maybe something for her little daughter. He was a bad Santa.

As he headed around the house back to the car something caught his attention. He listened hard, trying to figure out what he was hearing. He leaned his ear against the small exterior window. At this point he'd probably be arrested as a prowler and be thrown in jail for Christmas.

He *did* hear something. He listened again. It was a baby crying. It started out softly, but as he rounded the house it became much louder. He banged on the door. "Hello?" he yelled. *Hello, there's a lunatic at your door.* His banging made the baby scream louder.

Now, why didn't someone pick that poor child up? Nick twisted the door handle but it was locked. He ran around to the back door, which was also locked. But a good shove made the old wood on the French door splinter and the lock was freed. He stepped into the house. "Hello? Are you all right in there? I'm coming in."

There was not a sound but the pitiful crying of that baby. Nick didn't think twice after that moment, but barged right in and went toward the crying. The house was extremely cold. He flung open the bedroom door that the sound was coming from.

In her crib the baby sat hiccupping, tears streaming down her fat little cheeks. Nick had seen babies cry before and this little miss hadn't been at it too long, but long enough to make some red rims around those big blue eyes staring at him.

"Hi, honey, don't be scared, I'm here to help," he said softly. Her lower lip stuck out and she whimpered, but didn't holler.

Beside the crib he could see a figure wrapped in blankets on a small bed. This had to be Carol.

"Carol?" He knelt down beside the bed and shook her shoulder gently. She didn't move. Oh God, he was too late. Had he been sent here to save this woman's little girl? He smoothed away her wispy pale blonde hair and put his hand on her neck to feel for a pulse. She was warm; her heartbeat was faintly thumping. She was still alive.

Nick let himself breathe again. The baby looked over the crib railing at him as he removed the woman's hat and pulled back the quilt from around her face to take a look at her.

She was an absolutely beautiful woman. He was shocked to see how beautiful she was. It made him wonder what fool of a man got her pregnant and left her to raise her daughter alone. He'd like to punch the guy in the nose right about now. His insides twisted with concern for her.

Her skin was as pale as snow, but her forehead was burning so hot you could fry an egg on it. Her eyelids fluttered and her full, pale pink lips parted slightly.

"Joy," she whispered. The she started to cough and pulled herself back into a ball. At least she was breathing. But Carol Chandler was way, *way* sick.

"Well, baby, we're going to have to get your mommy some help, aren't we?" Nick pulled his cell phone out of his pocket and flipped it open. "Please, Holly, if you have any magic left in you, give me a signal." He saw one tiny bar light up on the display and called 911.

The emergency operator had instructed him to cool Carol down as much as possible so he peeled back the blankets and put a cold rag against her forehead. He figured little Joy was safe in her crib, and she'd stopped crying since he'd given her the stuffed dog that looked like it had dropped out of the crib.

The child still looked at him warily while he took some of the clothing off Carol. For cryin' out loud, she had two sweaters, double sweatpants, a pair of gloves and a scarf around her neck. He unpeeled her down to her long underwear and bared Carol's arms to wipe them down with cool water. Carol was limp as a rag doll and murmured words he couldn't understand the entire time he was undressing her.

"Hey there, Joy, don't you worry. We'll get Mommy all fixed up and back to normal in no time." He talked to the baby in soothing tones; she smiled at him and thumped the dog against her mattress.

While he was hustling around he thought to look in the fridge for a baby bottle and was rewarded. He came back to Carol, who was still not with it, and offered up the cold bottle to Joy.

"Sorry, baby, I'd only screw it up if I tried to warm it."

Joy flung her tiny arms open to him. He picked her up and sat down in the rocking chair across the room. He could watch Carol and make this kid feel better at the same time.

She grabbed the bottle out of his hands and skillfully fed herself, tipping backward in his arms. At no time did her eyes leave his face, and once she grinned at him, milk spilling out of the corner of her mouth. Her yellow footy sleepers felt a little damp, but he figured that was the least of their problems at the moment.

"Hey, cookie, you've got some kind of appetite, don't you?" He looked into her baby blue eyes and got very curious. This baby looked a whole lot like Holly with that mop of pale red hair and those blue eyes, but wait, Holly's eyes were green. Maybe Carol was related to Holly like he thought, and red hair ran in the family.

Or maybe Holly had been busier in Carmel than he figured. That would explain a whole lot regarding Holly's recent appearance in his life.

The sirens made Joy look frightened, but Nick was never so glad to hear anything in his life. He realized the front door was locked and jumped up to open it, carrying Joy with him like a squirming sack of potatoes.

Within seconds the paramedics were taking Carol's vital signs. They brought in a gurney and lifted her into place. She moaned when they moved her and cried out "Joy?" several times. The lady paramedic kept talking to her and told her the baby was fine.

When they'd taken her out, the woman turned to him. "Are you the husband?"

"No, just a friend,"

"Well, you probably saved her life. She's seriously dehydrated, and it looks like she's got pneumonia. I hope she pulls through."

"Is there a doubt?"

"We'll take her to Monterey General. It's the closest hospital. Do you know any relatives? Otherwise . . ."

Nick had seen enough television to know what they'd do if there were no relatives. They'd place Joy in temporary foster care. Somehow he just couldn't let that happen. "I'm related," he blurted out.

"Oh, I *see*," she said, and looked from him to the baby and back again. Let her think what she liked, he certainly wasn't sent across two states to let this woman's child, or whomever's child she was, be put in some strange place on Christmas Day.

Oh my God, it was Christmas Day.

"I'll keep her," he said. "Here, here's the mother's name and address. Nick pulled the Christmas card envelope out of his jeans pocket and handed it to her.

"Okay, we'll get more information later. I've got to get the mother transported. Just head north on highway 101 and you'll see the signs for the hospital."

"Thanks, I'll be there shortly. I've got to pack this munchkin a bag." He held the squirmy child firmly as she tried to escape his grasp. Nick smiled reassuringly.

The woman took one more look at him, grabbed her bag, and ran out the door.

Nick was alone with Joy, who wasn't too joyful anymore. She shrieked at him and tried to escape. He held her out in front of him and gave her a good talking to. "Now, Joy, your mom is sick and she's got to go to the hospital. Unfortunately that leaves me in charge. And hey, we're going to have to do something about those soggy drawers of yours. But first, let's heat this place up, shall we?

Joy yelled at him, followed by bubbled spit, then some screams that clearly broke the sound barrier. "Holy crap, that's some set of lungs you've got there." He carried her by his side, arm around her middle, and found the thermostat.

It looked to him like Carol had been trying to save money by taping the setting down to fifty-five. Well, this was an emergency. He hiked it up to seventy-five and strode down the hallway with his sidekick, who was kicking his side at the moment, flailing both her arms and legs.

There was a nice padded changing table in the bedroom he'd found Carol in, and he plopped Joy on top. Her little legs went out stiff and she looked like a redheaded devil about to show him who was boss. He made a funny face at her. She turned pink then let out a huge earsplitting shriek.

"Hey, hey, keep it down, I'm new at this!"

Nick handed her a squeaky duck. She took it then threw it so hard it hit the wall and squeaked a long, last squeak. As she yelled he saw a few little teeth in her mouth and decided to steer clear of that area. She looked dangerous.

Changing a baby. This was a completely new experience for him. One that his PhD in economics could not solve. He unzipped her sleeper and clumsily pulled her out of it as she made that as difficult as possible.

Thank God she was only wet. Her diaper looked like a balloon, though. He stripped it off and noticed the diaper wipes on the shelf below, plus a stack of disposable diapers.

This called for a consultation. He whipped out his cell phone and autodialed his mom.

"Merry Christmas, Mom."

"Honey! We've been dying to hear what you found in Carmel," his mother said.

"A very sick woman and a very difficult baby. I need emergency instructions on diapering, Mom."

His mother was more than happy to give him more child-care information than he'd use in a lifetime. He balanced the phone on his shoulder while she went over the direction that diaper tapes go and what to do if the baby had gas or spits up all over him. More information than he really wanted to know.

After some rather stupid attempts, he managed to

get the kid taped, wrapped, and tidied up, not necessarily in that order. Joy gave him a smirk and he again felt like he'd seen that face somewhere before.

"Okay, Mom, I'm going to drive to the hospital and find out how Carol is. Carol Chandler, the baby's mother. I don't know, it's just a miracle I made it down here when I did. That must be what our ghost was trying to tell us. Yes, that too, and strangely I'm okay with being unengaged. Bye Mom, I've got to run." Nick managed to get off the phone with his mom.

He picked up the diapered but naked child and held her with one arm while he rummaged through the nearby dressers to find her some clothes. For once she cooperated and looked curious. He came up with a red sleeper, just like the pale yellow one. Red for Christmas.

He also ran across a drawer full of Carol's undies, which were quite delicate, pale, and silky. Just like her.

He wriggled the baby into her red sleeper and gave her a pat on the diapered behind. "Ta-da. Now shall we see what Santa brought you?"

Joy clapped as if she understood, poor little darling. He took her into the tiny living room. Now that the morning sunlight streamed through the windows, he could see things more clearly. There was a small, fairly lame tree with tons of homemade ornaments and a pile of presents underneath, all for Joy. A toy kitchen with a big red bow on it sat to one side.

He laughed a bit at the mom that would put a kitchen together for a baby this young. It looked way to old for Joy. This must be her first child. Some presents are for the mothers anyway.

He set her on the floor and she crawled over to the

presents, then pulled herself up on the table that held the tree and stared at the paper snowflakes and glittered pinecones.

Maybe he should let her mother do this. Oh hell, the poor kid had been through too much already. Her mother was in good hands, and he couldn't really tell them anything more about her. Joy would be a handful in the hospital, and the kid hadn't eaten anything for breakfast yet. Hey, a little Christmas wouldn't delay them too much. "Here, let's tear into this stuff. I'll show you how." He got down on the floor and started ripping into the prettily wrapped boxes.

Joy babbled to him in her foreign, baby language and brought each item to him as it emerged, setting it into his lap. Pretty soon he had piles of plastic pots and fake food on him and around him. He was getting hungry enough to try the fake pork chop.

For a run-down beach shack, the little place was very clean, except for where he and Joy had made mounds of wrapping paper mess. There were vintage forties curtains and a sofa that probably had its best days back then as well. But it was homy and the paintings were truly wonderful. He looked closely at a couple of them and saw they were mostly by Carol, but one very amazing painting of cypress trees bending over the ocean in the wildest colors imaginable was signed *Holly Townsend*. It was *so* Holly.

Joy was now deeply involved in the box that the plastic pots came out of. She put it on her head and looked out at him from the cellophane window. Weird kid.

He freed himself from his pile of pretend pots and went into the small kitchen. It was yellow and white and very cheery. A collection of large white pitchers took up a corner china hutch. He opened up a few cupboards and found canned fruit, a box of oatmeal, some jars of applesauce, and not a whole lot of much of anything else.

He looked into the other room to check on Space Girl and saw her banging her plastic spatula against a pink pot. "Can you cook?" he asked. He picked her up and brought her where he could keep an eye on her. She hit him with her spatula a few times, but took the move fairly well. He deposited her in her high chair and she kept on with her spatula, beating the metal tray noisily.

There was bread in the refrigerator. "Raisin bread. Well, that's Christmasy, isn't it?" He made up six pieces of toast for the little one and himself and even found butter in the cupboard. No coffee, but tea. He also found cheese in the fridge and cut some in sticks for his pal Joy.

"Hey, Joy, let's eat raisin toast and cheese." She seemed quite agreeable to that and discarded her box-head to stuff fistfuls of squished raisin toast into her mouth. Probably not the best baby food, but hey, it was a holiday.

Nick watched her with interest. She was quite a corker. Joy really reminded him of Holly. Was it her baby? A wave of anger surged over him as he thought about Holly getting involved with someone so soon after their breakup. Someone who left her alone and pregnant with only her friend Carol to support her. He wished he knew the truth.

As he thought that, a tiny flame-up came out of the burner he had the teakettle on. A fizzle of smoke came from the spot.

"Oh, so we're back, are we? What did you do, fall for the first guy that handed you a latte line? And thanks for leaving your poor friend Carol with your wild-child. I got here just in time. You could have started haunting me a little earlier, you know. It would have saved me a whole lot on airfare." Nick looked around self-consciously to make sure no one heard him talking to the air. Joy looked at him calmly, as if people did this sort of thing all the time in her world.

Well, it wasn't Miss Messy's fault if her mother had been a little too free and easy. He supposed Joy *could* be Carol's child, but the more time he spent with her, the more Holly he saw in the little dynamo.

"Let's pack it up, Miss Thing, we're off to check up on Mommy." He mopped her off with a pile of damp paper towels and took the toddler with him to the bedroom, putting her in the crib to keep her confined. She held the sides and jumped up and down, singing some kind of baby song.

He hunted up a diaper bag, stuffing clean clothes and diapers in till it weighed as much as his briefcase back at the college.

He went back to their pile of Christmas toys and picked up a homemade doll that Carol must have made for Joy. It was colorful felt and rather amazing really, like an artist's version of a rag doll. He stuffed it in the bag to amuse Joy on the trip.

Damn, no car seat. Surely she owned one. He looked everywhere and finally found one in the laundry room out on the back porch. A few swear words later he'd wrestled the thing into his car, and the baby too, only having to completely stop once to change the stinking diaper Joy presented him with. "No more of that, young lady," he told her. She giggled at him, stuck out her tongue, and made raspberry noises. He put her in a clean sleeper with flowers on it and added two baby sweaters and a hat. "There, you're bundled to go."

Nick stood by Carol's bedside with Joy in his arms. He waited quietly for Carol to wake up. She was still as pale as the sheets but very beautiful, even with an oxygen mask on. He'd stopped by the gift shop and picked up a bouquet of red roses to brighten up her room. That, and a very large stuffed poodle for Joy, who was now busy chewing the ears.

The doctor had informed him they'd started Carol on IV fluids and meds just in time. She'd perked up nicely over the last few hours and showed signs of being very strong-willed.

He couldn't remember ever being so mesmerized by a woman before. She was Sleeping Beauty. He leaned over and kissed her cheek in a spontaneous moment of relief that she was alive and he'd gotten there in time.

As he straightened up, Joy gave him a sloppy kiss on the cheek.

"Thanks a bunch, Joy." He grabbed a tissue out of the nearby box and mopped his cheek. When he looked back at Carol, her eyes were open. Her beautiful pale hazel green eyes.

"I'm Nick Fredericks. Don't worry." He didn't know what to say. Holly sent me? I just happened to drive by your house on Christmas Day all the way from Seattle?

Her eyes. Nick was suddenly struck with the oddest thought. He took Joy over to the bathroom door to the small mirror hanging there and looked hard at the reflection. First Joy, then his own face.

Well, hell's bells, staring back at him were his own blue eyes, same as Joy's, same as his mother's. Cornflower blue. Joy even had his chin. But she had Holly's red hair and freckled nose.

"She's *my* Joy," he exclaimed. He carried her back over to Carol. "She's my baby, isn't she?" He couldn't believe he hadn't done the math. Him, the math whiz. But this wasn't a math moment, it was a moment of the heart.

Carol smiled at him and nodded. She reached her hand toward him. He took her hand and squeezed it gently. Joy balanced herself on his leg and bounced while he kept her from falling. She grabbed on to his hair and pulled it till Nick's eyes watered.

"Why didn't she tell me, Carol? Why didn't *you* tell me?"

Carol whispered, so he leaned over closer while Joy pulled on his hair.

"She made me promise. She was angry." Carol shook her head sadly.

Suddenly everything became clear as a Christmas bell to Nick. Holly had made a terrible mistake and she'd come back in spirit to fix it. She'd made her best friend promise never to tell him Joy was his, and Carol had taken on the burden of raising Joy alone.

As this flashed through his mind so did the familiar scent of Holly's perfume. The fluorescent lights in the room flickered. He heard the now-recognizable wind-chime laughter of Holly.

"Yeah, and I forgive you, too. Merry Christmas," he said to the air.

The sun filtered through the hospital curtains in the oddest way.

And here he was with his own Joy. He hugged her to him as she shrieked with laughter. Her Holly berry red hair and her Fredericks' blue eyes and chin were all his.

He closed his eyes and put his cheek against her little cheek. She tried to bite his nose. He was going to take care of this little angel for the rest of her life. He was going to take Carol out of her cold little cottage and give her a beautiful art studio and a warm, comfortable home. Well, if she'd let him. They'd have to work out the details. Joy needed Carol; he knew that. And Carol needed him. For the first time in his life he felt *needed*.

He looked at Carol, the beautiful Carol, who had helped Holly through her pregnancy and mothered his child for the last year, alone and brave. Who had reached out to him with a little hand-painted Christmas card, and done everything she could to make Joy's Christmas special.

Carol smiled at him and he saw tears in her eyes. He reached over and took her hand again.

"Everything is going to be fine now," he said. "I'll make sure of it. Merry Christmas, Carol."

A Very Vampy Christmas

Kerrelyn Sparks

"It's over, Don Orlando." Maggie O'Brian lowered her gaze. The tears that blurred her vision had little to do with the role she was playing—Jessica Goodwin, mortal doctor, hopelessly in love with a vampire. Like any good soap opera actress, Maggie turned her back to the person she was addressing and looked sadly at the camera. "You must never come here again."

"Don't say that!" Don Orlando rushed to her side and sank gracefully to one knee. He seized her hand and kissed it. "My darling Chiquita, I could never let you go."

Chiquita? What sort of cheesy person was writing this nonsense? Maggie inwardly cursed the writer while trying to ignore the way Don Orlando was brushing his lips against her knuckles. Sweet Mary, now he was nibbling her fingers.

But it meant nothing. He was only acting. Rumor had it he'd nibbled a lot more than women's hands in the last few years.

The tear that rolled down Maggie's cheek was worthy of a daytime Emmy. Unfortunately, her lack of a pulse during the day precluded her from attending the ceremony. And how could they give Emmys to a group of actors they didn't know existed? Only a few mortals employed at the Digital Vampire Network knew about vampire soap operas, and they were sworn to secrecy. The mortals knew if they blabbed, they would pay in blood. Literally.

Maggie yanked her hand from Don Orlando's grasp. "I'm sorry, but it was never meant to be."

As Don Orlando rose, he flipped his black silk cape over one shoulder, revealing half of his muscled torso and a thatch of very black, very thick chest hair. Maggie knew this movement caused Vamp viewers at home to sigh in ecstasy. She should know. She'd been one of them. And if Don Orlando executed the famous double flip, throwing both edges of his cape over his shoulders to reveal his entire chest in its muscle-rippling glory, his female fans were known to swoon. No doubt, a few male ones, too.

Maggie wandered to the empty desk of her pretend office. "How many times must I tell you? This is a hospital. You shouldn't come here without a shirt."

"I couldn't wait to be with you." His voice sounded as smooth as his black silk cape. "And the nurses never complain."

"You'll catch a terrible cold." She glanced at him over her shoulder. "Why, it's snowing outside. It's almost Christmas."

He shrugged his massive shoulders. "Mortal diseases do not frighten me. I will heal during my daily death-sleep."

Maggie pressed a hand against her chest and gazed at camera number two. "I swore an oath to protect life. How could I fall in love with one of the Undead?" She whirled to face him and pressed her hands on the desk behind her. This pose was designed to highlight her ample bosom. "That's how you seduced me, isn't it? You used some sort of insidious vampire mind control."

"It was you who seduced me with your pure and noble heart." His gaze lingered on her breasts. "I could not help myself."

"I must resist you. Somehow."

He bowed. "I am Don Orlando de Corazon, the greatest lover in the vampire world. No woman, alive or undead, can resist me."

"But I must!" Maggie strode toward camera number two. "I've worked so hard to get where I am today. Years of med school, endless hours in the ER. And now, I'm a famous brain surgeon. People need me."

"I am very proud of you, my Chiquita."

"Don't say that! I have a reputation to maintain. I need the respect of my peers. How can I have an affair with an undead trumpet player from a mariachi band?"

He lifted his chiseled chin. "I'm a very good trumpet player. And the greatest lover in the vampire world." He swaggered toward her, a hand on the low waistline of his tight black leather pants.

Maggie turned away with a gasp. "Don't tempt me, Don Orlando!"

"Come away with me!" He pulled her into his arms. "We will make beautiful music together."

"No, no, no!" She shook her head in rhythm to her cries.

"Yes, yes!"

She planted her hands on his chest to push him

away. The ring on her right pinky finger gleamed under the stage lights, bright gold against the coal black chest hair.

He embraced her tighter. "Kiss me and tell me you don't love me."

She turned her tear-streaked face to camera number one. "You're so cruel to make me suffer. Please let me go!" She shoved hard at his chest.

He stumbled back. "Aagh!"

"Aagh!" Maggie's higher-pitched scream joined his when she realized what had happened.

Grimacing in pain, Don Orlando pressed a hand against his now bare chest. And dangling from Maggie's right hand like a dead rat was the mat of black chest hair.

"Aagh!" She shook her hand. "Get it off!" It flopped wildly around her hand, tangled in her pinky ring.

"Dammit, woman!" Don Orlando winced as he rubbed the red welt on his hairless chest. "You nearly ripped my skin off."

"Cut!" Gordon, the director, yelled. "Makeup! We need Orlando's hair glued back on."

Maggie looked at Don Orlando's bare chest, then at the furry pelt dangling from her ring. It was fake? Sweet Mary, she should have known. How many men had body hair like an English sheepdog? She ripped it from her ring and offered it to its owner. "Sorry. I didn't mean to hurt you."

Don Orlando's mouth curled up, and he tapped the red splotch on his chest. "Want to kiss it and make it better?"

"No!" Maggie tossed the chest-toupee at him. "Why do you wear such a silly thing?"

He actually looked embarrassed. For about half a second. "They thought I would look sexier with more hair." He gave her a lopsided smile. "Though right now, I'd be happy if I just had some skin."

Maggie smiled back. For about half a second. Her amusement died when he checked out the makeup girl with a leering grin.

"*Hola,* pretty *senorita,*" he murmured to the makeup girl. She blushed as she painted his chest with adhesive.

"Shall we adjourn to my dressing room?" He winked. "We could bring the glue and get all sticky." She giggled.

Maggie clenched her fists to keep from slapping him. Sweet Mary and Joseph, she was angry. She'd been angry ever since she'd found out that her adored hero, Don Orlando de Corazon, was nothing more than a womanizing pig. And now, she realized it was even worse. He was a totally *fake* womanizing pig.

She stalked toward the refreshment table and poured herself a glass of Chocolood. The mixture of synthetic blood and chocolate was as close to comfort food as a lady vampire could get. She frowned at the black strand of hair still caught around the little gold cross on her pinky ring. She untangled the hair, remembering how her father had given her the ring at her First Communion when she was seven. Back then, in 1872, the ring had fit her fourth finger perfectly. She'd loved her pretty white dress, the first dress she'd ever owned that wasn't a hand-me-down from her older sisters.

As the eighth child out of twelve in an Irish immigrant family, Maggie had known hunger and poverty. But she hadn't known about the secret world of the Undead until she'd joined them involuntarily at the age of nineteen. Horrified, she'd tried to go home, but Da had reacted poorly. She'd shown him the ring and how the Holy Cross didn't harm her. Why would her beliefs change just because she was dead? She was still her father's darlin' Maggie May. But Da had disowned her, declaring her an unholy creature from hell.

Maggie sipped her Chocolood, ignoring the pain that still needled her. She didn't want to believe her father was right. She'd been attacked. How could a merciful God blame the victim?

But then, she'd learned that in order to survive, she would have to bite others. Victimize them. And the fear that her father was right grew like a festering wound. Thank God synthetic blood had been invented. It was so much easier to pretend she was a good person now. She wore the cross-shaped ring on her hand to convince herself her heart was still good, even if it stopped beating each day at dawn.

Five years earlier, something stupendous had finally put an end to Maggie's dreary existence. Some clever vampires had discovered that a Vamp's image could be recorded using digital technology, and the Digital Vampire Network had been born. Vampires all over the world were a much happier lot now that they were entertained with the vampire *Nightly News* and *Live with the Undead*, a celebrity gossip magazine hosted by Corky Courrant. DVN also introduced their wonderful soap operas—*As a Vampire Turns, All My Vampires,* and *General Morgue*.

Then, *he* had arrived. Four years ago, a new actor had appeared on *As a Vampire Turns,* and for the first time in Maggie's long life, she was hopelessly in love. Don Orlando de Corazon had burst onto the television screen with a flourish of his black silk cape and a gleam in his dark, passionate eyes, and Maggie was lost. He was the one. The only one for her. And if only he could meet her, he would instantly recognize her as his soul mate. It was her love for him that had given her the courage to audition at DVN. When she'd actually won a role on *As a Vampire Turns,* it had looked like her dream had come true.

But her dream had become a nightmare. Before her first day on the set, she'd learned the truth. Each night on her gossip magazine, Corky Courrant exposed Don Orlando for his raunchy, womanizing ways. And Maggie was stuck playing Dr. Jessica Goodwin, one of Don Orlando's many conquests.

She'd tried to focus on her acting skills and her new career. But each time she had a scene with him, her heart stuttered in her chest. How could she ever hope to get over him when he kept declaring his undying love for her? But it was all fake. Sweet Mary, even his chest hair was fake!

"Places!" the director yelled. "Let's finish the scene."

Maggie took a deep breath. This was it. In this scene, Don Orlando was supposed to kiss Dr. Jessica. Her first kiss from Don Orlando. *It's not real.* He probably didn't even know her real name. She stepped into her pretend hospital office, and the makeup girl quickly retouched her powder and lipstick.

"Let's start with 'Kiss me and tell me you don't love me,'" Gordon announced. "Roll 'em."

Maggie's breath hitched as Don Orlando strode toward her.

He swept her into his arms. "Kiss me and tell me you don't love me."

"You're so cruel to make me suffer," Maggie whispered, her knees growing weak. She clung to his shoulders. "Please let me go." *Please, kiss me. I've waited four years for this.*

He studied her face as he gathered her tighter in his arms. She closed her eyes and wilted against him. When his lips brushed hers, her body trembled. His mouth was warm and gentle. If only he could be the hero she had dreamed of. If only he could love her. If only he could see the goodness in her and cherish her the way she needed. If only miracles could really happen.

"That's great!" the director announced. "Cut and print!"

With a groan, Don Orlando deepened the kiss. He ran the tip of his tongue over her lips, then feathered soft kisses across her cheek to her ear.

"Cut!" Gordon yelled.

"Can you feel it?" Don Orlando whispered in her ear, then gently suckled her earlobe.

"I said *cut!* Come on, we've got other scenes to do."

Maggie could barely hear the director. Partly because Don Orlando's tongue was in her ear. And also because her heart was pounding incredibly loud. Sweet Mary, he was as wonderful as she'd imagined.

He nibbled down her neck. "You're so beautiful. My sweet . . . Jessica."

With a gasp, she stiffened. She shoved him back. "My name is Maggie!"

Don Orlando smiled. "Shall we adjourn to my dressing room, sweet . . . Maggie?"

She slapped him hard.

He stepped back, his eyes wide with surprise. "What—why?"

"Everything about you is a lie. You're not the world's greatest lover. You're the world's greatest fraud! You're a pig and a . . . a poser!" She spun and stomped off the set.

In his dressing room, Don Orlando grimaced as he peeled the mat of fake hair off his red, raw chest. *The world's greatest fraud.* Maggie had seen right through him, dammit.

The first time he'd met her, when she was auditioning, she had gazed at him with such adoration in her blue Irish eyes. She hadn't wanted to use him for her career or profit. Her undemanding acceptance had been the sweetest sensation he'd felt since becoming a vampire four and a half years earlier.

He'd asked the director to hire her and give her a role that fitted her. Someone with a pure and giving heart. Someone like Dr. Jessica Goodwin. Not only was the doctor the epitome of goodness, she was madly in love with him, Don Orlando.

But by the time Maggie took her job, she was cold and indifferent. She ignored his attempts at flirtation. He'd tried to show her tonight how he felt with the kiss. And what a kiss! The way she'd melted in his arms, he knew without a doubt that her indifference was feigned. She still adored him. He'd wanted to shout her name to the heavens, but he'd thought the cameras were still rolling, so he'd called her Jessica instead.

And now, she was upset. He needed to apologize and win her back. If only she would look at him once more with adoration in her eyes. It would make his phony existence so much easier to bear. He pulled on a black silk bathrobe over his bare chest and leather pants and strode down the hall to Maggie's dressing room. What could he say to impress her? Anything but the truth. He wanted her passion, not her pity. He knocked on the door.

"Come in." Maggie's face drooped with weary annoyance when he entered the small room.

Damn, he should have brought flowers. For the world's greatest lover, he could sure be an idiot.

Maggie remained sitting in front of her dressing table. "What do you want?"

I want you to love me. No, Don Orlando would never act like a needy wimp. He was macho and aggressive, and it worked. He had stacks of fan mail in his dressing room that confirmed it. Women loved Don Orlando de Corazon, and Maggie would, too. "I could not stay away. Margaret Mary O'Brian, you have bewitched me."

She snorted. "So you saw my name on the door. Should I be impressed that you know how to read?"

"Ever since we first met, your lovely name has been etched into my heart."

"That sounds painful." She leaned over to remove her high-heeled shoes. "You can cut the melodrama. The cameras are gone."

"But my passion continues to burn like a raging fire. I have vowed to make you mine."

Her eyes flashed with anger. "No woman in her right mind would want to be yours. The waiting line is too long."

He winced inwardly. Maggie must be listening to the lies Corky Courrant was spreading on her show *Live with the Undead.* "My heart belongs only to you, my sweet Chiquita."

"I'm not your banana!" She threw a shoe, aimed at his head.

With vampire speed, he dodged the missile. It clunked against the door. "*Ay, caramba,* such fiery passion! It sets my loins ablaze!"

"You set my stomach a-hurling!" She torpedoed the second shoe at him, and it hit him squarely in his chest.

"Ouch!" The stiletto heel had stabbed his raw skin. "Why are you so angry with me, Maggie?"

"Are you dense? Do you really expect me to be flattered by your slimy attempt at seduction?"

"Slimy?"

"What is this sick compulsion of yours to take every woman in the world to bed?"

"That's not true." He gave her his signature sexy look, the one that coupled a lopsided smile with an arched eyebrow. "There is no need for a bed. We can be . . . creative, no?"

"Aagh!" She jumped to her feet, grabbed a hairbrush off her dressing table, and tossed it at him.

He muttered a curse as he dodged the brush. Why didn't the act work on her? It did on everyone else. Realization struck him just as a flying, black demi-boot bounced off his head. "Dammit, you're different. You don't like Don Orlando."

With a sigh, Maggie slumped onto her chair. "I'm sorry. As old as I am, I should know not to throw things when I'm angry."

He stepped toward her. "Are you angry because I called you Jessica when we were kissing? I can explain. I thought the cameras were still rolling."

Maggie's cheeks turned pink as she looked away. "It's not about the kiss. It's . . . you and all the women—"

"You shouldn't listen to everything Corky says on her show. She's not telling the truth about me."

"Then it's not true that you had an affair with her?"

He winced. "Well, that part is true."

"And you cheated on her?"

"Well, yes, but there were good reasons."

Maggie snorted. "Reason number one being Tiffany? How many other *reasons* did you have?"

"It's not what you think." Dammit, he didn't want to tell her the truth. Who would believe it? "I have this problem . . ."

"I know. Your trousers. They keep falling off."

"No. It's . . . me. I don't like to be alone."

She snorted. "Pardon me while I cry."

"Maggie, I've been in New York for four years, and I was faithful to Corky till about six months ago. It was one time, when I was angry and frustrated, and Tiffany—"

"Wait a minute." Maggie stood. "Corky makes it sound like you've been with hundreds of women. Thousands."

"She's furious. She's exacting revenge on me."

"Why should I believe anything you say?" Maggie paced across the small room. "You're a total fraud."

He leaned back against the door. "I know Don Orlando isn't real. But he saved me. He gave me a reason for living. He made people love me." He sighed. "Even you loved me once."

Maggie slowed to a stop. "I thought I did, but it was all pretend."

He swallowed hard. "Pretend is all I have."

"Nonsense. There has to be a real you."

If only there was. He turned and grabbed the door-knob to leave. "I'm sorry. I . . . I wanted you to like me, but—"

"I might like you if I ever got to know you." Maggie strode toward him. "Who are you really?"

He leaned his brow against the door and squeezed his eyes shut. He couldn't do it. He couldn't let her see the gaping void inside him. "I'm Don Orlando de Corazon, the world's greatest—"

"Stop it. If you want me to like you, you have to be honest with me. You have to be your true self."

"There is no . . ." His eyes watered. He couldn't do it. He couldn't subject her to the emptiness. It was hard enough for him to bear. It was the reason he hated to be alone. It was like being with nothing.

Maggie touched his arm. "What's wrong?"

He took a deep breath. "I know Don Orlando is fake. Corky invented him so I could be a star. I'm sorry he offends you."

"Then don't be him," Maggie whispered. "Be yourself."

He snorted. "I wish I could. I wish I could be worthy of you. I wish I had a soul."

"Everyone has a soul."

"Not me. I'm nothing but an empty void."

She stepped back with a frightened look. Of course it scared her. It scared the hell out of him.

He shrugged. "Maybe Corky can explain it. If she's willing to be honest with you. She might enjoy spilling my ugly secret."

Maggie gave him a worried look. "What secret?"

"I can't be myself when I don't know who I am. The stupid role I play is all I have to keep me from slipping into a black hole of nothingness."

"You mean depression?"

"No." Don Orlando grasped the doorknob. "I have amnesia."

· 2 ·

After work, Maggie usually teleported to her friends' nightclub called Horny Devils. Her roommates had started the business after winning five million dollars on DVN's first reality show. But tonight, Maggie was too agitated to enjoy the fun. The pain she'd seen in Don Orlando's eyes just before he left haunted her. She paced about her dressing room, replaying the last scene in her head. Could he really have amnesia? Could Corky be lying about the hundreds of women he'd seduced? Maggie didn't know which was harder to believe—a faithful Don Orlando or a forgetful one.

She needed more information. And the source for all information at DVN was Corky Courrant, former torture expert at the Tower of London during the reign of Henry VIII, and now, the ruthless media queen of the vampire world.

Maggie headed toward the main offices of DVN. No matter how hard she tried to dismiss Don Orlando from her mind, the man continued to intrigue her. She'd always sensed an aura of mystery about him, and apparently, she was right. He *was* a mystery, even to himself. He acted cool and confident, but there was a sad vulnerability lurking beneath the facade.

With a sigh, Maggie realized she'd always been a sucker for lost souls. It had been that same compassion that had driven her to join the Salvation Army in 1884, which had resulted in the attack that had turned her into a vampire. Her friends called her soft heart a blessing, but she suspected it was more like a fatal flaw. Now, once again, her compassionate nature was leading her into the unknown.

She knocked on a door that boasted a huge sign— *Live with the Undead,* starring Corky Courrant.

"Come in!" Corky's strident voice screeched.

Maggie ventured inside.

"Oh, it's you!" Corky's eyes lit up. "Maggie something."

"O'Brian."

"Whatever. I was just watching you slap the shit out of Don Orlando. It's fabulous!"

"Excuse me?"

Corky aimed her remote control at a television and pushed a button. "One of the cameramen just gave me this footage." The scene Maggie had played earlier with Don Orlando came on the screen. They were kissing while the director was yelling *cut.*

Maggie's mouth fell open. "How did you—"

"Listen." Corky lifted a hand to hush her. On the TV, Maggie slapped Don Orlando, then started calling him names. Corky burst out laughing, her massive breasts bouncing. "*I love it!* I'm opening my show to-morrow night with it."

Heat rushed to Maggie's face. "But that shouldn't have been recorded. Gordon said cut—"

"So? The guys always keep recording when Don Orlando's in the scene. They know I pay good money to catch the bastard in an embarrassing situation." Corky used her remote to turn off the TV. "So, you want to be interviewed for tomorrow's show?"

"Well, I—"

"I don't interview just anybody. But you're smart enough to know what a scumbag Don Orlando is, so I'm giving you a chance."

"Thank you. That's very kind of you." Maggie suspected she'd get more information by playing along. "I think it's just disgusting the way he cheated on you."

"And after all I did for him!" Corky's eyes blazed with anger. "I made him famous. I made him rich. I made him a household name in the vampire world."

"Amazing."

"Yes, I am. He was nothing when I took him in. *Nothing!*" Corky's voice cracked with strain.

Maggie winced. "I heard he doesn't even have a real name."

"He doesn't! He was a worthless bum, wandering around New Orleans. He didn't even know what year it was."

"Then it's true. He has amnesia."

"So?" Corky waved a hand in dismissal. "I made him better than he could ever be on his own. I taught him how to dress, how to act, how to make love. He owes everything to me. If I hadn't come along, he'd still be lying in a gutter somewhere."

"How terrible."

"He was pathetic! But I brought him here and made him a star. All out of the goodness of my heart." Corky pressed a hand to her breasts, indicating there was a heart somewhere beneath the huge implants. "Plus forty percent of his gross earnings."

Maggie blinked. "Forty percent?"

"Why not? I put a lot of time into him. And it's in the contract. The bastard can cheat all he wants, but I still get my forty percent."

Maggie was beginning to see why Don Orlando was upset with Corky. She was using him like a slave. "I guess he's been cheating on you for a long time."

"Ha! I know everything that's going on around here. I can make or break careers, Missy, and believe me, I do." Corky smiled smugly. "No one but that stupid bitch Tiffany has ever laid a hand on my Don Orlando. They wouldn't dare."

Sweet Mary! He'd told her the truth! "Then he hasn't been with hundreds."

"No, of course not. That's . . . artistic license. Whenever I claim some bimbos have been with him, they play along. They like the attention. So, do you want that interview or not?"

"Oh, yes. I'd love it."

"I thought so." Corky smirked as she lounged back in her chair. "Be at Studio Two tomorrow night at eight. And be ready to spill all your nasty gossip about Don Orlando."

"Of course." Maggie opened the door to leave, then hesitated. "Do you ever wonder who he really is?"

"He's a lowlife pig. What else is there to know?"

Everything, Maggie thought. Where did he come

from? Did he have a family somewhere? "I know some guys from MacKay Security and Investigation. I bet they could find out who he is."

"Why bother?" Corky began leafing through a stack of papers, clearly bored with the turn of the conversation.

But Maggie had done enough acting to know what was needed. The proper motivation. "You want to humiliate him, right?"

"Yes." Corky took the bait, dropping the papers on her desk. "Do you know something embarrassing about him?"

"Not yet. But imagine how awful he would feel if you dredged up some terrible secrets from his past."

Corky's face lit up with a wide grin. "I love it! We could do an exposé, revealing his wretched past. Could you get one of those investigators to go to New Orleans for me?"

"Yes. And I could go as the director. I have experience. I was an assistant director on the reality show last summer." Maggie figured this would be the best way to control the content of the report, so it didn't deteriorate into a vicious character assassination. Don Orlando might want to know who he was, but he didn't deserve the sort of massacre Corky had in mind.

"Great!" Corky tapped her long fingernails on the desk. "I'll talk to Gordon so you can get a few weeks off."

Maggie grinned. It was really happening. She was going to New Orleans to unravel the mystery of Don Orlando. "I think Don Orlando should go, too. We might uncover something that will trigger his memory."

"Hmm." Corky frowned. "I don't know. I like to keep him working, so I can make money."

Slave driver. "But if we discover something really awful, we can record how embarrassed he looks."

Corky perked up. "Right. Okay, I'll make all the arrangements." She reached for the phone. "See you tomorrow."

Maggie smiled as she strode back to her dressing room. She would call Connor to see if he could spare one of his undead Highlanders from MacKay Security and Investigation. And she imagined how thrilled Don Orlando would be.

"It's a bad idea," Don Orlando protested the next night.

Maggie huffed. "Don't you want to know who you are?"

"Not with a cameraman following me around to record every miserable discovery, so Corky can ridicule me before the entire vampire world. No way. It's not happening." Don Orlando marched down the hall to Studio Four where *As a Vampire Turns* was recorded every night. His long black cape swirled around the tops of his black leather boots.

"But I'll be the director." Maggie followed him. "I won't allow you to be ridiculed."

He snorted. "Right. I saw you on Corky's show tonight."

"I had to play along. I did it for you."

He stopped and faced her. "For me? You spent ten minutes on her show, describing the joy of slapping me on the face."

Maggie blushed. "Corky had us on tape. I could hardly deny doing it."

"If you enjoy it so much, go for it." He turned his cheek. "You know I deserve it."

Maggie bit her lip to keep from smiling. "I'd rather find out who you are. And then, I might want to slap you again."

"I'm sure you will. I was a bum, Maggie. Hasn't it occurred to you that my wretched past may be better left alone?"

"Why are you assuming your past is wretched? You're a young vampire, aren't you?"

He opened the studio door and motioned for her to enter first. "I was transformed about four and a half years ago."

The refreshment table was crowded with people, so Maggie led him to a quiet corner. "Don't you see? As young as you are, you could still have family somewhere. Wouldn't it be wonderful to find them? You could even spend Christmas with them."

"Right. I can see it now. Merry Christmas, everybody! And by the way, did I tell you I'm a vampire? No need to pass the gravy, just bare your neck—"

"Don't be silly! You would never bite your own family."

"That's just it, Maggie. Maybe I would. Maybe we'll find out I'm a worthless piece of scum. At least now I only pretend to be one. What if reality is worse than the act?"

She made a grab for his arm, and ended up with a fistful of black silk. "I don't believe that for one minute. If you were truly an awful person, you wouldn't worry so much about it."

He tilted his head, studying her. "You believe I could be a good person?"

"Yes. And I believe your family would be over-joyed to find out you're still alive . . . sorta."

"And what if having an undead family member is more than they can handle?"

Maggie's hand dropped from his cape. *Get out of my house, you unholy creature!*

"Maggie, are you all right?"

She shook her head, trying to dispel the memories.

He touched her arm. "You look so pale all of a sud—" His eyes narrowed. "What happened to you and your family?"

She swallowed hard. "It was a long time ago. I . . . you have to believe everything will be fine. This is the twenty-first century. People are more open-minded now than they used to be."

He stepped closer. "Did your family turn you away?"

She winced. "I don't want to talk about it."

"Oh, Maggie, I'm sorry." He took her hand in his. "They should have realized what a kind heart you have."

Her heart started to pound. Did Don Orlando see what her father had missed?

He lifted her hand to his chest. "That's why you're helping me, isn't it? Because you have a sweet and generous spirit. I sensed it the first time we met."

Maggie couldn't think. She was melting under the soft, searching gaze of his golden brown eyes.

"Maggie," he whispered and raised her hand to his mouth.

"Oh, there you are!" Gordon strode toward them.

Maggie jerked her hand from Don Orlando's grip and spun to face the director. "Hello."

"Corky told me about your trip to New Orleans,"

Gordon said. "She wants you two to leave tomorrow night."

Don Orlando stiffened. "I haven't decided if I'm going—"

"You have to go." Maggie gave him a pleading look.

"I was just talking to the writers," Gordon continued, "and we have it worked out so you can leave. They'll get the new script to us in thirty minutes, and we'll shoot it tonight."

"How will they explain our absence?" Maggie asked.

"It was easy." Gordon crossed his arms. "Dr. Jessica is going to South America to disconnect a pair of twins who are attached at the head. Since you're a world-famous brain surgeon, they wanted you, and you agreed to do it free of charge."

Don Orlando nodded. "That makes sense. She has such a kind heart. She would always help someone in dire need." He lightly touched Maggie's hand with his fingers.

She glanced at him. Was he referring to her character or to her? Her breath caught when his fingertips gently stroked the length of her fingers. They were standing side by side, their hands hidden in the folds of his cape.

"What do you think, Maggie?" Gordon asked.

"It's . . . fine." She was finding it hard to concentrate. Don Orlando wasn't actually holding her hand. He was exploring it. "What will happen to Don Orlando?"

Gordon grimaced. "That was trickier. He gets so upset about you leaving, he crashes his car into the giant bull on Wall Street, and ends up in a coma."

Maggie blinked. "A coma? But wouldn't he recover during his death-sleep?"

Gordon shrugged. "It's television. Don't expect it to make sense. We can make the coma last a few days or it can go on for weeks, depending on how much time you need. And we can make the viewers frantic, worrying that he might die at any minute."

Don Orlando nodded. "I'm okay with it."

"Great! I'll see how the writers are doing." Gordon strode away.

Don Orlando turned to face her. "I don't want a cameraman."

Maggie smiled. "Then you're coming with me?"

"If it's just the two of us, yes. I trust you."

"Well, Ian MacPhie is coming, too. But you can trust him."

"I don't know him."

"He works for MacKay Security and Investigation. I knew him when I lived at Roman Draganesti's house. He looks like an innocent fifteen-year-old, but he's over four hundred, and he really knows what he's doing."

Don Orlando took a deep breath. "I can't believe I'm agreeing to this. If we find out something awful, Corky will broadcast it to the entire vampire world."

"She'll never know. Ian and I can keep a secret. Besides, there's not going to be anything awful to discover. It'll be wonderful, believe me."

"You're an angel, Maggie. I had given up all hope till I met you. And now, I have one hope."

"That you'll find your family?"

"That would be nice, but since I can't remember them, I don't miss them." He took her hand in his.

"Then what do you hope for?"

He lifted her hand to his lips. "I hope that when we find out who I am, I'll be worthy of you."

· 3 ·

Two nights later, Don Orlando arrived at Horny Devils with his duffel bag. By the time his eyes adjusted to the flashing lights of the nightclub, he was surrounded by a crowd of scantily clad lady Vamps who screeched to be heard over the loud music.

"Oh, Don Orlando! I just adore your show! And your cape!"

"Why are you wearing a shirt?"

"Can I have your autograph?"

A dozen cocktail napkins were thrust at his face. He reached into his inner coat pocket for a pen while he scanned the renovated warehouse for Maggie.

"Me first!" A napkin grazed his nose. A blond Vamp dressed like a cheerleader stepped in front of him, blocking his way.

He blinked. There was something disconcerting about a cheerleader with fangs.

She curled a hand around his arm, her long fingernails digging in like grappling hooks. "Do you need a girlfriend?"

"No, thank you." He wished he could publicly claim Maggie as his girlfriend, but she'd probably throw another shoe at his head. Still, she had to care about him, right? She'd arranged this trip to find out who he was. Where was she?

"Enough, ladies!" A striking woman with purple hair shouted over the loud music. "You don't want to miss our new dancer."

With a triumphant yell, the cheerleader released him and skipped toward the stage. The other women joined her, bouncing to the rhythm of a pounding drum. The stage curtains were whisked back to reveal a man wearing an Indian headdress, war paint, and little else. The women screamed.

Don Orlando breathed deeply. Thank God he was no longer the center of attention. He smiled at the purple-haired woman. "Are you one of Maggie's friends? I'm supposed to meet her here."

"She's in the office, waiting for you." The woman assessed him with narrowed eyes. "So, you're the famous Don Orlando."

"How do you do?" He extended a hand.

She took it and yanked him toward her so suddenly, the strap of the duffel bag slid off his shoulder. "My name is Vanda, and if you hurt Maggie, I'm coming after you."

"I would never hurt her." Not intentionally, though he was worried that she could find the truth about him disappointing. He shoved his duffel bag back onto his shoulder.

"Let me in!" A young voice bellowed at the front door.

"Get lost," the bouncer yelled. "You're underage."

"I'm 479 years old, ye moron."

"Hugo!" Vanda shouted. "He's okay. Let him in."

The huge guard stepped back, grumbling. "Well, he looks like he's twelve."

"Do not," the youthful-looking vampire hissed as he strode into the club.

No, he didn't. Don Orlando figured he looked more like fifteen. Black curly hair framed his smooth face, and a red plaid kilt swished about his knees as he walked toward them. "You must be Ian MacPhie."

"Aye, and ye must be Don Orlando." He shook hands, then turned to Vanda. "Ye're looking as lovely as ever." He took her hand and attempted to kiss it.

With a laugh, she pulled her hand away and ruffled his hair. "Come on. Maggie's waiting." She strode to the office.

"Thanks for helping with the investigation." Don Orlando noted the Scotsman's eyes were riveted on Vanda's swaying hips.

"I like to stay busy. It keeps my mind off . . . things." Ian glanced at the wiggling women in front of the stage.

Don Orlando suspected those "things" were women. It had to be hard to be stuck for all eternity with the raging hormones of a fifteen-year-old boy.

"I talked to the New Orleans coven master last night. He should be calling shortly. And I have the phone numbers of every coven master in America." Ian patted the leather pouch that hung from his waist. "We'll be able to teleport to any major city."

"That's good." Especially since Don Orlando had no idea where he was originally from.

Vanda stopped at a door with the words OFFICE painted on front. "Good luck finding out who you are." She turned to Ian. "You behave yourself in New Orleans, sweetie."

He gave her an exasperated look. "I'm older than you."

She laughed. "I know, but you look so sweet." She patted his cheek, then walked away.

Ian groaned, then pushed open the door.

"Don Orlando, Ian!" Maggie grinned as they entered the room. She was standing by the desk, holding the phone. "Colbert GrandPied just called. They're awake in New Orleans."

"Good. I'll go first." Ian stepped close to Maggie and leaned toward the phone. "Colbert, keep talking. I'm on my way."

Ian's form wavered, then vanished. Don Orlando understood the maneuver in theory. A Vamp could teleport long distances by using someone's voice as a beacon. Still, he had never executed the feat on his own before. He'd been half-starved and confused when Corky had teleported him to New York years earlier.

"Are you ready?" Maggie asked.

He hovered near the phone, listening to Colbert's French-accented voice. A wave of dread washed over him. What was he doing, going back to New Orleans? It was the home of his worst nightmare, where he'd lost his memory and mortality.

"Maggie," he whispered, "this is difficult."

Her pretty blue eyes widened with concern. "Don't worry." She lay the receiver down and punched on the speaker phone. Colbert's deep voice filled the room. Having run out of things to say, he was now singing "Au Claire de la Lune."

Maggie slipped a tote bag onto her shoulder, then took hold of Don Orlando's hands. "I'll go with you.

Every step of the way." She smiled. "You'll be sick of me before this is over."

"No, never." He tightened his grip on her hands and focused on Colbert's melodic voice. "I don't deserve you, Maggie."

"You deserve happiness." Her body slowly disappeared.

Happiness is being with you was his last thought before everything went black. He could still feel her presence and hear Colbert's voice becoming closer and louder. The thud of his feet on solid ground signaled his arrival. Ian was there, standing next to Colbert. Maggie's image shimmered, then sharpened into her real body, her hands still clasped in his own.

"Bonsoir, mon ami," Colbert nodded at him, then studied Maggie. *"Enchanté, ma petite.* And you are?"

Mine. A rush of possessiveness swept over Don Orlando. He knew Colbert was famous for seducing beautiful women, so he sidled close to Maggie and draped an arm around her shoulder.

Smiling, she glanced at him, then turned to Colbert. "I'm Maggie O'Brian. Thank you for letting us stay with your coven."

"My pleasure, *chérie.*" Colbert bowed gracefully. "Ian tells me you have come to discover Don Orlando's true identity."

"Yes." Don Orlando dropped his duffel bag on the floor as he glanced around. They appeared to be in an abandoned warehouse. Empty, broken crates littered the floor. The smell of coffee competed with the odors of mold and dust. This was far from the elegant wine cellar he remembered. "You moved?"

"Oui." Colbert sighed. "Our beloved wine cellar was flooded with the last hurricane. So much was ruined—many of our valuable antiques and all our lovely coffins."

"I'm so sorry," Maggie murmured.

"I was fortunate to find this old coffee warehouse." Colbert pointed at the far walls. "You can still see the watermark where the ground floor flooded, but we discovered the second floor was safe and dry. More importantly, it has no windows and no other exits. The government gave us a few cots and blankets, but it is not the same as the old days."

"Wait a minute," Don Orlando interrupted. "You received government aid?"

Colbert shrugged. "I filled out the proper paperwork." He gestured toward the second floor. A small balcony surrounded the closed door. "That is where we hide during the day."

Ian pointed at the heap of broken wood beneath the balcony. "Was that the staircase? Ye tore it down?"

"Oui. So no mortal can disturb us during our death-sleep."

Ian nodded. "A good plan. Now, if you doona mind, I'd like to get started with the investigation."

"But of course." Colbert smiled slightly at Don Orlando. "I must confess, I have long been curious about the identity of our Bootsie."

"Bootsie?" Maggie asked.

Don Orlando winced. This was going to be embarrassing.

"We didn't know what to call him," Colbert explained. "So we named him after the pair of boots he was wearing."

"What kind of boots?" Ian asked.

"Alligator, I believe."

"No, I mean what kind," Ian pressed. "Were they work boots, hiking boots—"

"Ah." Colbert nodded. "They were cowboy boots."

Don Orlando blinked. "I—I'm a cowboy?"

"You don't remember your boots?" Maggie asked.

He gritted his teeth. "No, if you recall, I have amnesia."

She huffed. "I know, but you must have been wearing them when you were transformed, after you already had amnesia."

"I see your point, *chérie,*" Colbert conceded. "But Scarlett and Tootsie didn't like the way Bootsie was dressed, so they changed his clothes before transforming him. He was unconscious at the time, so it is no wonder he cannot remember."

"Scarlett and Tootsie?" Maggie turned to Don Orlando with an irritated look. "Two women transformed you?"

Don Orlando groaned. "It's a long story."

"Wait," Ian interrupted. "Do ye still have his old clothes?"

Colbert rubbed his dimpled chin. "Perhaps. We grabbed as much as we could when we evacuated. I'll have to ask Giselle."

"Do that," Ian ordered. "We might discover some clues from his clothes. And I need to interview Scarlett and Tootsie."

"Must you?" Don Orlando grumbled.

"But of course." Colbert smiled at Don Orlando. "They've been eagerly awaiting your arrival. They're practically swooning from all the excitement."

"They're always about to swoon," Don Orlando growled.

Colbert laughed. "I'll fetch them and find Giselle. *A bientôt, mes amis.*" He levitated to the second-floor balcony, then opened the door. "Scarlett, Tootsie, he's here!"

High-pitched squeals responded.

Maggie shot Don Orlando an annoyed look. "You didn't tell me you had girlfriends here."

He considered climbing into one of the empty crates.

"He's here! Our little Bootsie is back!" A slim male Vamp ran onto the balcony. His eyes lit up when he spotted Don Orlando, and his scarlet-tinted lips broke into a wide grin.

Don Orlando grimaced. The hurricane hadn't destroyed Scarlett's clothes. He was wearing his usual white leather miniskirt and black fishnet stockings. His red satin bustier matched the red feather boa around his neck. His large feet were crammed into red patent leather pumps.

"Sweet Mary and Joseph," Maggie whispered. Her tote bag fell to the floor.

"Damn," Ian muttered, stepping back.

"Woo-hoo, Bootikins!" The Vamp waved at Don Orlando with the end of his boa. He glanced back. "Tootsie, stop worrying over your lipstick. You're keeping Bootsie waiting."

"I'm coming!" A deep male voice boomed from the upstairs room.

"Don't rush yourselves on my account," Don Orlando yelled.

Maggie turned to him, grinning. "Tootsie and Bootsie? You must have made a lovely couple."

"Don't go there," Don Orlando muttered. "Believe me, I didn't."

"Bootikins!" A male Vamp, wearing a red velvet costume, leaped onto the balcony. White fur trimmed the short skirt, neckline, and sleeves. A big white pom-pom hung from his red Santa hat, and his elf shoes were adorned on the tips with jingle bells. "Bootsie, you look gorgeous." He struck a pose. "Don't you love my new outfit? I look just like a Rockette."

"Yeah, right," Don Orlando grumbled.

Scarlett and Tootsie floated down to the first floor, the boa fluttering and bells jingling. They landed gracefully, then rushed toward Don Orlando. He stood still as they each embraced him and kissed his cheeks.

"What?" Scarlett whimpered. "No hugs or kisses for us?"

Don Orlando patted his shoulder. "It's good to see you again."

Tootsie dabbed at his eyes with a lacy hanky he'd pulled from his sleeve. "Our little boy has come home. I'm going to swoon, I just know it."

"There, there." Scarlett gave Tootsie a stern look. "We mustn't upset Bootikins now that he's home." He turned to Don Orlando with a trembling smile. "We're so proud of you! Our little Bootsie, a famous TV star."

Tootsie sniffled. "I just love your cape."

"Oh, me too!" Scarlett stepped close. "But we wanted to talk to you about that. Must you always wear black, sweetie? I think scarlet or plum silk would be so smashing."

"Excuse me." Ian raised a hand to get their attention. "We need to get down to business. Now, is it true that ye're the ones who transformed Don Orlando?"

"Oh, my!" Tootsie eyed Ian. "Your young friend with the sexy kilt and adorable accent is so serious and . . . aggressive." He shuddered. "I don't know whether to be appalled or excited."

Don Orlando cleared his throat. "Allow me to introduce my friends from New York. This is Ian Mac-Phie and Maggie O'Brian."

"Oh, yes!" Scarlett grabbed Maggie's hand and shook it. "You're Dr. Jessica from *As the Vampire Turns*. We think it's marvelous how you're going to South America to help those poor conjoined twins."

"But I—" Maggie started.

"I start crying every time I think about it." Tootsie wiped his eyes. "Tell me, was the surgery a success?"

Maggie gave Don Orlando a confused look. "Ah, yes, the twins are doing great."

"Oh, God bless them!" Scarlett pressed a hand to his flat chest.

"I'm so happy, I'm going to swoon from joy," Tootsie added.

"Could we get back to business?" Ian asked. "No swooning until I can interview you."

"Oh, he's so forceful." Tootsie shivered.

"You're such a lovely girl." Scarlett touched Maggie's chin-length black hair. "You know, not many of us can look good in a bob. But if I may suggest, some blue highlights would be so lovely for you. Don't you think so, Tootsie?"

"Yes, it would bring out the blue of her eyes."

"Business!" Ian shouted. "Before the sun rises, please."

"Oh, you're an animal," Tootsie purred as he slinked over to Ian. "Like a fierce young Scottish wildcat."

"Touch me and I'll break yer arm," Ian growled, folding his arms across his chest. "Now, we're here to discover the true identity of . . . Bootikins." His mouth twitched.

Maggie giggled.

Don Orlando glared at them both.

"Which one of ye found Bootsie first?" Ian asked.

"That would be me," Scarlett confessed. "Tootsie and I were taking our nightly stroll around Jackson Square. I'd already had some bottled blood for dinner, so I wasn't very hungry. But then I saw sweet little Bootsie sitting on the steps of the cathedral. He looked so sad and beautiful with his wavy black hair and big golden brown eyes, I couldn't help myself. I thought, perhaps, a little nibble wouldn't hurt—"

"You bit him?" Maggie looked appalled.

"Well . . . yes." Scarlett blushed a becoming shade of scarlet. "But Tootsie bit him, too."

Tootsie gave his companion a recriminating look. "Well, I couldn't let *you* have all the fun. Besides, he looked so marvelously tragic, like a dying Camille. How could we resist?"

Scarlett sighed. "I'm afraid we got a little carried away."

"A *little*?" Don Orlando glared at them. "You put me in a coma."

"But only because we liked you!" Tootsie exclaimed.

"We didn't do it right away." Scarlett blew red feathers away from his mouth. "You were fine when we tried to erase your memory. That's when we discovered you had no memory at all."

"And that's when Scarlett came up with the plan," Tootsie added.

"*My* plan?" Scarlett huffed. "You went along with it."

"What plan?" Ian demanded.

Tootsie hung his head. "I know we shouldn't have—"

"No, you shouldn't have," Don Orlando growled.

Scarlett's red lips trembled. "We said we were sorry."

Tootsie dabbed at his eyes with his hanky. "We begged you to forgive us, but you left for New York with that horrid woman and wouldn't forgive us. You wouldn't even talk to us."

"Oh, how sad." Maggie patted Tootsie's shoulder. "I'm sure he's forgiven you." She gave Don Orlando a reproachful look. "You have, haven't you?"

"Maggie, they murdered me!"

She shrugged. "So, you were having a bad day."

"*What?*"

"I don't mean to sound cold." She squeezed his arm. "But we were all murdered at some point. It's the nature of our existence. If you want to be happy, you need to get over it and forgive them. You could have a wonderful future ahead of you."

Tootsie nodded. "You should listen to her. She's a very wise doctor."

"Just look at how she saved those twins in South America," Scarlett added with a sniff.

Don Orlando sighed. Tootsie and Scarlett kept confusing Maggie with the doctor she played on TV, but they were right. In her own way, Maggie was healing him. And she was right. An eternity of bitterness would make him miserable.

He glanced at Tootsie and Scarlett. They were both sniffling, their bottom lips trembling, and their eyes watery with regret. "All right, I forgive you. In fact, I'm downright delighted to be a vampire."

"Really?" Scarlett wiped a tear from his rouged cheek.

"Yes." Don Orlando turned to Maggie and clasped her hands in his. "If I hadn't become a vampire, I would have never met this beautiful, courageous, and wise woman. Maggie, you were definitely worth dying for."

Her mouth fell open and her eyes widened. When he tugged her forward, she willingly came into his arms. He held her tight and kissed the top of her head. So what if he had no memories? He could build an eternity of memories with Maggie.

"Oh, my!" Scarlett fanned himself. "This is so romantic."

"Oh, yes!" Tootsie pressed a hand to his forehead. "I'm going to swoon."

"No ye're not," Ian ordered. "Ye never told us about the plan."

"Oh, you're so demanding." Tootsie shuddered. "You're like a Scottish terrier with a bone."

"Mmm, a very large bone." Scarlett smiled slyly as he regarded Ian's kilt.

"The plan?" Ian growled.

"Well, there's no need to get all huffy." Tootsie gave him an injured look. "We simply wanted to make Bootsie like us."

"Like a vampire?" Ian asked.

"No." Don Orlando glared at his makers. "They wanted to make me just like them. They took my comatose body back to the wine cellar and put me in a damned dress."

Tootsie scoffed. "You needn't growl at us. You said you've forgiven us."

"And it was a very nice dress," Scarlett added. "An ivory silk gown with extensive beadwork on the bodice."

"It was a freaking dress," Don Orlando growled. "I woke up the next night to find out I was undead and wearing a *dress*!"

Maggie covered her mouth to hide a smile.

"It wasn't funny," Don Orlando grumbled.

"I'm sure you looked very nice." Maggie wrapped her arms around his middle, and he forgot all about being angry.

"So." Ian gave the two male Vamps a disapproving frown. "Yer plan was to take a mortal with no memory, transform him, and convince him that he was a gay transvestite?"

Tootsie huffed. "You needn't make us sound so Machiavellian. We gave him our best gown."

"A Vera Wang," Scarlett added. "And the big brute ripped it when he tore it off."

Ian arched an eyebrow at Don Orlando. "I take it their little experiment dinna work?"

"No. Even without a memory, I knew I was straight."

Ian's gaze lifted to the balcony and his mouth fell

open. Don Orlando wasn't surprised. Giselle usually had that effect on men. She was standing on the balcony, dressed in a shimmering white gown, her white-blond hair cascading down her back. In her arms was a bundle of clothes.

"Bonsoir." She smiled as she floated down to the ground floor. "I have located Bootsie's old clothes." She sauntered past them to a small seating area.

Two Louis XVI chairs and a gold satin settee surrounded a scarred coffee table. Giselle dumped the clothes on the table, then perched on one of the chairs. Scarlett and Tootsie rushed over and sat together on the settee. Maggie and Ian followed them. Don Orlando gathered his duffel bag and Maggie's tote bag and set them on the floor next to the vacant chair.

"Thank ye for finding the clothes." Ian smiled and extended a hand to Giselle. "I'm Ian MacPhie from New York."

"Enchantée." She removed her hand from his grip before he could kiss it.

With a sigh, Ian turned to examine the clothes on the table.

Scarlett lifted a plaid Western shirt between his thumb and forefinger and shuddered. "How horrid."

Don Orlando picked up the boots. They were worn and scruffy. Had he really been a cowboy?

"This is interesting." Ian removed a belt from the pile and studied the buckle.

"It's huge." Maggie moved closer to Ian to get a better look. "What's that embossed on front? A wild horse?"

"A bronco." Don Orlando blinked when he realized

the word had escaped without forethought. He must really be a cowboy.

Ian turned the buckle over. "There's an inscription. FORT WORTH LIVESTOCK SHOW AND RODEO 1999. This could be useful." He turned to Giselle. "Is there a computer here I can use?"

"Yes, on the second floor." She rose. "I'll take you."

"Thank you." Ian followed Giselle to the balcony, then they levitated to the second floor. Scarlett and Tootsie dashed over at vampire speed to get a glimpse under Ian's kilt.

Don Orlando cleared his throat. They gave him sheepish looks.

Ian glanced down from the balcony. "Ye four should keep working. The clues are there, if ye think hard enough." He followed Giselle into the upstairs room and shut the door.

"What clues?" Tootsie's shoes jingled as he and Scarlett trudged back to the settee.

"I've always wondered how I got amnesia." Don Orlando sat in one of the antique chairs.

"His mind was a complete blank when you found him?" Maggie asked Tootsie and Scarlett. They nodded.

"Then the amnesia must have happened that night," Don Orlando concluded.

"Exactly," Maggie agreed. "It must have just happened or you would have had a little memory. And it must have happened very close to where you were found."

"Somewhere in the French Quarter?" Tootsie offered.

Maggie turned to the male Vamps on the settee. "Did Don Orlando have a head injury of any kind?"

"No, he was perfect." Scarlett grimaced. "I always suspected it had something to do with"—he lowered his voice to an ominous whisper—"the Dark Arts."

Tootsie gasped and pressed a hand to his chest. "Don't make me swoon."

Don Orlando sat back as a feeling of dread seeped into his pores.

"You mean magic?" Maggie asked. "Or witches?"

Scarlett and Tootsie exchanged a worried look and shuddered.

"They mean voodoo," Don Orlando whispered.

"Is that real?" Maggie asked.

"It's real if you believe in it," Tootsie whispered.

Maggie glanced at Don Orlando. "Do you believe in it?"

"I don't know. I can't remember."

"Well." Maggie lifted her chin. "I'm not afraid. And it stands to reason that if the amnesia is the result of some kind of spell, then there must be another spell that can undo it. We should locate the local practitioner and see what he can do."

Scarlett's mouth fell open. "You're not getting me to see a voodoo priestess."

Maggie gave him a stern look. "Not even for Bootsie?"

Tootsie grabbed Scarlett's hand and held tight. "We can take you to the French Quarter where the local shops are, but we don't want to go inside."

"Very well." Maggie stood. "Let's go."

Don Orlando smiled. What a fierce little fighter she was. He couldn't imagine living through eternity or even a single night without her. His smile faded as he realized the full impact of his feelings. He was in love with Maggie O'Brian.

She gave him a worried look. "Are you all right?"

"Never been better." He took her hand. "Let's go."

· **4** ·

"Sweet Mary, my feet hurt." Maggie leaned against an old streetlamp. It must be after three in the morning, and they'd been to one shop after another. Scarlett and Tootsie had abandoned them on Bourbon Street when they spotted a club with scantily clothed gentlemen dancing on the bar.

Don Orlando's gaze ran over her short black skirt, her legs encased in black hose, and her black high-heeled shoes. "You could cause a traffic accident with those legs."

She scoffed. "I'm too short."

"You're beautiful." His gaze locked onto her pink sweater.

The cad. Maggie was still surprised that he'd never had a girlfriend during his stay in New Orleans. Tootsie and Scarlett had confirmed that. She also understood why he'd run off to New York with Corky. The poor guy had simply wanted a life and an identity other than Bootsie, the failed social experiment.

Sweet Mary, she liked him. More than liked him. He was sweet and caring. Strong, yet vulnerable. And most of all, he thought she was special. Beautiful and kindhearted.

With a sigh, she glanced down the street. A recent

rain had left puddles in the uneven pavement. The air was warm and thick against her skin. She was worried now. Worried that she was hopelessly in love with Don Orlando. What if they found out he was married?

"I think we did all the shops on this street," she murmured. They'd been simple tourist shops, selling T-shirts, feather boas, beads, and masks. She pushed away from the streetlamp. "Where's a voodoo priestess when you need one?"

"Don't know." Don Orlando took her hand. "Let's find Tootsie and Scarlett." He led her down the sidewalk.

"Are we going the right way?" They'd ventured up and down so many streets, Maggie was all turned around.

"Yep. Bourbon Street's over there." Don Orlando pointed to the right. "Here's a side street where we can cut through."

They turned onto the dark narrow street, lit by one storefront window.

"Did we check this place?" Maggie slowed to examine the goods in the store window. The usual stuff—beads and boas. Little stuffed alligators wearing Santa hats. "Oh, look."

Don Orlando chuckled at the large box of voodoo dolls. "The economy pack. Twenty-four voodoo dolls at one low price."

"Sweet Mary. You could take care of all your enemies in one fell swoop. Let's go in."

He gave the door a shove, and it opened. A tiny bell tinkled overhead. "Hello?"

Maggie followed him inside. The door swung shut with another tinkling noise. The narrow store was dimly lit. One side held the usual touristy stuff, but the other wall was covered with glassed-in shelves. She eased closer for a better look.

"Ugh!" She stepped back. The shelves held glass jars filled with things that looked like pickled animals and body parts.

"Looks like we found the right place," Don Orlando said.

"That depends on what you seek," a male voice spoke from the back of the room.

Maggie gasped and edged closer to Don Orlando.

There was a scratch of a match, then a small flame traveled from one candle to another till three large ivory pillars illuminated the back of the room. The candles rested on a counter, and behind them, a bald black man stood.

Don Orlando cleared his throat. "Can you help us?"

The man bowed his head. "Those who come at three in the morning are generally in need of my help." His voice had a deep, hypnotic quality to it. "Come forward so I may see you."

Maggie followed Don Orlando as they neared the counter and the glowing pool of candlelight.

Suddenly, the black man stiffened. "Pierce?"

Don Orlando halted. "Are you talking to me?"

"Of course, man. Don't you remember—" The man's eyes widened. "Oh, God, you don't." He ran a hand over his bald head. "Store's closed. Come back tomorrow." He blew out a candle.

"Wait!" Don Orlando ran toward him. "You know who I am."

"No, no. I mistook you for someone else." He blew out a second candle. "Go now. The store is cl—"

"No!" Don Orlando grabbed the last lit candle

and held it away from the store owner. "Tell me who I am."

The man shook his head. "I told you, man, I don't know."

"You do." Don Orlando passed the candle to Maggie, then reached over the counter, grabbed a handful of the man's shirt, and lifted him off the floor. "You will tell me."

"Damn," the store owner wheezed. "How'd you get so strong? Okay. I'll tell you." He gasped for air when he landed back on the floor. "Sheesh, man. You don't even remember your name?"

"I remember nothing."

"Damn!" The store owner hit the counter with the flat of his hand. "I told her she was making the potion too strong, but does she ever listen to me? Nooooo. Three bat wings she put in the potion, not two like the book says. *Three!* And that eye of newt?" He raised his hands, shaking his head. "She should have never added that. I told her she was asking for trouble."

"Enough!" Don Orlando grabbed the candle from Maggie and set it down with a thud. The flame lurched and flickered wild shadows across the gruesome glass jugs. "Who am I?"

"You're Pierce. Pierce O'Callahan."

Don Orlando gave Maggie a stunned look. "I'm Irish?"

The store owner muttered another curse. "I told her she was making it too strong. She's always causing me trouble."

Don Orlando glared at him. "Who are you?"

"Durand Dérangé." With a sigh, he turned to the wall behind him and flipped on the lights.

The jars looked even more ghoulish under the flickering, purplish fluorescent light. Maggie could detect animal feet and eyeballs. "How did you erase Don Orlando's memory? I mean, Pierce." It would take a while to get used to his new name.

"More importantly," Pierce added, "can you make another potion to restore my memory?"

"Ah, man. I don't think so. Once it's gone, it's gone."

Pierce leaned over the counter. "The woman who made the potion, can *she* undo it?"

Durand's gaze flitted to his left. "I don't know where she is. She left before the hurricane and hasn't come back."

"Who is she?" Pierce ground out.

"My sister. Désirée." His gaze slipped to the left again.

Maggie glanced to his left and spotted a photo frame stuffed between two jars. She eased over for a closer look.

"Désirée is crazy, you know. Whatever she wants, she gets." Durand shrugged. "And she wanted you, man."

That figured. Maggie groaned inwardly. Even as a mortal, Don Orlando, or Pierce, would have attracted a ton of girls. The photo on the dusty shelf showed a beautiful young woman with glowing bronze skin, wearing a white sun dress. Beside her stood a little girl, also in a white dress. "Is this Désirée?"

"Don't look at that." Durand dashed over, grabbed the photo, and stuffed it under the counter. He glanced back at Pierce. "I told you who you are. You should go now."

What was he hiding? "Why don't you let Pierce see the photo?" Maggie asked. "It might jog his memory."

"No, no." Durand shook his head. "The photo cannot help. She erased herself completely from his memory."

"Why?" Pierce thumped the counter with his fist. "What could I have possibly done to deserve amnesia?"

"Nothing, man." Durand shrugged. "Désirée was visiting a cousin in Dallas, and they went to a rodeo. That's where she saw you and decided she had to have you. Don't ask me why. She's never wanted a cowboy before."

"Then I *was* a cowboy?" Pierce asked. "In a rodeo?"

"Sure, man. I hear you were really good."

"And Pierce started dating your sister?" Maggie asked.

"No, no." Durand shook his head. "Pierce didn't even know who she was till she slipped a love potion into his beer. Unfortunately, she always makes her potions too strong."

"So, she tricked Pierce into loving her?" Maggie balled her hands into fists. It was a good thing Désirée was out of town.

"Yeah," Durand continued. "Poor old Pierce was completely under her spell. When she got tired of him and came home, he followed her here. Eventually, she got so tired of him, she decided to erase herself from his memory."

Maggie clenched her fists tighter. How could any woman possibly grow tired of Don Orlando?

Pierce cursed under his breath. "She didn't erase just herself. She erased everything!"

"I'm sorry, man." Durand lowered his head. "I told her that eye of newt was too much."

"And you really don't know where she is?" Maggie considered slipping inside his mind to see if he spoke the truth.

"She left before the hurricane. Met some bigwig from Hollywood who said he'd make her a star." Durand scowled. "She left me to clean everything up. Left me all alone to work this damned store."

Pierce's laugh sounded pained. "Sounds like a great gal. I'm glad I don't remember her." He strode toward the front door.

Maggie started toward the door, but something prickled at her senses. She was missing something. She slowed to a stop and glanced back at Durand. "Who's the little girl in the photo?"

He gulped. "Don't know what you're talking about."

"The little girl in the photo, standing next to Désirée." Maggie wandered back toward Durand. "Who is she?"

"She—she's a cousin. We have so many." He grabbed a ring of keys from under the counter. "I need to lock up now."

Maggie focused her thoughts and concentrated on Durand's bald head. With a swoosh, she invaded his mind.

He gasped and stumbled back. The key ring fell and hit the floor with a jangle. Maggie walked toward him as she sifted through the images in his mind.

Durand retreated till he bumped into the back wall. "Oh, God. You're one of the nightwalkers."

"Then you know what we can do," Maggie whispered. She scoured his mind, finding images of Désirée with a baby.

"Damn." Durand glanced at Pierce. "You're one, too? That's how you picked me up." He grabbed a jar from the shelf behind him and poured a line of red dust along the counter.

Instantly, Maggie was shut out of his head. How had he managed that? "Who is the little girl?"

Pierce joined her. "Tell us the truth, Durand."

Durand lifted his chin. "You can't make me talk. You can't cross the brick dust, even with your minds. You can't hurt me."

"And you can't hide from us forever," Pierce growled. "Show me that photo."

"Damn." Durand shifted from one foot to another. "Désirée is always causing me trouble. You won't hurt her?"

"I have no interest in your sister," Pierce said softly. "Show me the photo."

With a resigned sigh, Durand handed Pierce the photo frame. "The little girl is named Lucy."

Maggie peered at the photo. "She's beautiful."

Pierce stroked a thumb gently over the little girl's face. Her facial features were very much like his. "Am I the father?"

Durand grimaced. "Yes, you are."

Back at the warehouse, Maggie was relieved to find that Colbert had installed two bathrooms on the second floor—one for males and one for females. As she showered, her thoughts centered on Don Orlando. Make that Pierce. Pierce O'Callahan who had a beautiful little girl named Lucy.

Her heart twisted. Oh, how she had wanted children! But it was impossible with a womb that was literally dead during the day. She lowered her head under the nozzle and let hot water pound on her. How could she be so selfish? She should be happy for Pierce. She turned off the water and toweled herself dry. After all, this had been the purpose of her mission, right? To discover his true identity and hopefully, find his family? She should be happy. Then why did she feel like crying?

Maggie removed her winter pajamas from her tote bag and put them on. Then, she combed her wet hair, grabbed her tote, and headed for the cot Colbert had assigned her.

She spotted Pierce with damp hair from his recent shower, seated at the computer and looking at something Ian had discovered on the Internet. Ian was standing nearby, talking to Giselle. He leaned close and whispered in her ear. Suddenly, she stepped back and slapped him.

Maggie gasped. Other Vamps exchanged amused grins.

"I do not consort with children!" Giselle stomped toward the ladies' restroom.

Maggie stepped aside to let her pass, then dashed toward Ian. "Are you all right?"

He shrugged like he didn't care, though his reddened face indicated differently. " 'Tis always the same. Either they're no' interested because they think I'm a child, or they *are* interested because they think I'm a child, which is even worse."

"I'm so sorry," Maggie murmured.

Pierce stood and patted him on the shoulder. "It's my fault. I should have warned you. Giselle is Colbert's woman. She would have slapped any guy who made a pass at her, no matter what his age."

"Oh." Ian straightened his shoulders. "Thank you."

Maggie smiled at Pierce, grateful for his attempt at making Ian feel better.

Ian took a deep breath. "Let's get back to business. I have confirmed that Pierce O'Callahan won the bareback riding competition at the Fort Worth rodeo in 1999."

Maggie gave Pierce a stunned look. "That's impressive."

He shrugged. "I don't remember it."

"And I've located the O'Callahan ranch in Texas," Ian continued. "'Tis about an hour's drive south of Dallas, so tomorrow night, we'll teleport to Dallas. The coven there is expecting us, and they've agreed to let Pierce borrow a car so he can drive to the ranch. Do ye remember how to drive?"

"I don't know." Pierce ran a hand through his damp hair, frowning.

"Ye'll probably remember once ye're behind the wheel," Ian said.

This was it, Maggie thought. No wonder she felt like crying. Tomorrow night, Pierce would drive to his family's ranch, and they'd welcome him back with open arms. Her job would be over. She would return to New York alone.

"Ian, could you help me find my daughter?" Pierce asked.

"Of course," Ian replied.

"I'm going to bed. Good night." Maggie wandered toward her cot while Pierce and Ian made plans to find the missing Lucy. She passed the coven's Christmas tree, noting the gaily wrapped presents underneath. And she felt all alone.

She settled onto her cot. Pierce no longer needed her. He had a daughter and a family. She snuggled deeper under her blankets. The sun must be close to rising. She could already feel the pull of death-sleep. Around the room, Vamps settled into their cots and turned off their bedside lamps. The only light left was the white star on top of the Christmas tree.

"Do you mind if I move closer?" Pierce whispered.

She rolled over to see him pushing his cot next to hers.

"I can't thank you enough, Maggie." He eased into his cot and pulled the blanket up to his waist. He dragged his shirt over his head and tossed it to the foot of his cot. His shoulders were broad, not that she was looking. The light was too dim. She had to squint to make out the brown, curly hair on his chest.

"You *do* have chest hair. Is brown your natural hair color?"

"Yes." He stretched out on his cot. "Corky thought I'd look sexier with my hair dyed black and a huge amount of chest hair."

Maggie yawned, feeling another tug from the encroaching death-sleep. "Corky's silly. I like you just the way you are." *Correction: I love you.*

"You're an angel, Maggie." He reached across to

her cot and clasped her hand. "You've given me my life back. And a purpose for living. I know now what I need to do. I need to find my family and daughter."

And there was no mention of her in his lofty goal. Maggie withdrew her hand. "I'm very happy for you." She rolled over so he wouldn't see the tears in her eyes.

For once, Maggie welcomed the painless oblivion of death-sleep.

· 5 ·

Pierce slanted a worried look at Maggie who sat in the passenger seat of the SUV he'd borrowed from the Dallas coven. She'd hardly spoken the entire trip, except to read Ian's directions or consult the map of Texas in her lap. Something was bothering her, he could feel it, but he didn't know what.

He checked the rearview mirror. For the last twenty minutes, they'd traveled alone on this Farm Road. "How much farther to go?"

She picked up Ian's directions. Thanks to a full moon and her superior Vamp vision, she was able to read. "We should be coming up on County Road Three any minute now. Once we turn right there, we'll be on the O'Callahan ranch."

"Great." Pierce reached between the bucket seats and opened the small ice chest. "We'd better eat first."

"Okay." She retrieved a cold bottle of Chocolood.

He opened a bottle of synthetic blood type O. "Cheers."

She didn't respond, just sipped her Chocolood and gazed out the window.

What the hell was wrong? Pierce guzzled down half his bottle, then plunked it into the cupholder. "Maggie, are you disappointed that I turned out to be a rodeo cowboy from Texas?"

"No. I—I'm very happy for you."

"You don't sound happy. I thought you'd like an Irish boy. I'm the sort of guy you could take home to meet your parents."

"Except that my parents died over a hundred years ago. And they would never approve of anyone who's undead. Even me."

"I'm sorry they rejected you. You—you never told me how you were transformed."

She sipped from her drink, refusing to look at him. "Here's the turn." She pointed at a narrow road up ahead.

"I hope you can tell me sometime." He hoped her transformation hadn't been a violent one. He wanted her to be able to trust and love. But he could wait till she was ready. That was one good thing about being a Vamp. He could wait a hundred years if he needed to.

He turned the SUV onto the County Road. Ian had been right. Once he sat behind the wheel, his driving skills had come back. He looked around the countryside, and a surge of pride swept through him. They were now on O'Callahan land.

"I was a volunteer with the Salvation Army," Maggie whispered. "We went into a bad area by the docks, and I got separated from the others. Night fell, and I was lost."

Pierce turned toward her. "You were attacked?"

"It was more like—" She gasped.

He looked forward and flinched. Something had dashed into the road. He stomped on the brake.

Maggie screamed. They screeched to a halt just as a large animal leaped into the thick brush on the right.

Pierce sat still for a while, waiting for his heart to stop pounding. "What the hell was that?"

Maggie took a deep breath. "I thought you were going to hit it."

He eased the SUV forward and spotted movement by a large oak tree. "Look! There it is!"

He'd seen the wolflike animal run on four legs, but now, it reared up on its hind legs and howled at the moon.

"It's huge," Maggie whispered.

The shaggy animal dropped to all fours and loped away.

Pierce shook his head. He could have sworn there were no wolves in this part of Texas. He drove forward, keeping an eye out for wild animals. A fence began on the left side of the road, the planks in sore need of a fresh coat of paint. Two brick columns flanked a narrow road. A rusty wrought-iron arch connected the two columns. Across the arch were two words—O'CALLAHAN RANCH.

This was it. *Home.* He turned onto the driveway and spotted a house at the end of the long drive.

It was a large, white Victorian with dark shutters and a three-story turreted tower on the left. The rest of the second floor was topped with a gabled roof. Lights from a Christmas tree twinkled in the wide bay window on the right. Steps led up to the front door and a wraparound porch. The whole house sat on top of a partially visible basement. Even in the moonlight, Pierce could tell the house needed a coat of paint, and one of the shutters was hanging crooked.

A sudden, dreadful feeling came over him that the ranch had suffered because of his disappearance. Would his family be angry when he reappeared after five years?

"It's beautiful," Maggie whispered.

She liked it? That was a relief. "You're okay with how this is turning out? I mean, me being a rodeo cowboy from Texas?"

"With a secret baby?" She glanced at him with a smile. "You know, it sounds like something from a DVN soap opera. And Pierce is a perfect name for a vampire. Very fangish."

"Yeah." He stopped in front of the house and studied the rundown building. "Maybe I get to save the ranch."

"Or maybe you're a long-lost prince from Europe."

He snorted as he removed the keys from the ignition. "Or maybe my father is actually an Arabian sheikh in hiding."

Maggie laughed. "And I bet you have an evil twin."

Right at that moment, the front door slammed open and a tall man strode onto the porch.

Maggie gasped. "Sweet Mary! He looks just like you."

A twin? Pierce's mouth fell open.

The man whisked a shotgun up to his shoulder and shouted, "Get the hell out of here!"

An evil twin? Pierce exchanged a shocked look with Maggie. "Duck down and stay low." He reached for the door handle.

"What are you doing?" Maggie scrunched down in her seat. "He'll shoot you."

"I don't think he can kill me." Pierce eased open the door. Though it would hurt like hell.

"I told you to go away!" The man cocked the shotgun.

"Wait!" Pierce edged around the front of the SUV. The headlights had yet to go off, so he stood in the pool of light. "Don't you know me?"

The man stumbled back with a gasp. The shotgun fell from his hands and discharged with a loud *kaboom*.

Pierce ducked behind the SUV. Maggie screamed.

"Sweet Jesus!" The man ran down the steps, then halted abruptly before reaching the ground. "Pierce, are you okay?"

An older, thin woman dashed onto the porch. "Patrick, what the hell are you doing? So help me, if you shoot Bob, I'll—"

"No!" Patrick pointed at the SUV. "It's Pierce! He's back!"

"What?" The woman stared at the SUV, her mouth agape.

Pierce straightened and gave a small wave. "Hi."

"Pierce!" the woman screeched. She turned back to Patrick and shoved him. "You shot at your own brother?"

"I didn't mean to. It was an accident."

"I'm okay. Really." Pierce headed toward the porch.

The woman charged down the steps and threw her arms around him. "Pierce! You're alive!"

Sorta. This didn't seem like the best time to dwell

on undead details. He returned the woman's hug. "Mother?"

She pushed back with a confused look. "I ain't your Ma."

"Oh, sorry." He stepped back.

"Don't you remember me? I'm your Aunt Betty."

"Ah, it's nice to meet you. You see, I have—"

"Well, I never." Aunt Betty planted her fists on her hips and glared at him. "First, you run off without a word to anyone, leaving us here in the lurch for five long years, and now, you act like you don't even know us. Of all the high-falutin'—"

"I have amnesia!"

His brother gasped.

His aunt scrunched up her long thin nose. "Is that like milk of Magnesia?"

"No, Aunt Betty," Patrick muttered. "*Amnesia*. It means he can't remember anything."

Maggie exited the SUV. "It's true. Pierce has suffered from amnesia for almost five years."

Aunt Betty narrowed her eyes. "And who the devil are you?"

Pierce wrapped an arm around Maggie's shoulders. "This is my good friend, Maggie O'Brian."

"Humph." Aunt Betty sniffed. "You remember *her* name."

Patrick opened the front door and yelled, "Ma! Pierce is back!" He let the door slam shut and waited on the porch.

Pierce wondered if there was bad blood between him and his brother. Patrick hadn't even bothered to shake his hand. "Are we twins?"

Patrick laughed.

Aunt Betty snorted. "Don't you know you're the oldest?"

"He has amnesia," Patrick reminded her. "You're three years older than me, Pierce, though you sure don't look like it."

Of course. When he'd become undead, he'd stopped aging.

A short, dark-haired woman ran onto the porch and gasped when she saw Pierce. *"Santa Maria!"* She dashed down the stairs. "Pierce Alejandro! I thought I'd never see you again." She pulled him into an embrace and burst into tears.

Pierce Alejandro? He gave Maggie a shocked look over his mother's head. He was part Hispanic, after all. Maggie grinned.

He patted his mother's back. "You *are* my mother, right?"

"Claro." She stepped back. "You don't remember?"

"He has amnesia," Patrick yelled from the porch.

His mother looked confused. "You don't remember us at all?"

"No, that's why I was gone for so long. I only found out yesterday that my name's Pierce O'Callahan."

His mother looked even more confused. "Then who were you before?"

"He doesn't remember!" Patrick shouted. "He has amnesia!"

"Actually, I do remember the last four and a half years. It's everything before that's a total blank."

Aunt Betty scowled at him. "So you've been cavortin' around the countryside while we were here starvin' to death?"

"We're not starving!" His mother protested, then

gave Pierce another hug. "Don't worry, *pobrecito*. You're home, and now, everything will be fine."

He patted his mother on the back. He was beginning to suspect they did expect him to save the ranch. But how could he when he remembered nothing about ranching?

"Y'all had better come in," Patrick yelled from the porch. "It's not safe out there."

Pierce reached for Maggie's hand. "Mother, I'd like you to meet Maggie O'Brian. She's been helping me find out who I am. Without her, I would have never made it home."

Maggie's eyes glistened with tears. "I was happy to help."

His mother grabbed her in a tight hug. "Thank you, thank you. You are an angel to bring my son back to me."

Maggie returned the woman's embrace.

"You must call me Dorotea," Pierce's mother announced. "And you are always welcome in my home. God bless you, child."

"Don't just stand there!" Patrick shouted from the porch. "Hurry, get in the house!"

There must be some kind of danger. Why else was his brother standing guard with a shotgun? Pierce led Maggie up the steps, following his mother and aunt. As soon as he reached the porch, his brother grabbed him in a bear hug.

"I'm so glad you're back." Patrick pounded him on the back.

Pierce grinned, relieved that he and his brother were on good terms after all. "What's the deal with the shotgun?"

"Nothing." Patrick slanted a nervous look toward his mother and aunt. "But you shouldn't be outside tonight."

Pierce exchanged a confused look with Maggie as they filed into the foyer. Then, they followed his mother and aunt into the living room on the right.

"Come, sit down." Dorotea gestured toward a long tan sofa with plump cushions.

Pierce and Maggie sat together on the couch. Patrick took a position next to the Christmas tree in front of the bay window. On the opposite wall, a large bookcase took up the whole wall, stuffed with books, knickknacks, and an old television. His mom and aunt sat across from him in two maroon wing-back chairs.

Maggie frowned at Patrick's gun. "Is there something wrong? We saw a strange creature on the road. Pierce almost hit it."

Dorotea gasped.

Aunt Betty jumped to her feet. "What kind of creature?"

"I'm not sure." Maggie twisted the cross-shaped ring on her little finger. "It was large and sorta wolfish looking."

"And you hit it?" Aunt Betty shrieked.

"No, no," Pierce assured her. "The animal was fine. It just gave us a shock."

"Oh." Aunt Betty sat back down, her face pale.

Patrick muttered a curse while gazing out the window.

"What's going on?" Pierce asked.

"You must be hungry." Dorotea stood and headed for the door. "I'll get you something to eat."

"No, thank you," Pierce replied. "We ate on the way."

Dorotea halted halfway to the door. "Something to drink?"

Maggie smiled. "We just finished some drinks in the car, but thank you very much."

"Oh." Dorotea returned to her chair. "So, tell me, Pierce. What have you been doing while you were gone?"

"I was in New York City."

"He's a famous actor," Maggie added.

Aunt Betty sniffed. "Not too famous. I've never seen him in anything."

"I play Don Orlando de Corazon on a soap opera on DVN."

"Oh, how wonderful!" Dorotea beamed at him. "I'm afraid we don't get that channel. We could never afford cable."

Pierce leaned forward, bracing his forearms on his knees. "Be honest with me. Is the ranch in trouble?"

His mother sighed. "We're having some difficult times, but it'll pass."

Patrick snorted. "It'll never pass."

Aunt Betty crossed her arms, frowning. "It ain't Bob's fault. He can't help it."

"Who's Bob?" Pierce asked.

"My husband, your uncle." Aunt Betty glared at him. "He taught you how to ride. Don't you remember anything?"

"Give him a break," Patrick growled. "He has amnesia."

"Well, I hope he remembers how to tend cattle." Aunt Betty glowered back. "What with you too afraid to leave the house."

Patrick stiffened. "I can't help it. It's the curse."

"Superstitious nonsense." Aunt Betty pursed her lips.

"A curse?" Pierce asked.

"Don't worry about it." Dorotea rushed over to Pierce and perched on the sofa arm next to him. "We're so grateful you're back. And just in time for Christmas!"

"I bet Pierce is too smart to believe in a curse," Aunt Betty muttered.

He wasn't so sure about that. After all, a potion from a voodoo priestess had wiped out his entire memory. "What curse?"

"A biting curse." Patrick lay his shotgun down on a deacon's bench against the wall. "Don't ever leave this house. If you do, I'm warning you, you'll get bitten."

Dorotea whispered loudly in Pierce's ear, "Your brother's afraid to leave the house."

"It's not fear." Patrick frowned at them all. "It's common sense. How did Dad die three years ago?"

Dorotea sighed. "He was bitten by a rattlesnake several miles from home. *Pobrecito*. He didn't make it home in time."

"I'm sorry." Pierce patted his mother's hand.

"And what happened to Uncle Bob and Rosalinda?" Patrick continued. "I'll tell you what. They were bitten!"

"Who's Rosalinda?" Pierce asked.

"Your sister." Dorotea frowned at him. "You don't remember her, either?"

"For God's sake, the guy has *amnesia*!" Patrick raised his hands in frustration.

"Sorry." Dorotea smoothed back Pierce's hair. "I keep forgetting." Suddenly, she removed her hand. "*Santa Maria*. Is it contagious?"

"No," Pierce assured her. "You're perfectly safe."

Patrick snorted. "Yeah, as long as we don't get bitten."

Pierce exchanged a worried look with Maggie. This was probably not the best time to admit they were vampires. "Where is Rosalinda? I'd like to meet her."

"She's gone . . . out," Dorotea mumbled.

"She'll be fine," Aunt Betty whispered. "She always makes it back home."

Patrick grabbed the shotgun and went back to the window. "We always stay up on nights like this."

What the hell was going on? "Where is she?" Pierce asked.

Dorotea shrugged, then her face brightened. "It's so wonderful to have you back for Christmas! Surely, things have turned around now, and God is blessing us."

Pierce glanced at the clock on the bookcase. Four-fifteen A.M. It would take an hour to drive back to Dallas. "Well, actually, we need to be going."

"No!" Dorotea stood. "You must stay for Christmas! And forever! There's no place like home. We won't let you leave."

"I'm really sorry," Maggie ventured, "but Pierce needs to give me a ride back."

"Nonsense!" Dorotea circled the coffee table to sit next to Maggie. "You must stay, too. You're the angel who brought my son back to me. You'll always be welcome in our house."

Maggie blinked. "Thank you. Thank you so much." She gave Pierce an apprehensive look.

He figured she was worried about finding a place for their daily death-sleep. The Dallas coven's underground headquarters would be much safer. "I'd better take you back." Her face paled. Were those tears in her eyes? Dammit, he'd said the wrong thing.

"You cannot go!" Dorotea stood once more.

"His daughter!" Aunt Betty jumped to her feet. "He must stay to see his daughter."

Pierce's mouth fell open. "My—my daughter? She's here?"

"Yes!" Dorotea grinned. "Can you bring her down, Betty?"

"Of course. Just a minute." Aunt Betty dashed into the foyer. Her steps pounded up the stairs.

Dorotea clasped her hands together at her ample bosom. "She's sound asleep, waiting for Santa Claus to come. But an even greater miracle has happened! Her father has come home." She frowned as Pierce rose to his feet. "You don't know you have a child? Shame on you. I raised you better than that."

"For God's sake!" Patrick shouted. "He has amnesia!"

"No, I do know about Lucy," Pierce confessed. "But I only found out last night. And I thought she was with her mother."

Dorotea grimaced. "That terrible woman. She doesn't deserve Lucy. She dropped off *la pobrecita* like an unwanted *gato*. Just because the man she was with didn't want a child."

Maggie gasped. "That's horrible!"

"I know." Dorotea cocked her head when steps sounded on the stairs. She held a finger to her lips. "We never talk about it in front of Lucy."

"Of course not." Pierce moved toward the foyer, anxious to meet his daughter for the first time. His heart leaped up his throat when he saw her on the stairs. Her curly black hair was disheveled, her big brown eyes drooped with sleepiness, her mouth was plugged with two fingers, and her Sesame Street pajamas were twisted askew. He'd never seen a more beautiful child in his life. His heart filled till it was heavy with love, then settled back into his chest with a sense of contentment.

Maggie and Lucy. He loved the most precious girls in the world.

Aunt Betty helped the sleepy little girl down the stairs. "We all adore her." Even Betty's pinched, narrow face had softened. "She's brought joy back into this house."

"I can believe that." Pierce knelt down to greet his daughter.

Lucy stopped in front of him and removed her fingers from her mouth. "You're not Santa Claus."

"No. I'm your father." And she was the only child he and Maggie could ever have. Their undead status precluded any more. "I think you're a miracle."

"No, I'm Lucy."

With a grin, he hugged her.

"Did you come with Santa Claus?"

"No." He straightened. "I came with an angel." He pointed at Maggie on the couch who was watching with tears in her eyes.

Lucy wandered into the living room and stopped in front of Maggie. "You're pretty."

A tear ran down Maggie's face. "I think you're beautiful."

"I'm sleepy." Lucy climbed onto the couch and rested her head in Maggie's lap.

Maggie gently stroked the girl's hair. Pierce felt his heart expand. For the first time in his memory, everything was right. He was blessed.

"What a lovely picture you two make." Dorotea headed for the bookcase. "I should get the camera."

"No!" Pierce rushed toward the couch. Shit! If his mother had a 35 mm camera, he and Maggie wouldn't show up in it.

Maggie gave him a frantic look.

"The—uh, the flash might wake up Lucy," he grappled for an excuse.

"Yes." Maggie nodded. "Perhaps we can look at your old photos? Maybe it'll jog Pierce's memory."

"Good idea!" Dorotea grabbed a photo album from the bookcase.

Pierce exhaled with relief and sat next to Maggie.

Dorotea perched on the sofa arm and thumbed through the photo album. "Ah, here's one of my favorites." She lifted the album so Pierce and Maggie could see. "Halloween. Rosalinda was a princess. Patrick was Robin, and Pierce was Batman."

Maggie slanted an amused glance at Pierce. "A black cape?"

"Yes." Dorotea smiled. "Pierce was always fond of capes."

Maggie grinned. "How interesting."

Pierce wondered if somehow his subconscious had held on to certain things. Like capes. And a natural preference for short women with dark hair. Like his mother and Maggie.

Patrick wandered over to look at the picture. "I remember those costumes. We used to wear them when we played in the cave. Pierce would say, 'To the bat cave, Robin.' "

Dorotea scoffed. "And the two of you would come home stinking of bat guano. You ruined those costumes." She flipped pages in the album till she located another picture. "Here they are the next year. Patrick was Spiderman, and Pierce was Zorro."

Maggie laughed. "Another black cape?"

Dorotea continued through the album. "Most of these are Pierce with his horses. He was winning medals by the age of ten. Then in high school, he discovered another passion."

Maggie's grin faded. "You mean girls?"

"Oh, no," Dorotea chuckled. "He was shy around the girls. It was the marching band he loved. And music."

Pierce blinked with surprise. "I know how to play an instrument?"

"Of course." Dorotea tipped the album toward them. "Here he is in his band uniform. Doesn't he look handsome?"

"Very handsome." Maggie leaned closer. "Sweet Mary, you're holding a trumpet."

A trumpet? Pierce exchanged a surprised look with Maggie. No wonder Don Orlando had played the trumpet in a mariachi band.

Dorotea continued to show them photos while Lucy slept soundly, cuddled up to Maggie.

"It's getting late," Maggie whispered, then projected her thoughts into his head. *We could teleport to Dallas, but that would be hard to explain to your family.*

You're right. He glanced at the clock. Five-fifteen. "Maggie and I are tired from our journey. Is there a place we can sleep? A dark place with no windows?"

"No windows?" Dorotea closed the photo album on her lap.

"There's a bed in the basement," Aunt Betty offered. "But only one." She pursed her lips in disapproval.

"There are a few windows in the basement." Dorotea returned the albums to the bookcase. "But they're very small. I'm sure they won't bother you."

"I—I have a skin condition," Maggie explained. "Any exposure to sunlight would be very painful."

Betty snorted. "I thought you looked too pale. In fact, both of you look too pale. A little sun would do you good."

Pierce winced. "This may sound strange, but we both have an illness that requires a lot of rest and complete darkness."

Betty scoffed. "Sounds like hanky-panky to me."

Patrick chuckled. "There's always the cave."

"Don't be silly," Dorotea fussed. "There are a million bats in that cave. And mounds of stinky bat guano."

Patrick nodded. "With our luck, one of those bats would bite them."

Dorotea's face lit up. "The storm cellar! It's very dark."

"That sounds good." Pierce stood. "Where is it?"

"Close to the garage. It's where we go if there's a tornado warning." Dorotea wrinkled her nose. "But it's not a fit place to sleep. There's no electricity or heat."

"It'll be fine," Maggie insisted. "Thank you."

Pierce gently lifted Lucy's head so that Maggie could get up. He slid a pillow under Lucy's head and kissed her brow. "See you tomorrow night, little one."

Dorotea shook her head. "This is terrible. How can we let you sleep in that cold hole in the ground when we have perfectly good beds in the house?"

Aunt Betty harrumphed. "I doubt they'll be cold."

"We'll be fine, Mother," Pierce assured her. "We really do need total darkness. And we need to sleep all day tomorrow undisturbed."

"All day?" Dorotea asked. "But tomorrow's Christmas. You should watch Lucy open her presents. And dinner will be at three in the afternoon."

Pierce gave Maggie a worried look. "We're . . . very tired."

Aunt Betty snorted.

"I'm serious," Pierce insisted. "I want your word that none of you will enter the storm cellar until after sunset."

Dorotea ran a hand through her graying black hair. "Very well. We'll have Christmas dinner at seven in the evening."

"Thank you." Pierce kissed his mother's cheek. "Now, take us to the storm cellar."

· 6 ·

Maggie stopped by the SUV while Pierce and his mom went to the storm cellar. She stuffed two bottles from the ice chest into her tote bag. She knew Ian and the Dallas coven would be worried, so she called Ian on her cell phone.

"Don't worry about locating Lucy. She's here." Maggie spotted Patrick watching her from the bay window. "There's something weird going on here."

"Like what?" Ian's voice sharpened.

"I don't know. Can you check the local papers for anything like a strange creature on the loose?" She turned toward the SUV just in time to see a furry animal jump out from behind a rear wheel. "Sweet Mary!" Maggie retreated with a gasp.

"What is it?" Ian demanded. "Is it the bloody creature?"

Maggie pressed a hand to her chest. "No, it's a rabbit."

The rabbit hopped toward her, wriggling its nose and studying her with big brown eyes.

"Ye frightened me over a wee bunny?" Ian asked. "I was ready to teleport there and slay a vicious monster."

Maggie laughed. "It startled me." She stepped toward the bunny, but it scampered to the house and wedged through some broken latticework underneath the front steps.

The house was in need of repair, and Maggie knew Pierce would be determined to help his family. But she wanted to help, too. She wanted to belong here like he did. Dorotea had welcomed her, but Pierce was the one who needed to ask her to stay. And all he'd done so far was offer to take her back to Dallas.

She needed to prove her worth, and an idea had occurred to her in the house. "Ian, can you check the price on bat guano?"

"Bat guano?"

"Yes. Let me know tomorrow night." She hung up and hurried to the storm cellar. A howl in the distance made her shiver. No wonder the bunny went into hiding.

Dorotea was standing by the hatch and gave Maggie a hug. "Are you sure about this?"

"Yes. We'll be fine." Maggie swung her tote bag onto her shoulder and stepped onto the ladder. Below, Pierce lit her way with a flashlight. Halfway down, Dorotea closed the hatch.

"Alone at last." Pierce set the flashlight on a shelf.

Maggie set her tote bag on the cold linoleum floor and removed the bottles of blood. "I brought us a snack."

"Great." Pierce opened a bottle and drank. "You're the best, Maggie." He set his bottle on the shelf next to the flashlight and began unrolling the sleeping bags.

Did he really believe she was the best? If he did, why didn't he proclaim his love and ask her to marry him? No, he just squatted there on the floor, unzipping sleeping bags.

Oh well, it *was* late. She could already feel a slight tug from the death-sleep. He was right to get things ready.

She looked around the small cellar. Along one wall, there were shelves filled with jugs of water. On the opposite wall, a unit of shelves jutted out to provide a small space behind it. The shelves were filled with canned goods and supplies.

She slipped behind the shelving unit and removed her pajamas from the tote bag. They were damp from the cold bottles she'd stashed there. She wrinkled her nose. If she had any nerve at all, she'd prance out from behind these shelves completely nude and show Pierce she really was the best.

She groaned inwardly. She knew nothing about seduction. Her one encounter with seduction had been over a century ago when a male vampire had used mind control to steal her blood, her virginity, and finally, her mortality. He'd been gentle enough, but still, he'd controlled her. He'd made her think it was pleasurable, but the next night, when she awoke, she was undead and appalled. It hadn't seemed so pleasurable then.

Over the next hundred years, she'd engaged in psychic vampire sex a few times, but she'd never wanted to make love again in the physical way. She'd never wanted to risk that sort of emotional vulnerability with a man. Until now.

She quickly undressed and slid on the damp pajama bottoms. What if Pierce rejected her? He was always thanking her, but she wanted his love, not his gratitude. He also referred to her as an angel. Did that mean he didn't desire her as a woman?

She felt another pull from death-sleep. If she was going to seduce him, she'd better do it quick. She slipped on her pajama top and peered through two huge cans of baked beans to see what he was doing.

He was sitting on the sleeping bags, watching her.

She gasped, her old-fashioned upbringing reappearing. "How dare you!"

He grinned. "Don't worry. There's a big box of toilet paper in the way, and I completely missed the good parts."

Maggie's heart raced. He *was* interested in her as a woman. She eased out from behind the shelving unit.

His gaze drifted over her. "You look beautiful, Maggie."

"In flannel pajamas?" She smoothed her hand over a damp patch. "They're a little wet."

"Then you should take them off so you don't catch cold."

She snorted. "Now that sounds too much like Don Orlando."

Pierce shook his head. "Don Orlando is gone." He stood. "There's just you and me."

Her heart beat faster. She looked down at the floor and saw what he'd done. He'd opened all the sleeping bags and stacked them flat on each other to create one mattress. Two pillows rested at the head, and blankets at the foot.

A wave of heat poured lazily through her. "Are you planning to seduce me?"

"Yes." He unzipped his jeans and dropped them to the floor. "I know you deserve better, Maggie. You deserve the finest suite at the Plaza or the Ritz."

"I'm okay." More than okay. She watched his muscles bunch and ripple when he yanked his T-shirt over his head.

"And you deserve better than a poor cowboy who apparently has a strange family."

"I like your family." Her breath caught when she spotted the huge bulge in his cotton briefs. Sweet Mary and Joseph, he wasn't thinking of her as an angel now.

He stuck his thumbs in the elastic waistband and tugged the briefs down slowly. "I don't mean to rush you, darling, but we don't have much time before the death-sleep takes us."

She licked her lips. Yes, she wanted him, but what about love? Why couldn't he say what she needed to hear? She turned away just as his briefs hit the floor. "Do you love me?"

"God, yes." He grabbed her and turned her to face him. "I have always loved you, Maggie. I loved you as Don Orlando. And I adore you as Pierce. I don't know how I could face eternity without you. Hell, I couldn't face one night without you."

"Oh, Pierce." She cradled his face in her hands. "You had me with *'God, yes.'* And I love you so much."

His mouth came down on hers with a hunger that took her breath away and melted her knees. Before she knew it, they were stretched out on the makeshift mattress, and Pierce was covering her face and neck with kisses. She smoothed her hands down his back, loving the heat of his skin and the bulge of his muscles.

"We have to hurry." He unbuttoned her pajama top.

"I understand."

"So beautiful." He took a nipple into his mouth.

It *was* beautiful. Maggie had never realized how beautiful real love-making could be. She could hardly breathe. Hardly think. Her skin burned wherever he touched her. And heat, demanding heat sizzled between her legs. "Hurry."

He pulled off her pajama bottoms and settled between her legs. "Forgive me for taking you so fast." He plunged a finger into her core and stroked her.

Maggie squealed. "Oh, God, you're forgiven."

"You're so wet." He spread her moisture around the sensitive folds, then tasted her.

She jolted, raising her hips into the air. Sweet Mary, he *was* the greatest vampire lover in the world. She spiraled out of control. His tongue continued to torture and delight her, feast on her and devour her. She screamed when the climax shattered her, immersing her in a flood of sweet throbbing sensations.

"Pierce me." She wrapped her arms around his shoulders and her legs around his waist.

He entered her. "I wish we had all night." A look of fatigue crossed his face.

She felt it, too. Death-sleep was coming, tugging at her consciousness. "Just a little more. Please."

He gritted his teeth and plunged again and again.

She lifted her hips to meet each thrust. *Just a little more time. Please.* She felt the spiraling sensation building within.

He quickened his pace, his breathing harsh. Then suddenly, with a deep plunge, he stiffened and groaned. He collapsed, his head beside hers. "God, I love you."

"I love you, too." As death-sleep pulled her under, she felt one final sweet throb where their bodies were still joined.

Pierce awoke with the usual jolt that reverberated through his body. He opened his eyes as Maggie shuddered back to life.

A scream erupted behind them.

Maggie's eyes flew open, and she screamed, too. Pierce looked over his shoulder. A young woman at the foot of their bed squealed, then grabbed his mother. Dorotea screamed.

"Enough!" Pierce pulled the blanket up to cover himself and Maggie as he flipped over into a sitting position. Dammit. They must have come in before sunset.

"I thought you were dead!" The young woman pointed at him.

Dorotea pressed her palms together in prayer. "It's a miracle!" She dropped to her knees and burst into tears.

The young woman knelt beside Dorotea, hugging her. She shot Pierce a confused look. "I could have sworn you were dead."

"Who are you?" Pierce demanded.

"Your sister, Rosalinda. Mother told me not to come till after sunset, but I couldn't wait. I had to see you again, but then, I thought you were dead." She covered her face and sobbed.

Great. He'd started his new life by traumatizing his family. He glanced at Maggie to see how she was doing. Her face was pale, and she was busily buttoning her pajamas. His mother and sister were so upset, he could hear their hearts pounding, smell the blood racing through them. He glanced at the half-empty bottle on the nearby shelf. He needed to eat soon.

"Why are you screaming down there?" Aunt Betty yelled from the hatch opening.

"They're alive!" Rosalinda stood, still crying.

"What?" Aunt Betty yelled. "They're not dead anymore?"

"They're alive!" Rosalinda moved to the base of the ladder and looked up at her aunt. "Call nine-one-one and cancel the ambulance."

"It's a miracle." Dorotea crossed herself as she struggled to her feet. "A Christmas miracle."

"I can explain." Pierce groaned inwardly. Could he really?

"No need." Rosalinda laughed, wiping the tears from her face. "It's pretty obvious what you've been up to all day."

Maggie winced. "Actually, we were . . . asleep most of the day."

"Yeah, right." Rosalinda snorted.

"We were unconscious," Pierce added.

"For thirty minutes?" Her eyes suddenly widened. "Wow. I wish I had orgasms like that."

Dorotea gasped. "Rosalinda!"

A pang of hunger shot through Pierce. He needed to get them out of here quick. "Please, go to the house. Maggie and I will be there soon, and we'll explain everything."

"Very well." Dorotea exchanged a pointed look with her daughter. "We all have some explaining to do."

After they left, Pierce grabbed the bottle from the shelf. He guzzled it down while Maggie drank from her bottle. With the edge off their hunger, they began to dress.

He zipped up his jeans. "I don't know how to tell them."

Maggie took his hand and squeezed it. "I'll be there with you. For good or bad."

"Thank you." He kissed her hand. "Ready to go?"

"Yes." She swung her tote bag onto her shoulder and followed him up the ladder.

As they walked toward the house, Pierce spotted his brother on the porch.

"You're okay?" Patrick ran down the steps, but halted on the last one. A look of shame crossed his face. "I wish I wasn't so damned afraid. You two come in. Dinner's ready."

"Just a minute." Maggie ran to the SUV and retrieved the last two bottles of blood.

As soon as they entered the foyer, Lucy ran up to them with a big grin. "You want to see what Santa Claus brought me?"

"In a little while." Pierce picked her up and kissed her cheek.

Lucy giggled. "You sleep too much."

"I'm afraid so." Pierce carried her into the dining room. She wiggled down from his arms and climbed into a chair with a booster seat.

A tall man in overalls came forward. "I'm your Uncle Bob. I'm glad you're back."

"I'm glad to be back." Pierce shook his hand. "And this is Maggie." He wrapped an arm around her.

Dorotea, Rosalinda, and Aunt Betty finished loading the table with food—turkey, dressing, mashed potatoes, and salad.

Uncle Bob took a seat at the end of the table. "I hope you two are hungry. The gals have been cooking all day."

Pierce exchanged a worried look with Maggie. She quietly set their bottles of blood beside two plates on the table.

"Everyone sit down." Dorotea sat at the other end of the table with Lucy on one side and Rosalinda on the other. Patrick sat between his sister and aunt. Pierce took the seat next to Lucy, and Maggie sat beside him.

"Let's say the blessing," Dorotea announced, and everyone reached out to hold hands. "Thank you, Lord, for giving us Lucy who has brought so much joy into this house. And thank you for sending us Pierce and Maggie. My son, who was lost, has been returned. Amen." Dorotea crossed herself with tears in her eyes.

"Now, everyone eat." Uncle Bob piled his plate with turkey meat, then passed the platter to Maggie. She passed it on to Pierce who put some meat on Lucy's plate.

"What's wrong?" Dorotea asked. "Aren't you two eating?"

"We're on a special diet," Maggie murmured as she opened her bottle of Chocolood. She poured some into her glass.

"Well, I never," Aunt Betty muttered. "After all the work we did, slaving over the stove."

"Food's great." Uncle Bob wolfed down an entire turkey breast in two gulps.

Pierce opened his bottle and took a sip. "The night I lost my memory, something else happened, too. I was attacked."

Patrick looked up from his plate. "You were bitten?"

"Yes."

"Damn!" Patrick hit the table with his fist. "I knew it. It's that damned curse."

"Please don't curse at the table," Dorotea murmured. "Go on, Pierce. What happened?"

He swallowed hard. This was it. "I was transformed. Into a vampire." He glanced quickly around the table, but was met with nothing but blank looks. At least, they weren't screaming. Or trying to stab him with the silverware.

"Are you sure, dear?" Dorotea asked.

"I didn't think such a thing existed," Rosalinda mumbled with her mouth full.

"It's true," Maggie said. "Pierce and I are both vampires."

Silence descended around the table as everyone stopped eating. Pierce wondered when the screaming would begin.

"Ah, well." Dorotea shrugged. "Nobody's perfect."

"That's the truth," Aunt Betty muttered.

"Pass the potatoes," Uncle Bob said.

Pierce blinked, then passed the bowl to his uncle. "You're not upset? Maggie and I are sorta . . . dead during the day."

"Ha!" Rosalinda smiled smugly. "I knew I was right."

Patrick frowned. "You're not going to bite us, are you?"

"No. We drink synthetic blood." Pierce demonstrated by taking a swig from his bottle.

A ringing sound came from Maggie's tote bag. She retrieved her cell phone and excused herself from the table. Even though she was talking quietly in the foyer, Pierce could tell with his super vamp hearing that she was talking to Ian.

Everyone else resumed their eating. Uncle Bob was gnawing on a turkey leg. Rosalinda was nibbling at a salad.

"I suppose we should fix up the storm cellar and make it more comfy for you," Dorotea said as she cut up her meat.

"That would be nice. Thank you." Pierce took a deep breath, greatly relieved. "You're all taking the news very well."

Aunt Betty shrugged. "We're family."

"And we thank God you made it home," Dorotea added.

"I have some money saved up," Pierce said. "We could use it for repairs."

"Oh, that's wonderful!" Dorotea exclaimed.

"Or we could buy more cattle," Aunt Betty offered.

"Why should we?" Patrick muttered. "They'll just

get eaten like all the others. We're doomed. Nothing can save us."

"Don't say that." Betty sniffled. "He can't help it."

Uncle Bob hit the table with his fist. "I've worked this ranch since I was a young boy. I helped build it with my bare hands. Do you think I enjoy being the one to destroy us?"

"There, there." Betty embraced her husband.

"What's going on?" Pierce asked.

His family grew silent.

"Good news!" Maggie returned, smiling. "I know how you can save the ranch. You can make a bundle selling bat guano for fertilizer."

"Maggie, you're brilliant!" Pierce grinned at her. "Can still love me when I'm a guano farmer?"

She laughed. "Of course."

Uncle Bob cleared his throat. "I'll be happy to help you shovel that guano."

"Thanks." Pierce turned to Patrick. "You could help, too."

Patrick turned pale. "It's not safe to leave the house."

"I won't let anything hurt you, Patrick. Trust me." Pierce grabbed the fork beside his plate and bent it into a circle.

Patrick's eyes widened. He tried to bend his fork, but couldn't. "Wow, you're really strong."

"I have superior strength, vision, and hearing. I can levitate, teleport, and control people's minds if I have to. You would be safe with me, Patrick."

He glanced at Uncle Bob. "Can you control an animal?"

"I suppose. Will you help me, Patrick?"

He gulped. "I—I'll try. But we can't do any work on the night of a full moon."

"Why not?" Pierce asked.

"Because whenever there's a full moon, we lose another cow," Uncle Bob said sadly.

"You can't help it," Betty whispered. "If you didn't take one of ours, you'd go to the neighbors, and they'd shoot you for sure."

Uncle Bob was killing the cows? Pierce tilted his head, confused, then suddenly remembered the wolflike creature. Maggie gasped and looked at him. She was thinking the same thing. They turned to stare at Uncle Bob.

He sighed. "That was me you almost hit on the road. I change every time there's a full moon."

"I didn't think werewolves existed," Maggie whispered.

"I didn't think vampires existed," Bob replied. "But I'm not really a werewolf. There ain't no wolves in this part of Texas. It was a coyote that bit me."

Pierce blinked. "You're a were-coyote?"

"Yep." Uncle Bob nodded.

"It's the curse," Patrick moaned. "We'll all get bitten. Rosalinda was bit, too."

Maggie gasped. "You're a coyote, too?"

She put down the carrot stick she'd been munching on. "Actually, it was a jack-rabbit that bit me."

Maggie gasped again. "You're the rabbit from last night?"

Rosalinda nodded with a smile. "I was curious about you."

"Now, all our secrets are out." Dorotea gave Pierce

a worried look. "Are you still happy you found your family?"

"Yes. I'm happy you can accept me the way I am."

His mother smiled sadly. "We love you, no matter what. That's how it is in a family."

Pierce stood and pushed back his chair. "Then I hope there's room for one more in this family." He knelt beside Maggie's chair and took her hand in his. "I love you, Maggie. Can you give up the glamorous life of a television star to be the wife of a poor guano farmer?"

"Yes!" She slipped out of the chair and into his arms. "Yes, I can."

Epilogue

One month later

"It's over, Don Orlando." Maggie stood over the fake hospital bed on the set at DVN. Pierce lay there silently, pretending to be in a coma.

"I can never see you again." She turned away from the bed and faced camera two. "I've decided to leave the country. There are so many sick people in South America. They need me."

Maggie spun around to face Don Orlando. "But before I leave, there's one thing I must do." She took his hand and leaned over the bed. "I have to tell you how I truly feel. It was always impossible for us. You're the greatest vampire lover in the world, while I'm a famous, mortal brain surgeon. Our love could never be."

She sat beside him, clutching his hand to her breast. "But I will always love you, Don Orlando."

He moaned and turned his head.

Maggie leaped to her feet, releasing his hand. "Oh my God. It's a miracle! He's coming out of the coma!"

"Dr. Jessica," he whispered, opening his eyes. "You've come back to me." He grabbed her hand.

She swayed away from him, directing a forlorn look at camera one. "I must go. I'm leaving for South America tonight."

"Then I will come with you." He sat up in bed.

"And leave your mariachi band?"

"They can come with me. I hear there is a shortage of mariachi bands in South America."

She sat next to him on the bed. "But you're famous here. You would give that up for me?"

"I love you, Dr. Jessica. Wherever you go, I shall go with you." He pulled her into his arms.

"I love you, too, Don Orlando."

"Then my life is complete." His mouth covered hers.

Maggie wrapped her arms around him and savored this last kiss with Don Orlando.

"That's great!" the director yelled. "Cut!"

Pierce deepened the kiss, invading her mouth with his tongue. Maggie moaned and snuggled closer.

"I said cut!"

Pierce planted kisses down her neck and nuzzled her ear. "I love you, Mrs. Maggie O'Callahan."

She sighed with contentment.

He pulled back and gave her a rakish Don Orlando look, one dark brow raised. "Shall we adjourn to my dressing room?"

With a laugh, Maggie walked off the set with her husband, the greatest lover in the vampire world.